Miss Harrie Elliott

MARIAN O'NEILL

TOWN
HOUSE
DUBLIN

First published in 1999
by
Town House and Country House
Trinity House, Charleston Rd
Ranelagh, Dublin 6

ISBN: 1-86059-097-7

A CIP catalogue record for this book is available from the
British Library

Typeset by Typeform Repro
Printed by ColourBooks, Dublin

Cover: Miss Iris Tree
by Augustus John
reproduced by kind permission of the copyright holder
and the Hugh Lane Municipal Gallery of Modern Art, Dublin

For my mother and father, Seán and Brid

Acknowledgments
I would like to thank my family and friends for
their enthusiastic support,
Siobhán, Treasa and Bríd of Town House for their
dedication and professionalism
and Stephen for absolutely everything

Chapter 1

Yesterday afternoon I overheard little Miss Kelly, my salaried friend, on the telephone. She was complaining about me. She said that in my old age I used my wealth to exploit others just as I had used my beauty to exploit them in my youth. Of course, she was in no way as concise: she spent half an hour trying to explain that simple concept.

I took it as the most tremendous compliment, even if it did come from little Miss Kelly. At eighty, one takes one's compliments where one can find them. In my case they usually lurk behind insults. I prefer it that way. Penniless old people find their insults behind shouted, hearty compliments. But even still, over sixty years on, I can't take full credit for that compliment. After all, little Miss Kelly never knew Harrie. If she had she would have grown beyond my employ.

I see a lot of myself in my little Miss Kelly, my pre-Harrie self of course. I was a little Miss Moore before I met Harrie and without her I am sure that I would have stayed as such. I never had the charms necessary to attract. As a baby I never attracted gushing compliments and as a child I never attracted friends. I had no reason to suppose that as an adult I would attract a husband.

I was very young when we first met, Harrie and I. I had left formal education as soon as it was deemed seemly to do so. My parents insisted on that, and they insisted that I move to the city to work. It was mostly my father that did the insisting. He didn't hold with educated women. He said the more learning you stuffed into a woman the more life you squeezed out of her. By 'life' my father meant charm, and all the willowy grace that is associated with it.

I saw myself as living proof of his inability to assess specific situations. Although I had just completed years of formal education, a variety of teachers and teaching methods had failed to stuff any learning of note into me, and yet, there I was, as lifeless as a corpse and as charmless as a grave.

My mother blamed my looks, holding my father directly responsible: 'If you had my hair it would be one thing, but no, you take after your father. His was mousy before he lost it.' Or 'I'm proud to say I've still got all my own teeth, but your father's family! Well your randmother only ever knew how cook soup, there was never a need for anything else. You must take after them. I'm sure theirs were discoloured before they were removed.'

Because of her continuous fault-finding, I was, from a young age, astonished by her choice of husband. She seemed to be constantly admitting to involving herself with a very dubious gene pool. Not only was my father's family deficient in hair and teeth durability, they were also plagued with bad skin, a tendency to slouch and an irritatingly weak constitution.

Not that I ever blamed my mother for her choices or for her continual nagging, she couldn't really help herself. She was a slight, simple woman with a slight, simple approach to life. She knew what was important to her sex and what was unseemly for a woman to concern herself with.

To be seen to be virtuous was important; making the best of oneself was important; the etiquette of social eating was important; one's Sunday outfit was important; the respect of one's neighbours was important (for respect I always read envy). It was unseemly for a woman to actively attract attention to herself; it was unseemly for a woman to be seen to be hungry; it was unseemly for a woman to concern herself with issues; it was unseemly for a wife to have intimate knowledge of her husband's finances.

My father was even more innocent in his treatment of me. His approach to life was even simpler than my mother's: men did things and women applauded them for it; men provided goods and women thanked them for it.

Children fitted rather clumsily into this equation. Or, to be more precise, ugly daughters didn't fit into the equation at all. A son would have slotted in neatly. A son would have learned from his father and would have loved his mother. It wouldn't have mattered if a son was mousy or dim, his potential manhood would have validated him.

A pretty daughter would have been given a place as well. A lesser place but a secure one. A pretty daughter would have learned from her mother and would have respected her father. A very pretty daughter would have flung their expectations back at them with girlish glee. She would have subverted their rule system, re-inventing it to suit her specifications, and such a mother and such a father would have stood back, defeated in admiration.

I saw Harrie as such a daughter. She knew what was proper and what was unseemly. She knew what was expected of her and the limitations of her sex. But she did as she pleased and delighted all those who should have been appalled.

But I was the ugly daughter, one who was seen as an embarrassment to future generations. I was tall and strong-featured, when such attributes were considered merely masculine, a failure to femininity. It didn't help that I was flat-chested and hipless.

If I had been diluted by a large family I would have had my uses. I could have nursed my parents and excelled at house management. I could have minded my nephews and nieces and been rewarded with pressing annual invitations.

But luckily, as I doubt that I would have had the strength of character necessary to break away from such a role, I was an only child. I stood stark and ugly, a monument to my parents' failure at reproduction. I think, perhaps, that after me, my parents hadn't the courage to try for a second child. Though officially a condition of my mother's was the reason given for my lack of siblings. What exact condition she had was never made clear – back then one didn't pry into such matters. But it was a versatile condition: centred in her belly, it spread to her head, excusing any lapses of intellect she might suffer from, and through her limbs, excusing her from any unwelcome activities she might have foisted on her.

But I am sure that even before her condition settled her mind she could never have been intelligent. If she had been, some of it would have to have been passed on and I would have had the option of going into professional nursing, or teaching. I would, of course, have done these things far from home, but I would have written interesting, articulate letters. Letters that my parents would have been proud to show to their friends. And there would always have been the chance that some old or unusual man would take me for a wife on the strength of my mind.

However, as well as being masculine and ugly, I was dim. I stuttered in public, I blushed, I bumped into things, I refused to memorise, I confused the trifles of everyday living and I betrayed my parents with every failure.

So, at seventeen, I was sent to the city and given a job in the haberdashery department of Hall's Central Stores. My mother's mother was a Hall and my mother made all the arrangements. I suppose she didn't think me capable of securing even such a lowly position as a shop girl without assistance. And the tragedy is that she was probably right.

It was also arranged that I was to stay in a boarding house that a sensible someone had recommended to my parents. There was some talk of them visiting the establishment before I was sent there, but in the end a trip to the city proved to be too strenuous for them. My mother pleaded her condition and my father pleaded the heat, but they both took the time to voice as much concern for my future as I could hope for.

My mother lectured me, at length and in detail, about the family connection that I was indebted to, the family honour that I was to live up to and the personal effort she had made to launch me into the world of commerce.

'We Halls have always been diligent, honest and hard-working and it is expected that you will carry on the tradition. I have no doubt that that is why they offered you this position. So please remember that the family expects a standard from you. Try to stand tall and please make an effort not to fumble and drop things so often. Remember also that I am known personally by your employer and when a child, especially a girl, leaves the home, she stands as a testament to her mother. You know I have always done the best for you – not many parents would stick their necks out like I have – and now it is your chance to shine for me.'

Even my usually removed father kindly offered to lecture me on boarding house etiquette: 'Benson's is a good house and an expensive one. I will supplement your rent until you are earning a little more. Now, don't get me wrong. I don't begrudge the expense, but I know the difference between necessary and unnecessary expenditure – no man knows that better than I. I will not have my necessary expenditure wasted, so I insist that you treat Mrs Benson's establishment with the respect it is due. Obey the house rules – they are there for your good as much as anyone's – and always keep your landlady informed as to your whereabouts, in case of emergencies or some such. She is to be regarded as a type of surrogate mother.'

My parents explained my departure to their friends as wilfulness on my part. They sighed and told the village that 'Mary was always very determined to be independent. I suppose it is the modern way.' The neighbours must have had a good laugh amongst themselves at the thought of mousy Mary Moore harbouring determination. But at some stage they must have forgotten the reality of me, because I seemingly went down in local lore as a trail-blazing feminist.

I left my childhood and my family quietly one Saturday morning. My father put me on the train and left before it took off. I had a feeling that he was eager to return to his real life, the one that he shared with his wife. It was a life that had never really stretched to include me.

It was a long enough journey, about five hours on that old train, but emotionally it was much longer. Emotionally it was a journey into the unknown and a journey into the realisation of loneliness. When I finally arrived in the centre of the city, on a Saturday afternoon, I stepped into a life of complete and enforced independence.

I can still remember the liquid feeling of fear and excitement that melted my stomach and dampened my armpits. I was only seventeen and had never visited a city of any kind before. I mistook the straggling crowd for bustle and the glitz of second-rate shops for glamour.

I had with me a large suitcase, one I could barely carry. My father had insisted that the weight must not be beyond my strength. 'Mark my words, girl,' he had said to me, interrupting my packing, 'a taxi cab is excessive expenditure.' I also had a ridiculous winter coat that I had to carry. It was June and far too warm for black wool with astrakhan trimmings. It had looked foolish folded beside me on the train and it looked ridiculous now, draped across my arm, but my father had insisted, and so I had to take it. He explained that it wasn't that he didn't expect to see me before winter set in, it was just that boarding houses were renowned for draughts. A winter coat on a bed seemingly saved quite a few chests over the years, and 'Precautionary medicine saved many an unnecessary doctor's bill.'

Besides my suitcase and my coat, I had a dainty handbag, an oversized hat that threatened to blow away with the slightest gust of wind, a streetplan and a huge hand-drawn map showing the exact position of Hall's Central Stores in relation to every landmark in the city. My father had included banks, other retail outlets and trees over a certain age as landmarks.

I stood outside the railway station for a long few minutes. I held my bag and coat close against the villainy of city-dwellers, my hat down against the gentle cross-wind and my maps tight to my chest against the terrifying eventuality of losing them.

The straggling crowd stepped around me, sporadically gathering momentum and bumping into me. I half shuffled and was half jostled into the shelter of a doorway. Once there, I trusted my bags and my coat to villainy and my hat to the elements and concentrated on my maps. I needed to find Marsh Lane and Mrs Benson's lodging house. I longed to be indoors, away from the sidelong glances and the imagined comments.

My father had obviously, and typically, thought it more important that I find my way to work than to my new home. There was no hand-drawn map to Marsh Lane. Written in the margin of my streetplan were two numbers, 42 and 26. I remembered that one was the number of the house and the other the number of the tram that was to get me there. I had forgotten which was which. I had also forgotten the loose instructions that had been thrown at me that morning, on the way to the station.

That was the first time that I consciously remember cursing my father. I don't know what words I used – I doubt that I knew any suitable ones, but the intent was there. I wanted him damned for leaving me alone, on a strange street corner, in a strange city, just because my home town was too small to offer me a husband and too small-minded to offer me an alternative.

It was also the first time that I consciously remember disobeying my father. I squashed my maps into my dainty handbag, pulled my hat low over my forehead, picked up my case, shifted the weight of my coat into the crook of my arm and marched over to what I thought was a steady stream of traffic with the intention of hailing a taxi. It was a very innocent intention. Blinded by the comparative largeness of the city, I assumed that its population would have the means to sustain a full-time fleet of taxis, but my train had long since emptied, and the taxis that had been there to meet it had all departed. I knew nothing of such urban subtleties. I had never ridden in a taxi before and any knowledge I had of their workings came directly from films. So, imagining myself on a busy New York sidewalk, I made an elaborate pantomime out of waving my arm. If I could have, I have no doubt that I would have whistled.

I had been swinging my arm about for quite a while when finally a large, black, shiny car slid up to the kerb in front of me.

It wasn't a taxi. It was a kindly concerned old gentleman, but that didn't deter me. I was willing to believe that in big cities, taxi drivers could be of any age and could be dressed in any style they deemed suitable. I had noticed that this driver was very well dressed, before settling myself and my case in his back seat.

'Marsh Lane,' I barked in my best tough-cookie voice. The toughness was there to mask my nerves and also because the movies had led me to believe that even the surliest of drivers took it upon themselves to handle a lady's luggage. There was a pause before the car slipped back into the easy flow of traffic.

'So are you all right then, dear? Is there an emergency of some sort?'

'Fine, thank you and no, it is just that my case is heavy.'

I answered as briefly as I could. I thought my mother would not consider it seemly of me to encourage a conversation with a driver, and I thought his questions peculiar and far too personal.

'You're not running away from anything are you?'

'No.'

'Do you have friends in Marsh Lane? Is there some one waiting for you there?'

'I am expected.'

'So there is nothing wrong with you?'

'Nothing.'

'I thought perhaps you were in need of medical assistance.'

'No.'

And slowly the horrible truth began to dawn on me. I had a brief and clear picture of myself, half off the path, swinging my arm above my head in desperation. No wonder the poor man had expected a life and death situation. I did intend to explain myself but the truth seemed too embarrassing to admit to and it was too late to make up a suitably dramatic story, so I stayed silent and let the kindly old man think me completely mad.

And he obviously did. He drove at an increasingly fast speed and almost skidded to a halt half way down Marsh Lane. I got out as quickly as I could, dragging my case behind me and before I got a chance to thank him he had pulled my door shut and sped off.

Number 26 Marsh Lane – there was no number 42 – was a sad disappointment to any delusions of glamour that I had harboured. There were no flights of steps, no colonnades, no concessions to taste or proportion. The houses on the street, all thirty of them, looked soft with damp. They crowded in on each other, throwing the road into continual shade. No wonder it was called a lane.

Number 26 was just the same as all the others. It was narrow and tall, three storeys over basement. Its windows were dull with grime and its brickwork loose with neglect. The door opened straight on to the street. I never got over my first impression of that door. Every evening and every night when I faced its blistered, peeling, blood-red paintwork, I was reminded of an old, toothless mouth. Every night that same mouth swallowed me and, as time wore on, I took comfort in the image. Mrs Benson suited her lodging house as perfectly as some women suit their pets. She was tall and narrow with a grey face and a slash of half-worn scarlet lipstick. Another disappointment – I had hoped for the universal mother, welcoming me with outstretched, floury arms and clucks of approval. Mrs Benson welcomed me with a slight bow of her head and an overly formal greeting. The car had left the lane before she opened the door. Our relationship, I'm sure, would have been completely different if she had seen me step out of such luxury.

'Miss Moore, I presume. Charmed.'

She held out her hand and I took it. The severity of her dress and the regal arch of her eyebrow dissolved my adolescent powers of reasoning. Still holding her hand I curtsied. Half way down I realised my mistake and bobbed back up as quickly as I could. Mrs Benson didn't say anything – she didn't need to. She didn't offer to help me with my luggage and she didn't offer me any refreshment. My curtsey had denied me such adult privileges.

'If you would be so kind as to follow me, Miss Moore, I will show you to your room.'

I followed her. I followed her dainty head bound tight in a brown silk scarf, her elongated neck and her rigidly thin body with its covering of starched cotton and soft wool. I followed her up three flights of stairs in slow, stately, silence, dying a little on every step. The house was dying too.

The hall was clean and grand in a heavy Victorian way. It had an umbrella stand, a cupboard for coats, a central table with a dusty spider plant as a centrepiece, an overstuffed sofa and a curious smell of stale lavender. Everything was in its place and everything was terribly proper.

To the right, through a half closed door, I glimpsed a similar parlour. I saw just enough to form an impression of a jumble of highly polished furniture and oppressively framed prints. But, as we climbed higher, we left such comforts behind. After one flight of stairs the carpet disappeared, after two the linoleum did the same. The paintwork went from white to beige and from beige to grey and the light fittings went from tasselled shades to plain glass bowls to bare bulbs.

Mrs Benson finally stopped, at the top of the house. I was obviously a low-paying tenant. My father must have considered such trappings as carpets and light shades unnecessary. She opened a dark-brown door and walked before me into my room. I immediately liked that door. Its thick paint had run before it had dried. It was a friend, as miserable as I was, tears streaking the length of it.

'Your room faces the front.'

She turned, handed me my keys, and left me with no further explanation. No explanation was necessary, a long and detailed list of house rules hung on the back of the door.

Breakfast is served from 7.00 to 8.00 a.m. ONLY.
  Mid-day and evening meals are NOT provided.
Unless alternative arrangements have been made.

> *Tenants are allowed consume non-alcoholic, liquid refreshments ONLY in their rooms.*
>
> *Bathroom rota is affixed to bathroom door and MUST be adhered to.*
>
> *Tenants are responsible for the cleanliness of their own rooms unless alternative arrangements have been made.*
>
> *A standard level of hygiene is expected and the management have the right to inspect rooms without warning.*
>
> *Same sex visitors ONLY allowed in rooms and ONLY before 10 p.m.*
>
> *Tenants are requested to maintain a discretionary silence from 10 p.m to 7.00 a.m.*

The list went on and on. I stopped reading half way through and never went back to it. I had, after all, a room to explore. It was brighter than I had hoped. Being on the top of the house, its windows looked over the opposite terrace and on to rows of parallel chimney stacks. The view was elevating, but the room itself was deeply depressing. It was brown. The walls were cream but discoloured by a thick layer of age and dirt. The ceiling was oppressively low, weighed down with nicotine stains, and the furniture was veneer painted an unconvincing mahogany colour. Chocolate-brown cretonne curtains hung heavy with dust and matched the brown of the counterpane perfectly. Neither matched the elaborately patterned but badly worn orange of the carpet at all. The overall effect was of a three-dimensional coffee stain.

I had a bed, a small wardrobe, a clumsy tall-boy, a table, a stool, an armchair and a gilt-framed picture of the Sacred Heart. I unpacked slowly. I put the stool by the bed, the armchair by the window and the picture in the wardrobe. I drew the curtains back as far as they would go and took off the counterpane. I had done all I could in only half an hour and I was at a loss as to what to do next.

It was getting on for six o'clock and I was beginning to feel hungry. I rightly guessed that my father had not made any 'alternative arrangements'. I had a feeling that 'alternative arrangements' could be classed as an 'unnecessary expenditure', so I had no option but to go out.

I found the bathroom on the floor beneath mine and the toilet across from it. Both were empty. I read that I was allowed access to the facilities between 7.15 and 7.30 a.m. and again between 10.00 and 10.15 p.m. I inferred that there was free access during the uncharted interim.

I washed the grime of travel off in cold water – I had no shillings for the meter – brushed my hair and brushed my teeth. Back in my room I changed into my lightest, prettiest summer frock. I packed my dainty handbag with my keys, my comb, my lipstick, my purse and a fresh handkerchief. I put on my new white jacket – a belted, sophisticated affair that came with a matching skirt, which I considered flared beyond the fashion dictates of the season – and sat in my armchair looking out on the regular strips of chimney stacks.

I sat there, willing myself to move, and then I sat there imagining myself in a variety of cheap restaurants ordering my tea. I imagined my walk home, stopping outside shops, whose names I had always known, admiring their displays. I imagined a kind gentleman bending to pick up my dainty handbag after he had inadvertently bumped into me. I would be civil to him but I would make it clear, in a polite way, that I was not the sort of girl who usually talks to strange men and he would make it clear that I was the most beautiful woman he had ever seen.

And there I sat, little Miss Kelly's beauty, until it was dark enough to go to bed.

Chapter 2

I remember everything. Women, even young women, constantly complain about their lack of recall. It's always women. Men would never admit to such a dependent failing.

Old women gather together and laugh bravely at their lapses. They stand in the rain in slippered feet, they go shopping without money, they carefully pull their doors shut against the threat of drug addicts, before they remember the key left on the mantelpiece. They say they can remember thirty years ago but they can't remember yesterday. They remember their husbands as heroes and themselves as beauties.

Sometimes I envy them. I envy them their ability to glorify their youth and negate the tedium of their dotage. I am cursed with the ability to remember the gritty realism of all my yesterdays. And the past few have been deadly dull. Nothing but Scrabble and no-one but little Miss Kelly, and the two don't mix. The day before yesterday she used a blank and most of the S's for a score of fourteen. I think the word was 'misses', though it could have been 'masses' or 'messes'. I didn't bother to ask. I just shifted my priorities and amused myself by trying to let her win. I didn't succeed and it rained all day.

But, twenty thousand days before yesterday, it was sunny and sharp. It was the first day of my days with Harrie.

It was Sunday morning. My first full day at Benson's. I had hardly slept, the bed was too hard and I was too hungry. I was wide awake at six but I held on until my allotted time of 7.15 before I washed, brushed and dressed myself. I was still young enough to respect, without question, the authority of rules.

At 7.40 I arrived downstairs dressed in my lightest, prettiest summer frock, which was only slightly creased from its evening in an armchair.

I stood in the hall for a while and then I stood in the parlour for a while. It wasn't what I had expected. There was no clatter of meal noise to guide me, no friendly face to direct me, no smells, no carefully written notices.

I stood still and quiet in the parlour surrounded by its layers of lace and its delicate, highly polished clutter of furniture. I could almost feel the dust of the room settle on me, and I stared at an aspidistra pressed tight against a lace curtain. I didn't know what else to do, my mind was blank with the pressure of this new life. That's where Mrs Benson found me.

She swung in through the half open door to the hall, and stopped dead. She stared at me and then slowly followed my gaze to her aspidistra. While still looking at the plant she addressed me with dishonest nonchalance.

'Is anything the matter, Miss Moore?'

'No, nothing. I was just looking for the breakfast room.'

I answered politely, confident of a prompt and informative reply, but my confidence was short-lived. Mrs Benson snapped her head around to face me. The small of my back and my armpits melted under the full force of her regally arched eyebrows.

'The breakfast room is to your right as you step off the staircase. The door is slightly behind the staircase and, though panelled in the same wood as the rest of the hall, is not, in my opinion, totally obscured.'

I went to shuffle past her, but she stopped me with a firm, if minute, gesture of her hand.

'I had thought that the rules of residence made certain facts clear.'

She paused and I presumed she was waiting for an answer.

'Oh yes, very, yes.' I answered, even though I was a little unsure about what exactly she meant by 'rules of residence'.

'So you read them?'

'Oh yes, indeed, yes.' And I remembered the list hanging on the back of my door.

'So can you explain how you came to be in my private quarters without invitation?'

I couldn't. After an excruciating wait Mrs Benson continued.

'I was wary of taking in so young a girl, especially one with such tenuous references. I have a duty to my other guests as well as to myself and the memory and belongings of my late husband....'

It was then that I first saw Harrie. She was on her way to breakfast and had heard Mrs Benson's tone rather than her words. The parlour door had been left open a crack.

Harrie peeped in, and, after ascertaining that Mrs Benson's back was to her, she eased the door open and stepped silently into the room. Mrs Benson was too lost in her own rhetoric to notice and I was quick enough to interpret Harrie's wink as a request to say nothing.

I stayed silent all through Mrs Benson's tirade against furtiveness and dishonesty, and her long list of reasons for demanding privacy. Towards the end I was forced to hang my head and blink back tears. I was perilously close to uncontrolled laughter.

Harrie had started by standing directly behind Mrs Benson, arching her eyebrows into her baby blonde fringe and drawing her whole face up into a question mark. She sucked her lips tight together opening them sporadically to spit out the occasional, overly mimed expletive. Some of which I couldn't make out having never heard them before. But it didn't matter, the whole effect was too funny to question.

Harrie's pretty, childish face with its harsh, middle-aged expression was amusing, but it was the incongruity of her militaristic stance and her pink silk dressing gown that finally overwhelmed me.

She had grown tired of standing and mimicking and had disappeared into the hall, returning with an umbrella. She flung it over her shoulder and marched stiffly up to Mrs Benson's back. Once there she carried out an array of complicated manoeuvres ending in a simple, but accomplished baton-twirling exercise. I couldn't believe that this would go unnoticed – the wind from the flying umbrella would surely be enough to alert Mrs Benson.

It was then that I started to blink back tears, my mouth contorted and I lowered my head. I managed to muffle a snort of laughter with my handkerchief and it was taken for a sob.

Mrs Benson obviously felt that she might have gone too far. She concluded her lecture on a slightly softer note, telling me that for just this morning she would delay clearing the breakfast things for a quarter of an hour so as to give me time to eat in comfort.

Harrie took her cue from this change of tone and ran. She was nowhere to be seen when Mrs Benson led me across the hall and through the unmarked, panelled door at the far side. Though she was felt everywhere. The aged air of the hall had been unsettled. Its dead smell had been cut open with a fragrant slice youth.

The breakfast room was at the back of the house, down a short flight of steps but still below ground level. It was small and dark and smelled of basement damp. It was also clinically sparse. Mrs Benson obviously didn't feel the need to cheer her guests' mornings with friendly clutter or to confuse them with a varied selection of food.

There was a long table down the centre of the room and another to the side. The side table was laden down with crockery and lightly decorated with a choice of cereals (cornflakes or cold oatmeal), breads (white or grey) and preserves (black or yellow).

On either end of the long centre table there was a large, black teapot and a silent old lady. Harrie sat in the middle, within easy access of both teapots and both women.

The room was quiet when we came in. All three diners seemed remote from one another, gathered into their separate selves, but both old women jumped guiltily from their plates when they saw Mrs Benson.

She nodded at them and bent her lips upwards with effort,

but, when she turned to greet Harrie, she smiled with ease. Harrie, apparently oblivious to everything but her bread, ate on. I was surprised to note that she didn't even look flushed. She didn't look up during Mrs Benson's speech but I could see that she was composed and the side of her face, visible through the curtain of her hair, was as pale as it was smooth.

'May I present our new guest, Miss Moore. As this is Miss Moore's first morning, and as she is as yet unused to our ways,' here there was a pause to remind me of my crime of trespass, 'I have extended this morning's breakfast hour until 8.15. It will give you time to get acquainted. Miss Moore, may I present Mrs Boothe, Miss Charter Thomas and Miss Elliott.'

One old lady acknowledged me with a sidelong glance through her bush of grey hair and a hissed greeting of sorts. The other smiled at me with too much enthusiasm and launched into a welcoming gush.

'Fanny Boothe at your service. Call me Fanny. I'm on the first floor return. Drop in any time. Always willing and able for a chat, though when I was your age I couldn't sit still long enough for an introduction let alone a chat....'

But Harrie just smiled at me. She slowly raised her head and she smiled directly at the core of me. She smiled at my clumsiness, my blundering, my social awkwardness and she smiled with warmth. No-one had ever smiled at me before.

I smiled back. I smiled with all my might and, ignoring Fanny Boothe's prattle, sat next to Harrie and held out my hand.

'I'm Mary,' I said. As if that should explain everything, and then the mood shattered. Harrie laughed.

'Oh what a shame and what a name!'

She stood up and, with a sweep of her arm, cleared her lap of crumbs and caught her dressing gown tight around her hips. I watched her go, feeling suddenly and awfully lonely. Fanny Boothe shuffled up a couple of seats and settled herself directly opposite.

'So you're the new girl? My but you are a length of a girl. Tell me where are you from and do they all grow to that height around your parts? Not that there's anything wrong with a bit of height, I've had many a long friend myself. I'm sure you'll settle here as snug as you'd want, we're a friendly crew really even if there's some of us that are a bit odd.'

And she nodded over at the other elderly lady, Miss Charter Thomas, who was pulling at strands of her hair and muttering to herself quite fiercely.

I tried to avoid staring and I answered what I was asked and drank as much tea as I was offered, but did not eat anything. It was back in the days when good Catholics fasted on Sunday mornings, before going to mass and communion.

As well as being a good Catholic, I was a good girl, so I politely waited until Mrs Boothe seemed exhausted with talk before I left. I managed to get away before Mrs Benson returned to clear the meal, leaving the two old ladies alone in their silence.

I walked slowly back to my room, weighed down with the hours and minutes and seconds I had to fill before I could sleep again. That is one of the things that I miss with age, the agitation of youth.

Harrie was waiting for me outside my room. Still wrapped in pink silk.

'I'm so sorry for leaving you with the gnome but I find it hard to be civil in the morning and I do want us to be friends. I'd also rather not hurt the gnome's feelings. She is terribly sweet when she's not being terribly annoying.'

'The gnome?' was all I could think to answer. It was always that way in conversation with Harrie. She was always in control.

'Fanny Boothe, of course. You must have noticed how her chin almost meets her nose?'

I laughed and opened the door. I didn't know what else to do. It was a way of talking that I had no experience of. Where I came from young people were never disrespectful to adults. I hadn't seen anything to criticise in Fanny Boothe's face. I didn't know one was allowed to look for such things.

'You're shocked now, and so you should be. Fanny Boothe is a lovely old woman and I'm nothing but a cow. I take it all back.

The woman looks nothing like a gnome. In fact she is quite a beauty. And Miss Charter Thomas is as sane as a banker.'

I had closed the door and stood with my back to it. I was listening with all my senses. There was a sensuous taste of freedom about the way Harrie spoke. She dragged her limbs when she moved, even when she moved quickly, and she drawled her words when she spoke, even when she was excited.

She had walked before me into the room and was touring it, stopping every now and then to finger something. She did a full circle of inspection before she came back to me and the door.

'It's a bit gloomy, isn't it? You should ask old Benson to let you paint it. Paint it all white, I don't hold with colours on walls. White walls and large windows and let the sun take care of the rest.'

'Mrs Benson!' And I burst out laughing. I remember seeing a silver spray of my saliva glisten for a moment in the sun before it settled on Harrie. I was horrified. But Harrie just smiled.

'You should never take old Benson seriously. She drinks too much to stay balanced on a moral high ground. I'm on the floor below you. I'll keep my door open. Come and see me when I'm dressed.'

She walked past me and I caught a stronger sense of the smell that had lingered after her, earlier, in the hall. It was a smell I can still remember, a pure smell of youth and vibrancy.

I waited nervously. How long would it take a girl like Harrie to dress? I visualised the longest routine I could imagine. She would surely wash slowly. I couldn't imagine her hurrying over something so potentially luxurious. Then there would follow a complicated ritual involving creams and lotions, eau-de-colognes and talcum powder. And there would have to be – in my innocence I believed it to be a necessary badge of sophistication – a dab of powder, maybe some rouge and a natural shade of lipstick.

I sat back, relaxed into my armchair. I had just imagined Harrie groomed now. I tried to imagine her dressing. I reasoned that someone like her was bound to have mountains of clothes.

One would only buy a silk dressing gown if one had plenty of everything else. So I allowed time for choosing and preening, accessorising and co-ordinating. I was visualising a pantomime of shoe selection when Harrie burst in on me.

'Come on! I was sick waiting. What have you been doing?'

Chapter 3

That first morning with Harrie is the text on which I base my religion. We all of us like to think that we are here for a reason; the closer we get to death the bigger that reason becomes. I see my peers claw at their gods, their liverish hands pressed tight together in supplication and their mouths twisted around the mutterings of prayer and desperation. But not me. I've known for a long time that we are small creatures and we are here for small reasons. It is enough for me that I was born to live that morning with Harrie. It is a bonus that I have lived long enough to remember it well and it is a blessing that that morning lasted for most of the summer.

Harrie dressed was a surprise. I had thought of glamour, I had expected a lady dressed in adult confidence, but Harrie was different. She was wearing yellow, a fluffy Easter shade. Her dress clung to her, highlighting the fullness of her hips and the roundness of her chest. Her figure was fuller than fashion dictated, but fashion never applied to Harrie. She just was.

And there she was in front of me, pinning a battered brown skull-cap on to her blonde, curly head, and wriggling her yellow body into a sensible, tan raincoat. Her hair was barely brushed and her night's sleep was still gathered in the corners of her eyes.

I was even wrong about her use of make-up. Her skin was its natural colour, thin and pure white. It seemed that all her life blood had been sucked to the scarlet of her lips.

'Aren't you ready yet? Where's your hat? Where's your coat? Oh me! Here I go again. I'm bad and bossy. You might be busy. I never even asked you what you were doing or what you wanted to do. Well, here are your choices – you can do whatever you were thinking you might do, or you can do whatever I think you should do. I warn you I come with the second option but if your first choice sounds exciting I might come with that as well. Actually, to be honest, I think this morning you are stuck with me whether you like it or not.'

I did like it. I liked it very much and I laughed out my answer.

'I didn't know what I was going to do. I'd like to do what you think I'd like, with you. What's your name?'

And Harrie laughed.

I put on my white jacket over my pretty navy blue light frock. I pulled my flat brown hair back into my new straw hat with its bright blue ribbon. (I always disliked that hat. I considered it childish, and indeed I was right: broad rims on hats are there to frame the round faces of youth. My face, even then, could never be described as round.) I coloured my lips in coral pink and I packed my dainty handbag with keys, handkerchief, money, comb and lipstick. I did all this as quickly as I could, self-conscious in Harrie's presence.

And Harrie watched and laughed.

'Henrietta would you believe. The name belonged to my grandmother, and there it should have stayed. She should have taken it to the grave with her but she was too wealthy, so she left me her name and my mother her fortune.'

I was shocked. I had never heard anyone speak so openly about death or money. I had always believed such topics were vulgar, about as vulgar as scarlet lipstick on a young girl, and I had always believed that vulgarity was a vice. Until there was Harrie.

I laughed.

'They, the parents, took pity on me after she died and they were rich, so they shortened it, the name, to Harriet and when I reached the age of reason I took it that one step shorter and refused to answer to anything except Harrie and it worked, though I hadn't expected it to. If I had, I probably would have gone a horribly adolescent step too far and insisted on calling myself something gruesome like Lorelei and you would have nothing more to do with me.

'Ready? My, but you are smart and organised. I use my pockets and my winter mac.'

I was ready. I stood facing Harrie, well, looking down on her actually. She was about four inches shorter than I. I stood tall and awkward. I suddenly felt overdone. I wanted a mac, an old shoddy coat with huge pockets filled with nonsense.

Harrie laughed and linked my arm.

'I do envy you. You look so elegant.'

And we two walked down and out into the morning.

It was Sunday, at a time when everyone took their religion seriously and when almost everyone limited their socialising to those with the same birth-given religion. My father had chosen Benson's, so it followed that Mrs Benson and her tenants were Catholic. My mother would have considered anything else unseemly. And so Harrie and I had to start our day by attending mass.

Harrie took me to a church in the centre of town. She said the priest was so sweet it was a pity not to support him. This time I was deeply shocked. To the me of seventeen religion was sacred.

'Harrie!' I said. It was the first time I said it and the name fizzed on my tongue. My indignation was diluted by the thrill of the exclamation, but still noticeable.

'But he is sweet and terribly old. If we don't go this week he may not be there next week. He's also very quick. He does everything in such a rush, I'd swear he's on a gallop from death. And he's right too. I think death always comes quicker to those who stand still.'

I had no option but to laugh. She had replaced all that was sacred with an innocent, worldly humour. An attitude far more attractive to June and youth than morbid devotion.

To me Sundays had always come with oppression. One had to wear clothes that cramped movement, one had to sit in silence through the solemnity of Latin chants, one had to be reminded of a vengeful God and an imminent death, and then, one had to digest a lard-laden dinner at the unusual hour of three o'clock in the unusual company of aged relatives. My mother was always specific about the correctness of a late luncheon on a Sunday afternoon and the duty one had to one's less fortunate family.

But on that June day, I sat with Harrie at the back of the church, dressed in my lightest, prettiest summer frock under my new white jacket and giggled. We giggled at the old man sitting three pews up who kept falling asleep, and we giggled at his wife who began by poking him and ended up hitting him. We giggled at the altar boy who couldn't quite get into the swing of the incense, and I finally took a deep breath and giggled at the priest.

Harrie had been right. He was almost bent double with age and his voice was faltering badly. Most of what he said was muttered at his feet, but every now and then a forceful bellow would jerk everyone into awareness. There was, however, no sign of age about his movements. He bobbed and hopped and raced and ran through the mass. Another hour gained on death.

I nudged Harrie and Harrie whispered in my ear and both of us giggled and neither of us was struck dead. By the time we left the church. I was almost hysterical with evil-doing.

'And now to eat,' said Harrie, and I was confident enough to link her arm. 'There's a hotel nearby that does the best breakfast. It has a reputation for feeding the wrong sort of people, but in this day and age it is only them that are thriving so it must be feeding them well. Are you hungry?'

I nodded. I was very hungry, but I was shocked again. I was close to sobering up, reverting back to my own reality of Sunday. There was surely something sinful about the comfort of my clothes and there was no denying that a late breakfast was bound to ruin my appetite for a lard-laden luncheon. Besides, the mention of food had reminded me that Harrie had taken communion even though she had eaten earlier. And now she was taking us to a hotel of ill-repute.

I was on the verge of disentangling myself and making some

excuse, when a light, warm gust of wind hit me from behind. It twirled my skirt high around my knees and ruffled some loose hair gently against my cheek. It was a natural kiss of freedom. It was a reminder of youth and warmth and immortality. For the first time I was confident of my new decision-making capabilities. I chose to eat in a hotel of ill-repute and I chose Harrie. We walked on.

Harrie told me that she worked in a law firm as a secretary. She dismissed her job as boring and her qualifications as negligible, even though they did include a working knowledge of German and fluency in French.

'Oh ze French iz nozing, one must just know how to speek wiz ze zilly accent. And the rest of it! Don't remind me – it's too close to Monday. All week it's nothing but typing and suits. Lawyers turn fifty when they turn thirty, except for maybe one,' and her smile slipped sideways into a suggestion of a leer.

'But you! Hall's! You're lucky. You get to spend all day in heaven. Do you think it's worth my while asking for a job there? I doubt it, I'd say everyone who works there has to be tall and elegant like you.'

I walked on feeling taller, prettier and better employed than the qualified beauty by my side. It was always that way with Harrie – she created you in her own image.

We walked through the empty Sunday streets, weaving in and out of the occasional morning strollers, with our arms linked and our heads close in conversation. Harrie pointed out her office building. I asked to see her window, but we were on the wrong side.

She showed me the Metropole and the Savoy, landmarks of entertainment. We stood for a while outside the Savoy studying the posters and arguing the merits of Garbo's beauty. Harrie thought it embodied all that was perfect in femininity and I shyly argued the case for the rounder figure, the smaller woman and the softer hair.

Harrie laughed and tucked a loose curl behind her ear and we walked on. The hotel was just around the corner, shrouded in the heavy smells of cheap cuts frying in butter. My stomach growled into action and Harrie's must have felt as empty, because she suddenly broke free from me and raced ahead.

I hardly hesitated before I caught up with her and, with ease, outstripped her. It had been years since I had been so careless as to run on the street. When I had turned thirteen my mother had taken the time to tell me that such behaviour was no longer seemly.

We both arrived at the hotel panting and had to take the time to compose ourselves before we braved the formality of the reception area. It was a formality that I would never have been brave enough to face alone.

I followed Harrie through the heavy rotating door, past the splendidly uniformed men and down some steps to the right, and all the while I tried my best not to gape. I knew that I had to stare – I had never been part of such glamour before – but I also knew that I had a tendency to stare with my mouth opened as wide as my eyes. It was an expression that my mother called my 'simple ape gape' and it was one that I couldn't let Harrie see.

The Sunday breakfast room was the evening grill room, and was located in the basement, at a distance from the purity of the silver-service dining-room. It might not have been of a silver-service standard and its windows did only look out on a flight of basement steps, but it was the finest restaurant I had ever seen.

The tables were large, round and luxuriously spaced. Each was swamped in white, starched linen and had as a centrepiece a silver vase with either a red or a yellow rose and a sprig of greenery and, overhead, heavy chandeliers tinkled and sparkled with gleaming droplets of crystal, brought to life by the rising currents of hot air.

Even so, despite all the linen and all the glass, the place was filled with suspicious-looking types. Not that I would have noticed this myself, but Harrie's vicious humour and amazing powers of exaggeration combined to condemn them all.

Harrie had smiled at the waiter, so we were given good seats in the crowded room. We were sitting by a window that was wedged comfortably open and we were facing the action of thirty people eating. Harrie told me that most of them were creatures of the night and that this was their supper. And I believed everything Harrie told me.

'You can always tell a prostitute,' she said, 'by the drabness of their hats, coats and gloves and the brightness of their nail varnish. You see, they don't want to stand out for the police, but they want their men to know what they are. So, they wear scarlet nail varnish on the longest nails they can grow and flash them about, but, if they see anyone who might not be a client, they slip on their gloves and hey presto! they magic themselves into nothing more sinister than a late-night stroller.'

There were three women at a table close to ours. They were all wearing plain, if expensive, summer bonnets and they had no gloves, due to the season, but they did have obvious nails. Nails that were perfectly manicured and brilliantly coloured.

Harrie saw me stare and stopped speaking while I strained to catch what they were saying. The conversation seemed to be about prices, but such innocence did nothing to dissuade Harrie and if Harrie wasn't convinced of their legality neither was I.

'They seem to be talking about the price of bacon,' I whispered across the table.

'Why that proves it,' Harrie replied in full conversational volume. 'Bacon is a street word for hotels that charge by the hour.'

I had no idea what she meant by that, but her tone implied that I should and so I didn't ask and Harrie moved swiftly on.

'You can always tell a gangster by the wideness of his tie and the brightness of his suit. Young gangsters wear dark suits and old ones wear light ones but they both wear loud, fat ties. There's no doubt about it, that man, the one by the door, is a young gangster. Probably a rich one too – the unsuccessful ones have scars.'

'A gangster! What does a gangster do?'

'Why, everything that is dangerous and bad, though they are terribly glamorous. They would never harm a lady or a gentleman but they are ruthless to their own who break the code.'

'Do you know any?'

'No, I wouldn't know any. None of them work in law firms.' Harrie laughed. It was always that way with Harrie. When there was nothing else to laugh at, she laughed at you. But I didn't know that then. I thought I had stumbled into a social underworld as complex and sinister as Chicago's.

'And how do they get their scars?'

'Why, if they're found out doing the dirty on each other, of course. There are some crimes that demand a fate worse than death and disloyalty is amongst them.' She spoke flippantly but her words rang clear in my head. They still do.

I was gaping around, absorbing as much of the seedier side of life as I could, when the waiter came to take our order. He spoke with terrifying politeness.

'Good morning, ladies, may I help you?'

Harrie hmmed a little, but chose with confidence. When he turned to me I snapped my menu shut, and with a cinematic twang said, 'That sounds good.'

'What sounds good?'

'What Harrie... what she said.'

I felt as if I had been caught out in a lesson undone. The menu had been too elaborate to read and the formality and the proximity of the waiter made it impossible for me to concentrate.

'So it is a full breakfast twice. And would madam like tea or coffee?'

I hadn't expected to be questioned at all but I think I might have managed if he hadn't thrown in the madam. There was no need to call a seventeen-year-old child madam. It was cruel.

'Oh, I don't mind. Whatever is easie..'

'We'll have a pot of tea for two.' Harrie spoke abruptly, dismissing the waiter with her tone and she had the grace not to laugh. She just twirled the conversation on beyond embarrassment.

'See that old man in the corner, the one in the light checked suit? Don't look now.'

But I looked and nodded.

'He's a master gangster, a king of the underworld. They call him the butcher because of the amount of bacon he owns.'

And I gaped even harder and Harrie, for some reason unknown to me then, laughed and laughed.

'What's so funny?' I asked earnestly, and perhaps my sincerity sobered her into giving me a reason for her laughter that I could understand.

'What do you think of Mrs Benson?'

She screwed her face up into a tight-lipped parody of our landlady's, and she spat the question out in mock anger. We both laughed then and I added, as best I could, to her caricature. I took my hat off and scraped my hair up into a bun then, holding it in place I arched my eyebrows as high as they would go.

'Miss Moore,' I said perfectly enunciating each syllable. 'My reasons for privacy are threefold, namely, one, to preserve my sense of identity, two, to maintain a discreet but necessary distance from my paying guests and three, to ensure that those same paying guests are not tempted by my trinkets. Some of which are obviously of considerable, and not only sentimental, value.'

'My, but you're marvellous,' Harrie enthused and I, flushed with her praise, persisted with my imitation long after I had run out of material.

But it didn't matter. That meal, for me anyway, was as satisfying as it was exciting. I ate a marvellous amount of food, fried brown and crisp, I studied the eating habits of prostitutes and gangsters, I experienced the giddy excitement of making Harrie laugh and I listened carefully to everything she told me.

She told me that Fanny Boothe read racy romances, had a very public crush on the doctor and had a pastime that was too bizarre to mention so early in the morning.

'She's either the walking dead or a hypochondriac. No-one could need medical advice so frequently and still live. And she may insist that she is a religious woman but no woman of prayer could survive the blushes brought on by even one paragraph of one of her many books.

'And no I can't tell you what she does all day – you won't believe me, and, even if I prove to you later that I am right, our friendship will never recover from your first impression of me as a liar. Trust me, first impressions, no matter how untrue, have a tendency to linger.'

She told me that Miss Charter Thomas came from a very wealthy family but they had farmed her out because she was a little simple and a lot embarrassing.

'Old Benson keeps her sedated and threatened with the mad house. And a good job too. If she was left to her own devices, God knows what she would get up to. Seemingly,' and I shuffled closer, bending my head to catch the whisper. 'Seemingly, the last straw for her family was when she ran naked into the dining-room, at dinner time, screaming "My skin is my fur." But I don't think that that is the worst thing she's done – at least she did that in the comfort, and relative privacy, of her own home. No the worst thing she did by my reckoning was take up watercolours. Lord, you would never believe that a paintbrush could cause such pain. I only saw her work once and my eyes still sting with the memory.'

As for Mrs Benson, well, according to Harrie, she drank all day and sang all night. 'Honestly, any time after midnight, you can hear her singing as hardy as a sailor. It's almost impossible to keep a straight face when she's giving out to you the morning after you've heard her sing a few choruses of "The Girl with Come-All-Ye Eyes". Remember that next time. But you would have to feel sorry for her, she tries so desperately hard to be proper.'

We, well, Harrie, ordered another pot of tea and a plate of tiny, delicate cakes. We stayed talking for almost two hours and only left when the staff started pointedly setting out places for the grill-room's special Sunday lunch.

'We had better go,' said Harrie suddenly, glancing at her

watch. 'The staff are close to kicking us out and I suppose we can't really blame them. It wouldn't do at all if they allowed their lunch guests to mingle with their breakfast guests. Politicians and prostitutes never see eye to eye in daylight.'

We paid a cashier on the way out and I mortified myself by yelping at the price. My share was more than I had with me and far more than I ever imagined a meal could cost. I hadn't realised that the hotel was the most exclusive in the city. Harrie must have noticed my alarm. She paid the full amount without question and left while I was still struggling with my coat. She was waiting for me outside.

'I can give you half a crown now and I'll give you the rest when we get back.'

I held out a sweaty coin and thrust it at Harrie's cool, white hand.

'You'll do no such thing. I asked you out and I insist on paying. It was a special welcoming treat and I did force you out of the comfort of your morning. Let's just say that you owe me a date when you get your first pay packet.'

She sounded so reasonable, I put my coin away without further argument. It was always that way with Harrie. She made you feel generous by taking.

'Now Em dear, you don't mind if I call you that do you? It's so much cuter than Mary, it suits you much better.'

I shook my head, delighted. It was my first breakfast out and it was my first petname. I felt re-invented.

'If you follow this road to that second junction and turn right you'll be in sight of Benson's. If I'm home early enough I'll call in to you.'

I must have missed something. She was leaving me. My face obviously sagged.

'Oh, didn't I mention it? I have a date that I just can't get out of. No offence, but even though it is perfect weather for a girlfriend and an ice-cream, this is one date that I really don't *want* to get out of.'

And she was gone. It was always that way with Harrie. She eased you into dependency but she never let you trust her.

Chapter 4

There's nothing more to say about that first Sunday. I walked home quickly, back to the security of Benson's. Without Harrie's guidance I was suddenly afraid of the threat of prostitutes and gangsters. I kept my hands out of my pockets and, when lingering by the side of the road waiting to cross, I made an elaborate show of displaying the purity of my naked nails.

Once home I stayed there. I sat alone in my room for the rest of the day and all the long, lonely evening and all the dark, empty night. I stared, mesmerised by the tiered, clustered pattern of chimney stacks that stood bold against the blue sky and later, melted into the dirty, city dusk. Even now if I close my eyes I can recall the shape of that view and remember the giddy feeling of hope and height that went with it.

Harrie never called in to see me. Even though I stayed awake until after twelve. Even though I sat with my light on.

Harrie had been right about Mrs Benson. Long after the street had settled down to sleep I could hear the thumping strains of rousing songs coming from what I deduced was her parlour. And, while I sat up in my bed, desperately trying to keep awake, I heard the songs melt into the whine of maudlin tunes. I took some comfort in the knowledge of how horrified my father would be if he could hear the carry on of my 'surrogate mother', but it was cold comfort with no-one to share it with.

Mrs Benson's wailing merged with the spasmodic groans from the old house and the sepia light that was all my single bulb was capable of, so that when I finally fell asleep, I was haunted by every nightmare cliché. I woke grey and weary, having been hounded into the dawn.

I was to be at Hall's Central Stores at eight-thirty to attend a charade of an interview. The job was mine already, that had been arranged, but Miss Walsh, the manageress of haberdashery, had insisted on an opportunity to look me over. If I had two heads and a limp she was under obligation to take me on, but no-one had taken the time to tell me this, so, when the reality of what day it was hit me, my initial sense of greyness spread to my stomach.

I washed in lukewarm water, after wasting a shilling in the meter, and dressed in my best frock. I was hoping to see Harrie at breakfast but there was no-one in the dining-room when I arrived, and though I stayed for as long as I could, no-one showed up. I was to learn that this was the norm.

Mrs Benson always laid out the breakfast table the night before. She made an effort not to drink on a Saturday night – she thought it sinful to stay in bed late on Sunday – but she had no such qualms about weekdays. Mrs Boothe and Miss Charter Thomas only ate breakfast at weekends, They liked to keep up the pretence of a social life and they had only energy enough to pretend on the weekends. During the rest of the week, they were happy to stay in their beds until noon.

And Harrie? Well, she did have a social life, so was always up and eager on the days she didn't work, but on working days she clung to her bed until the last possible moment and then ran straight to her office.

I could never do this, though I did try. I thought that such behaviour was the height of sophistication. But I needed a breakfast to settle my stomach in the mornings and I needed time to dress with care and to pinch my cheeks into life. Harrie always looked beautiful freshly tumbled out of bed. She never had to worry about the secrets of grooming.

After that first morning I never bothered waiting for her, I never expected her, but on that first morning I needed her badly and was deeply disappointed when she didn't appear. I was almost tempted to call to her room but I hadn't the nerve or the emotional strength to weather even the politest of rejections. After the magic of the previous day I was back to myself. I bruised my hip on the side of the table, knocked over the dregs of my tea and chipped the side of the sugar bowl. After that final, and probably billable, offence I ran back to my room, terrified of being seen by Mrs Benson.

I left to walk to Hall's Central Stores, giving myself plenty of time. But I walked at a great pace, my nerves driving me on, and I arrived almost twenty minutes early. My father's map had been far too precise to allow for error and I had allowed myself time to get lost as often as I expected I would.

For twenty minutes I lurked around the waking streets. I bumped into delivery men, blocked the scurrying commuters with my aimless wandering and I was sure I alerted the attention of the two traffic police on duty. I could see them point and I could almost feel the hum of their voiced suspicions, even though I did make a point of fluttering my natural-coloured nails in their direction.

It didn't help that it was a warm morning and that it was gathering itself into the haze of a scorching day. My dress, already limp from the heat, was becoming moist with my confusion. I stood at a distance from Halls, staring at a window display of Aran knitwear and even the wool warmed me, it seemed to reflect an extra dimension of heat on to my face.

It was twenty-five past eight and there was a crowd of girls and boys gathering outside the shop. They called to each other and broke into groups, lighting each other's cigarettes and playfully jostling their more beautiful companions. They all looked beautiful to me. Young and vibrant and confident. They were to be my colleagues. I waited, wishing them gone. I was far too shy to approach them but I was terribly nervous of being late. What if they all stayed there until nine o'clock? What if I was supposed to go in early through a back door or something?

I was just about to brave all and approach a singularly unjostled girl when the situation was saved by the arrival of a sombre, young man dressed impeccably and carrying an umbrella at a sombre, mature angle. He was, obviously, not one to take a chance on the weather, even on a day like this, and he was not one to engage in the frivolity of twirling his umbrella, or even swinging it in time with his gait. He was wearing a dark suit with a broad, bright tie, and, despite his conservatism, and my eventual lack of naiveté, I always thought of him as a successful gangster.

He opened the main glass doors of Hall's Central Stores and the crowd of girls and boys surged around him and melted into the building. I took a deep breath, cleared my mind and began walking. The same sombre gentleman stopped me before I managed to get through the door.

'We are not open. We do not open until nine o'clock. Our opening times are clearly stated to your left. Good morning.'

He spoke abruptly and went to close the door on my opened mouth. He didn't respect me as a customer. Even in my best summer frock and my new white jacket, I wasn't considered grand enough to shop in Hall's Central Stores. And I didn't blame him. I thought that I would never be lady enough to face such a shop with confidence. Four huge plate-glass windows and two glass doors with brass trimmings were enough to dwarf any seventeen-year-old.

I spoke quickly, without thinking. I had to, the weight of the door was bearing down on me, picking up momentum, swinging itself shut at great speed: 'I'm to work. Miss Walsh. I'm to be interviewed.'

The sombre gentleman caught the door before it snapped shut. 'Why didn't you say so? You must be Miss Moore. Come along in. There's a lot to do before opening. Miss Lawrence will show you to your locker and your department. You were to be here at half eight.' He produced a watch from the folds of his suit and snapped it open. 'Seven minutes late on your first day is not a start that augers well, now, is it?'

I didn't get an opportunity to answer but I doubt that I would

have had the nerve to point out that that being the case he must
have been five minutes late himself.

To signify that our discussion was over he snapped his fingers
high above his head and miraculously and immediately Miss
Lawrence appeared. I had never seen anyone so cowed by
authority as poor Miss Lawrence. She almost made me feel self-
assured. She ran up to us, and, pausing to bob at the sombre
gentleman, ran on. I presumed I was to follow.

She led me through the sumptuous arrangements of handbags
and scarves and around the still shrouded counters filled with
soft leather gloves, huge linen handkerchiefs, shiny diamond
pins, crystal bottles of scent, deep puffs nestled into smooth
compacts of powder and plain black or gold tubes filled with
thick, matt lipstick. We walked in silence, our steps muffled by
the deep pile carpet and any inclination to converse smothered
by the smooth hum of activity surrounding us.

The babbling crowd of youth that I had seen gathered outside
the shop was transformed into a hive of sedate and responsible
workers. They slowly drifted out from various side doors,
uniformly dressed in brown and white, and went about their
business with perfectly co-ordinated ease. It all seemed very far
beyond me.

Once we left the shop floor Miss Lawrence slowed down a
little and took the time to turn and smile at me.

'It's a bit of climb', she said. 'Five flights up to the lockers.'

She must have known from experience not to say any more.
The stairs were steep and long. By the time we reached the top
we were both breathless, but I was gasping. There was no lift for
the staff. The public lift only went as high as the four trading
floors and we were not encouraged to use it.

Once she had caught her breath, Miss Lawrence told me this
and a lot more in a surprisingly bitter tone. I had expected her
conversation to match the meekness of her appearance. I
followed her listening carefully, eager to know anything that
could ease my situation.

'Of course Mr Hall has his office on the fourth floor, wouldn't catch him mixing with us or breaking a sweat. Oh that was him that let you in, didn't you guess? Ol' stuffed shirt! But he doesn't scare me. I use the lift when I want and if he gets in and sniffs at me – you'll get to know his sniffs – I just say that I can't use the stairs on account of my monthly weakness and you should see the colour he goes, red as a cherry in season.'

I burst out laughing. I could not imagine Miss Lawrence opening her mouth to the deity who was her boss, let alone insulting him with biological details.

'Yeah, as red as a... as a nun in a brothel.' She misunderstood the reason for my laughter and I didn't correct her. I was tactful enough to know that she might not be so happy about being laughed at.

'Here's your locker and here's your uniform. You owe for that. They take the money out of your first week and if you harm it they charge you double for a new one. They pay you back the money when you leave and give them back the clothes if, of course, they're in mint condition. But what's the use of that? The way Hall works us, and with the pennies he pays us, we're none of us leaving except in a cardboard box.

'And here's the staff room. Hall gives us a cup each, some broken ol' ashtrays and every month enough tea to last a week and he thinks he's a lord to do that much. And here's the ladies'. It's always smelly. Mrs Hopkins the cleaner thinks she's too good for cleaning toilets. She does the managers' one and leaves ours, so they don't care and if we complain they'd probably just hand us a bucket and mop and tell us to get busy, I wouldn't put it past them.'

I walked mutely behind her, holding on to my brown uniform dress with its white clip-on collar and cuffs, trying to assimilate as much as I could.

'What's the matter with me? And what are you doing letting me babble on when I don't even know your name? I'm Anne, Annie to my friends. And you?'

'Em, it's short for Mary but everyone calls me Em.' From then on I made sure that everyone did.

We shook hands as potential friends do and she left me to get dressed. I never did get to call her Annie. I don't think we ever spoke again, or at least never so freely. I don't know how it got out, I never said a word, but by the end of that first day it was common knowledge all over the shop that I was related to the Halls. And anyone connected to the Halls was not to be trusted.

Not that they weren't friendly, they were, but they were just polite to me. They were absorbed in each other. They met by arrangement to gossip on the back stairs at all times of the day, they chose their best friends to link and go to lunch with and loud, squealing groups of them poured out of the building every evening and into the cinemas and coffee shops. Some of the lads went drinking, returning to pick up a date for the night. I was aware of their couplings and jealousies and victories and defeats, but was never included in them. Perhaps if I had tried I would eventually have been winked on to the back stairs to hear the latest news. But I never tried – I didn't mind my isolation, because I had Harrie.

I changed quickly into my uniform, and was surprised by how well it suited me. I had never thought to wear brown before. I had always seen it as a middle-aged colour. At seventeen, fool that I was, I fancied it made me look sophisticated. Carried away by delusion I sailed on to the third floor and stopped the first girl I met.

'I'm looking for Miss Walsh of haberdashery.'

'Well you've found her.'

On closer inspection the girl had shrivelled into a woman. Her tone and her lingering body-length look deflated me completely. It was my first taste of what it was to work.

'...and you will do well to match your tone to your situation. If you wish to pose a question you do so, you do not demand by statement.'

I spent the whole day close by Miss Walsh. She didn't like me. Maybe it had been my initial tone, but I suspect that she had been made aware of my connections. And I suspect that it was she who made everyone else aware. She started on me immediately.

'A few ground rules, Miss Moore. Dress is very important to Hall's image, so I have to insist that you straighten your collar and invest in some darker, more respectable stockings.

'Your hours are from eight-thirty to five-thirty with a forty-minute lunch break and two ten-minute tea breaks. Your time-keeping this morning has been noted. Any further lapses will be deducted from your salary.

'You will be given a card which will record your movements. Any attempts to clock in for a friend or have someone do the same for you will be punished with immediate dismissal.

'As well as your half Saturdays, you have one half Wednesday a month. These hours may be varied coming up to Christmas.

'Sick leave must always be accompanied by a doctor's account and you are entitled to no more than six weeks' paid sick leave a year.

'These are the pins. They are displayed by descending width. You are to keep the widths separate at all times and you must acquaint yourself with their uses so as to be of optimum help to the customer.

'The ribbons are sold by a price per yard. Prices vary and are listed here. Should a customer want only a fraction of a yard I presume you will be able to calculate the cost....'

She circled the free-standing, waist-high haberdashery counter as she spoke, fingering and pointing and straightening displays as she went. I followed and did try to concentrate but I suppose I only heard about a third of what she said. By eleven o'clock I had only energy enough to concentrate on my headache, for very little fresh air made its way to the third floor. She did finally let me take a tea break but she accompanied me and continued her lecture.

'Tea is provided by the management once a month and no more. Management is not liable for any crockery that you choose to leave in the canteen.

'You are expected to clean up after yourself, dispose of any waste and wash any delph you use. The overall cleaning of surfaces is the responsibility of the junior staff and is organised by rota. You are expected to check the rota weekly.'

When I think of it, she continued her lecture for the whole six months I worked with her. It never did her or her beloved haberdashery department any good, though. I never did learn the uses of pins or the available colours of ribbons. I always messed the displays of thread and one horrible morning I upset a whole tray of needles. I was never enthused by thimbles and I never learnt how to roll a professional-looking ball of twine.

I also never got used to the complicated network of overhead pulleys that connected every counter with the floor cashier, and the cashier, a Mr Newby, never got used to my haphazard way of dealing with moneys and receipts. My customers would always have to wait while I ran off to do the transaction by hand. It led to large queues at the haberdashery counter, making it look more popular than it was. My mother once told me, years later, that Mr Hall noticed this and mentioned it to Miss Walsh. I doubt she had the courage to put him straight. After all, I was her responsibility, so any failure of mine reflected on her. So at least the powers of Hall's Central Stores considered me a success, even if the middle management knew me for the incompetent I was.

In time I took a kind of pride in my uselessness, it upset Miss Walsh so much. I also took pleasure in the fact that she was unmarried and must have been all of thirty, that she was stringy rather than slim, that she had the beginnings of facial hair and that her lower jaw was very prominent. It helped me to think of these things during her daily, usually public, rant at me.

It was through Harrie that I learnt to survive like this. It was for Harrie that I worked each new humiliation into a funny story, thereby distancing myself. Without her I would have bowed lower with each blow. And where would I be now? And what about poor little Miss Kelly? Where would she find some one else willing to pay for her furry little presence?

Chapter 5

I wonder if I am being fair to the me of seventeen, to the pre-Harrie me. It is hard to be objective about a memory of oneself, especially when one has no respect for the subject of those memories. But I think I am doing all right. I have described myself as gauche, plain, inept, talentless and timid. I could drag in some subsidiary failings, but they would probably cloud the issue, and I refuse to fall into that old-lady trap of clouding the issue.

When dealing with the past, clarity and honesty are essential. Otherwise we are merely dealing with the fantasies of the aged. I can swear by my clarity – I remember everything only too well – but honesty is always difficult when dealing with subjective material.

However, it is honest to say that after my first day at Hall's Central Stores, I arrived at 26 Marsh Lane at 5.50pm in tears. I remember the time because my watch fell into my dainty handbag while I was searching for my key, and I remember the tears because I stopped searching to watch them fall and discolour the red felt that lined my bag. Harrie found me there at approximately, and I say approximately as a concession to honesty, 5.53pm.

'Oh goodness was it that bad? No, don't answer – it was a stupid question. Obviously something was that bad.'

She linked my arm and opened the door. She led me through it, across the hall and up the stairs talking soothingly to me all the time. Between her arm and her flow of conversation I was mentally and physically supported to my room.

'I remember *my* first day at work as a complete nightmare. All that typing that I had sworn I could do! I spent all my time trying to work with my back to everyone else so that they wouldn't see me using two fingers. Of course they found out and there was one hell of a scene. It ended with me threatening to take my skills elsewhere and them laughing and asking me what skills I was talking about and of course I couldn't answer that question so I just stormed out in what I hoped was flurry of drama. Now that I look back on it, it was probably more like a dramatic sulk.'

'But what...?'

'Oh, I got another job soon enough and so will you. There are other shops, maybe none bigger than Hall's, but there must be a few that are better.'

'But I don't need a new job. I didn't walk out.'

'There, then life isn't so bad. Here we are at your humble little palace. You go and wash your face and what not and I'll expect you in my room in fifteen minutes. I have in my bag the cure for Mondays and luckily I have enough to give you a double dose.'

I laughed and she ran back to her room. It was always that way with Harrie, she always put your problems into perspective.

I washed my face and I combed my hair. I carefully applied some coral lipstick, pouting and stretching my lips to ensure that no natural colour was showing. Then I stepped out of my best frock and into my Easter dress of two years previous. It was a little dated and a little babyish, but it was yellow.

I patted my hair and I patted my lips. I swirled in front of the mirror and I ran down to Harrie. Miss Walsh seemed very far away, sandwiched between the past and the future. I no longer believed in her.

Harrie's room was at the back of the house. I had expected a room similar to mine but decorated in style and filled with beautiful things. I had been right, but I didn't have the imagination or the experience necessary to visualise the impact of Harrie's concept of beauty and style.

Her room overlooked the garden, which was long and narrow and overgrown, but was filled with that hectic buzz of nature one only finds in the city. Birds and bees and ants and spiders and

mice and foxes and trees and brambles and roses and weeds all
clambered for life in this dense patch of greenery. Harrie's room
was on the second floor and the clamour reached that high. Her
window was open and her room was filled with busy sounds and
heavy smells.

Her room was like mine in that it was large and square. But it
was so bright it seemed to have exploded outwards. The walls
were white and the furniture was painted a deep, creamy ivory.

Her bed was swamped in a white throw and accentuated, in a
sexual way, with a selection of white and scarlet cushions. They
were scattered over the length of the bed, tumbled against each
other, looking invitingly comfortable. The norm, at the time, in
bed-sitting rooms was to arrange your cushions, if you had any,
in a neat row against the wall, thus disguising your bed as a
settee. A bed was considered too personal a piece of furniture to
be on view.

Aside from the bed, she had a wardrobe and a dressing-table
along one wall and, in front of the window, there were two
armchairs and a low table. She was kneeling at the table, busy,
with her back to me when I came in, and she didn't turn around
for a moment. I stood silent behind her, staring.

Her curtains were thick velvet. They were white, but fell into
the depth of green and yellow folds. They were far too big for
the window. They spread wide on either side of it and collapsed
into an arranged, tumbled mess on the floor.

The wardrobe and the dressing table both had huge, crystal
clear mirrors, and there was another on the wall opposite them.
The mirrors reflected each other and the space and the objects
between them.

There was a white vase in front of the mirror on the dressing-
table. It was filled with the thick greenery of offensive weeds and
its image echoed around the room. Harrie said that she never
picked flowers, that they were too delicate and that they died too
quickly.

'And who can have respect for anything so wishy-washy? I
pick weeds because the flowers need all the help they can get to

survive and because I find it exciting to have something so masculine in my bedroom.'

I have since tried this argument, and many variations of it, on little Miss Kelly and all the Miss Kellys before her, but it never sinks in. I have always been cursed with rooms filled with dahlias or some such nonsense.

Still with her back to me, Harrie asked, 'Do you like it?'

'I love it. I can't believe it.'

She turned then and smiled and drew my attention to the details that I had initially overlooked. The silver brush set, the lace nightie draped over her pillow, the delicacy of the stitching on the silk kimono that hung on the back of the door, the silver perfume bottle with its mermaid top and the two thick, long beeswax candles in their deep-blue glass holders. Finally she stepped clear of the low table and I gasped again.

It was covered in a heavy linen cloth with a band of gold trim. It was an altar to tea. Despite Mrs Benson's rules, it was filled with food.

'And now,' she said as she stepped clear of the table, 'may I present my cure for Mondays. Sardine paste on white rolls and chocolate cake with plenty of strong tea.'

We both laughed. It was always that way with Harrie. She could make a ceremony out of the most mundane event.

It wasn't the food that had made me gasp. It was the setting. A round silver teapot sat squarely on a tripod, above a lighted gas canister. That was the centrepiece. The meal was spread around it.

The rolls and the cake were arranged on strawberry pink plates with gold floral trimmings, plates that glowed transparent when held up to the light. The butter and the sardines and the cream and the sugar were all in different coloured bowls of a variety of sizes. The two tins of sardines were almost lost in a blue bowl big enough to mix a cake in, and the milk covered the bottom of a deep red pitcher that must have been two pints high. The summer sun, golden and lying low beyond the garden shone directly on to the table lighting up the colours of that meal.

That is why I gasped and I laughed because the simplicity of the food was so incongruous with its setting.

I ate more than my fair share. All I had eaten all day had been a slice of Mrs Benson's day-old bread at breakfast time. I hadn't had the courage to follow the confident, babbling workers into one of the cafés and I didn't want to sit in the staff canteen staring at the chatting, munching groups. So I had spent my lunchtime wandering in a nearby park. Adrenalin had kept me over-active all day, but once I relaxed hunger caught up with me. In between mouthfuls I gushed my enthusiasm and praise for the food, the setting and the company.

'Isn't some food just perfect? I never knew that it was possible to fit foods to days until now and I love your room. My mother always used to say that white walls look unfinished, but they don't, do they? And she was always so careful to have everything matching but it's so much more colourful when nothing does. And you're so nice to ask me again, especially after yesterday, and it was supposed to be my turn to ask you somewhere.'

Harrie watched and laughed.

'You needed your cure,' she said and I blushed with the realisation that I had been greedy and ungrateful and I guiltily remembered my mother's rules of seemly behaviour.

'I'm so sorry,' I began, but Harrie stopped me. It was always that way with Harrie, she never could tolerate apologies, she always understood your motivation. Even at the end I'm sure she understood why I did what I did.

'You know,' she said, 'we should meet for lunch tomorrow. I'm sick of sandwiches with dusty old ladies. Our canteen is full of dusty old ladies and if I don't eat with them I have to eat on my own, and I hate eating on my own. If it's fine we can eat in the park and if it's wet we'll eat in the best tea rooms in town. Maybe we should eat there anyway. Do you think that would be a better cure for Mondays?'

I laughed at the thought of being hungry again and at the thought of anything tasting better than sardine paste and chocolate cake.

'No,' I answered, 'nothing has ever cured me as thoroughly as this meal.'

'Well, just to be sure,' she said. 'Come on and finish that cake. Then I think we should visit Fanny Boothe. She needs a chat a day and you would love her room. You still don't even know what she does.'

I finished my cake and followed Harrie, but I wasn't happy. I didn't see the need to involve an old lady in our evening, even one who had a fascinatingly secret hobby. I had been secretly hoping to go to the pictures. I was even planning on making the suggestion myself.

I wasn't to know that Harrie disapproved of the cinema. Not in a moral or even in a serious way, but in a Harrie way.

'Don't you find all that glamour just a little tedious?' She would say. 'Don't the movies make you ache for a ketchup sandwich and a pair of wellies? Except, of course, for westerns and they just make you ache to be elsewhere.'

I would laugh and spend my evenings with Harrie in parks or coffee shops or deep in books. And I am pleased that I did. Now I have the memories of all those evenings, all those conversations, instead of only the empty memories of films.

Mrs Boothe's room was worth a visit. I should have trusted Harrie. In time I did. In time I came to follow her without question. Mrs Boothe herself wasn't quite so interesting. She talked. She talked with all the tedious detail of lonely, unbridled age. Perhaps I am guilty of that now, but at least I have the manners to keep my conversation to myself, occasionally inflicting it on Miss Kelly, but then she is paid to look interested. Harrie wasn't, but still she listened and encouraged and I fiddled and stared.

The room was as large as any in the house but Mrs Boothe had inverted her space. It was the opposite of Harrie's and of all I had just decided was proper in the world of taste. It was an old woman's room, cluttered and fusty and messy and slightly smelly. It smelled of soap and face powder and gin and urine, but I got over that. I lost myself in its contents. It was a museum of a life.

Every inch of floor space was covered with occasional tables covered with doilies covered with pictures peeping from behind ornaments. The walls were textured with curling, faded postcards and ragged-edged pictures of Victorian sweetness. Mrs Boothe ripped calendars apart as a hobby. Perhaps she even thought of it as an art form.

But what was most interesting about Mrs Boothe and her nest was spread all over a sizeable centre table. Mrs Boothe was sitting at it when we came in and she gestured to Harrie to sit opposite her. I stood awkwardly for a while before I sat away from them, on the bed. I didn't mind. I was too far away to be expected to contribute much to the conversation, but I was close enough to see everything Mrs Boothe was doing.

She was sculpting in wax. Her table was spread with newspapers and cloths, a selection of stunted-looking knives and lumps of cheap waxy candles. She was moulding and hacking them into shapes of inanimate objects, and moulding and hacking them very badly. Almost everything she made looked like a box but she held them up for view and described them as all sorts.

There was a box chair, a box radio, a box teapot, even a box scissors. Harrie applauded them all with obvious sincerity, and I did as Harrie did, though I am sure that I must have sounded as patronising as I felt. Mrs Boothe was delighted with Harrie's praise and she barely registered mine. She chattered on, blooming under the warmth of Harrie's attention and I eventually sat silent and jealous, watching.

'But you couldn't say it was hot for this time of year,' she said, 'now could you? Or could you? Maybe it's only old bones. The sun doesn't reach them so easy. Now this is a clock, a mantel clock. The summer of '92 now that was a summer, or was it '93? And this is an inkwell. My mother tried painting the porch and the paint just wouldn't dry. And this I did yesterday – it's a teacup....'

We stayed for half an hour and then Harrie gracefully closed the visit.

'Goodness! Fanny, you are too polite. You should have told us the time and turned us out. The pair of us sitting here as selfish as you please taking up all your time and depending on you to entertain us for your trouble. You have to be harder next time, and next time we'll call earlier and not be keeping you up half the night.'

We left Mrs Boothe staring in confusion at her clock and the still warm sky out her window. It was only half-eight but the power of Harrie was such that I wouldn't have been surprised if Mrs Boothe hadn't gone to bed, convinced it was midnight and cursing her god for mismanaging his days.

Once outside the room, I laughed. I laughed because everything was suddenly young and fresh again, because I was alone with Harrie again and I laughed because I saw Fanny Boothe as ridiculous. But Harrie didn't laugh.

'She's a lovely woman,' Harrie said. 'She has had a long fall from a privileged youth and she has ended up soft and sweet when she could have ended up bitter.'

I stopped laughing and suddenly felt small and dirty and angry at Harrie. I wasn't to know that. All I had seen was a daft old lady fumbling about in her daft old world. But Harrie broke my mood before it gathered strength. It was always that way with Harrie – she could divert you before you were aware of your own direction. She linked me and squeezed my arm.

'You know her sculptures?'

I nodded eagerly, it was just me and Harrie again. Just us two.

'She only ever does things because she believes in the power of voodoo. She says that the soul is a delicate thing and can very easily be robbed. She thinks that a wax model of a person or an animal can entrap their spiritual beings, and she says that she wouldn't feel comfortable living with a collection of wax cages.'

This time I waited for Harrie before I laughed.

She disentangled herself before we reached her room and I

took this as a dismissal. I turned to go back up the stairs, but Harrie stopped me.

'Oh stay a while,' she said. 'I feel flat and dull and in need of company. You know,' she said. 'I have black moods. They're darker than those blues that people sing about, and I feel one coming on now.'

I swelled with pride and followed Harrie into her room. I talked and Harrie questioned and she seemed gay and happy all evening. I prided myself that I had kept the blackness at bay and I worked hard to do so. I started with my impersonation of Mrs Benson and I worked my way through my parents and a few singularly nasty teachers. I grew hoarse with the effort and Harrie grew hoarse from laughing.

'Oh Em dear,' she finally stopped me, 'I can't take much more, and I don't believe for a minute that anyone, let alone a respected teacher, could be guilty of such a grating voice and such a severe squint. Though now that I say it, I do remember meeting a woman like that once. I think she was Dutch, she had the most marvellous English and the prettiest face in repose but once she started talking her eyes squeezed almost tight shut. Seemingly she had a great big dark secret that she had sworn to herself never to reveal to anyone but she didn't trust the words to stay inside, so, whenever she had to talk, she screwed her face up tight in an effort to keep the secret in.'

'And did it ever come out?'

'Oh, I'm sure it did. Secrets are only ever made for telling and promises are only ever made for breaking. It proves their existence. It is like that age-old riddle, if no-one can hear it, does a tree falling in a forest make a noise? Does a secret never betrayed really exist? Was a promise never broken ever made? We'll never know because respected secrets and binding promises are never spoken of.'

I didn't answer, of course I didn't – I was only seventeen. It didn't dawn on me that I was supposed to laugh. We sat on together after that in companionable silence, curled tight into her armchairs and, when our limbs seized with cramp and exhaustion, we stretched out on the bed.

It was strange, that silence. It was deep and happy and belonging to a much older relationship, but it settled on us easily. Bound in the comfort of our own silence we listened to the world around us.

Harrie's room, being a floor lower than mine, was a floor closer to Mrs Benson's apartments. We lay on the bed, surrounded by Harrie's heap of scarlet cushions and listened to the rise of our landlady's voice. Every now and then we deciphered some lyrics and giggled.

I was happier then than I had ever hoped I would be. I lay quiet by Harrie and felt her weight trust itself to me. She shook me before I fell asleep and threw me back to my own room. I didn't see the necessity of parting, but I did as I was told. Most of the time I did exactly what Harrie told me to do.

Chapter 6

Hall's Central Stores, Miss Walsh, haberdashery and my brash colleagues had all disappeared during my evening with Harrie. By morning they were back, diminished, but they were back. As I dressed, in yellow, and as I ate my slice of stiff bread and drank my cup of strong tea, they grew. As I walked past the hordes of bicycles and curling trams they loomed large and solid.

It was to be that way every morning. It was to be that way every moment without Harrie. And, do you know, it may still be that way. It has been a long, long time since I have allowed myself the luxury to remember Harrie in this much detail. The memories cost too much. They turn my heart inside out. It is not the sort of thing one confesses to the little Miss Kellys of this world, but inside this shell of propriety and position, inside this old lady, there beats the heart of a scared old woman. It is ridiculous to think that deep inside that experienced heart there is, somewhere, a little girl who believes that lack of nail varnish is sufficient proof of virtue.

My second day at Hall's was much as my first, and my first was much as my last. There is a grinding repetitiveness about menial jobs that eventually denies one the ability to catalogue memories successfully. Fortunately I wasn't at Hall's long enough to have this happen to me. No matter how cluttered my head is with the tedious details of my days in haberdashery I find that preferable to waking up at sixty-five and realising that the last clear memory one had was forty years old.

On that second day in Hall's, Miss Walsh greeted me with pursed lips when I arrived on the floor. I was three minutes late. I never bothered to check my pay slips but I wouldn't be at all surprised if Miss Walsh hadn't tried to deduct three minutes' worth of wages.

And being late wasn't my only crime. I had left a counter uncovered the previous night and my collar was more crooked than yesterday. I didn't think it worth my while to try and explain that no-one had told me to cover the counter and that I couldn't find a mirror to check my collar in. The other girls kept mirrors in their lockers.

Gillian from soft furnishings listened to every syllable of Miss Walsh's tirade and when it was over winked at me in sympathy. I would have preferred it if she had just minded her own business. She was still around, and still listening, when Mr Newby, the cashier, questioned me at length about a woman who had rung complaining that she had been short-changed.

I stood with my head bowed listening and agreeing, concentrating on working the situation into a suitably funny story for Harrie at lunch in the park. It helped that Mr Newby was slightly hunched, and that Miss Walsh was slightly furry, but it wasn't enough.

I could feel the familiar flush as my blood heated with shame. My eyes watered and my mind froze before the fear of failure, and fail I did.

I spent that morning in a panic of incompetence. I miscounted pins and muddled threads. I ran back and forth to the cashier box, delaying every transaction. I broke an overhead pulley and I inadvertently kicked Miss Walsh, blackening her stockings.

But I was whistling when I ran upstairs to grab my dainty handbag – it was too hot for my new swing coat – before racing off to the park. Gillian stopped me on the stairs, calling after me. She asked me to lunch and I answered, rather abruptly, that I had a date. She had followed me down to my step at this stage and clumsily patted my shoulder.

'Don't let them get you down,' she said. 'They always do it to the new girl. They're just knocking you into shape.'

It was an offer of friendship that I would have leapt at once. But now it was different – now I had Harrie. I drew away, rather abruptly, and answered, rather abruptly, 'Thank you. I'm afraid I'm in a bit of a hurry.'

She stepped back, looking offended. I don't think I meant to be rude. It was just that I had no interest in her now that I had Harrie, but I didn't admit that much to myself. I blamed her winks for my rudeness.

Harrie was waiting for me by the main entrance to the park, which was grand and arched. She was absorbed in licking a large ice-cream. She had squared it and was trying to keep it symmetrical. It was all she had for lunch, and it seemed such a young and glamorous choice it turned me quite off my plans for a full dinner in one of the cafés I had passed.

She didn't see me until I was close. She wasn't looking at anyone, but I was. I could see how the passing men took the time to watch her and how the women patted their hair as they passed her, or straightened their skirts, or stood a little taller. They subconsciously recognised Harrie as competition.

Not me, though. I knew that I could never compete with blonde curls, rosebud features and feminine curves. I wasn't in the running.

'Em! You scared me.' Harrie looked up suddenly, probably drawn by my stares. 'What a day for a park and what a waste for an office. How was your morning? Any better? No, obviously not. Come on with me and tell all.'

It was a large park filled with city workers starved of sunlight. They lay where they fell, gazing up at the sky. It scared me. I had never seen such abandonment in adults before. I had never seen such lengths of leg or so many bared arms, and I was never overly fond of the flesh of strangers.

Harrie led me past all that. I followed her through a maze of narrow pathways and away from the crowds. She stopped at an old bandstand. It was rusted and rotten and surrounded by the overgrown remains of a once formal garden. Very few people took the time to walk so far to drape themselves around such an eyesore. But Harrie did, and so did I.

She ran on to it, and, catching on to one of its poles, swirled herself into the centre in that cinematic musical way. She broke into a mimic of a love song, twirling her voice around the clichés of 'love' and 'dove', 'June' and 'croon', clutching her hands tight to her breast and rolling her eyes in an ecstasy of passion.

I laughed and followed her. I ran to the steps and dramatically stopped still. I held out my arms and echoed her nonsense in a double-chinned baritone. I ran up three steps and ran down two and stopped again. Then I ran straight up to her. We sang her nonsense in unison and I waltzed her around the full circle of the bandstand. We broke apart panting and laughing, and squealing when we saw that we had been observed by three ladies and two gentlemen. But it was our bandstand and our day so it didn't really matter.

'And now,' I said in my best forthcoming-attractions voice. 'The terrifying tale of a morning in haberdashery.'

I crouched down and shuffled, Quasimodo-style, to centre stage. 'Miss Moore, a word,' I hissed. 'It is the policy of Hall's Central Stores to try to avoid practising fraud when handling the moneys of our customers. You can take the time to practise fraud at home but don't try it in Hall's Central Stores unless you have the art perfected....'

I did them all, down to Mr Hall and his umbrella and Gillian, with her oversized ears and elaborate wink. Harrie laughed and clapped and howled for more.

I was prepared to do as much as she wanted, and I was just building up to my Miss Walsh finale, when I stopped. I noticed that two of the three ladies had fallen silent and were obviously listening and I had an uneasy feeling that they were capable of complaining about my behaviour. I had mentioned Hall's and haberdashery frequently and loudly and I couldn't chance any more complaints, not even for Harrie. So, I closed my show, and joined Harrie on her step.

'What'll we do tonight?' I asked. 'Will we go for a walk? Will you show me the river?'

'No,' she stood up and brushed herself down. 'I have a date, and rather a nice one too.'

Her tone didn't encourage further questions and so I didn't ask any. It was time to go back to work. We walked together to the arched exit in silence. My good humour had melted into my hunger and the horror of the afternoon ahead of me and, after that, the tedium of an evening of loneliness, but Harrie swung along by my side unaware of any tension. It was always that way with Harrie – she tried to charm her life by only confronting the pleasant things in it, an enviable if not very realistic approach.

We stopped at the arch before going our separate ways and Harrie must have seen my expression. She squeezed my upper arm and kissed my right cheek.

'I hope tonight's date is as nice as my lunch date,' she said, and I laughed politely and truly believed that it couldn't be.

But it must have been even nicer. It was such a nice date that Harrie stayed out longer than I could keep awake. Though maybe I fell asleep sooner than I thought. I was exhausted.

My afternoon had been much the same as my morning, a series of minor mistakes, until, just before closing, I was sent to serve a hot, fat woman. I think her name was Jones. I should remember for sure, because she was a frequent customer, but I can only remember her hats. They were wide-brimmed and ridiculously ornate. She wore them with pride and she trimmed them herself. That's why she was such a frequent customer.

That day she was looking for ribbons in shades of cerise. Well I can laugh about it now, or I could if I had someone to share the story with, but back then it wasn't considered funny that I had never heard of cerise. To the me of seventeen, cerise sounded remarkably like a Greek island.

'What do you have in cerise?' said Mrs Jones.

I replied in my best 'madam is always right' voice, 'Hall's is a family store with only one branch. As of yet we have no plans to expand into Greece.'

I spoke slowly, assuming that the old bat in the mad hat asking stupid questions must be a bit slow. She didn't give me the same respect. She assumed that I was being intentionally cheeky and insisted on carrying the matter further. She shouted for a manager and Miss Walsh came running. Gillian shuffled closer and the remaining customers were silenced by her imperious tone.

'I need to speak to someone in charge. Who is this child's superior?'

Miss Walsh seemed all too pleased to accept the responsibility and she seemed genuinely delighted when the situation had been explained to her, and beyond her, to the collected shoppers and the winking Gillian.

'Miss Moore, you will apologise and you will report at once to Mr Hall. This sort of behaviour is clearly in breach of the statutes of your probation period.'

'But I didn't know,' I wailed. 'I thought it was an island.'

Fear of facing my mother having lost my job stripped me of any self-respect. My sincerity must have been blatant and Mrs Jones had heart enough to withdraw her complaint. She laughed it loudly away and insisted that Miss Walsh did the same.

'Leave the poor girl be,' she said through her gasps for breath. 'Sure we can't hold her responsible for what she's ignorant of.'

'Well, if you are sure,' said Miss Walsh very reluctantly.

'Oh, I'm sure all right. Just look at the young thing.' Everyone did and I looked at my shoes. 'She meant no harm. You can tell by her blushes. One thing a woman never can fake is her blushes and if she could there'd be many more men taken to the altar than are already sacrificed.'

'It is very good of you to take such an approach.' Miss Walsh creamed out the words. 'But please be assured that we at Hall's pride ourselves on the calibre of our staff. Miss Moore is new amongst us and has a lot to learn. Obviously a lot more than we initially thought.'

'And isn't she in the right place for learning? Don't worry, dear, I never learnt a thing before I turned twenty that was worth remembering.'

I mumbled a 'thank you' to her for highlighting my ignorance in public and returned to serving her. Eventually the listening crowd returned to their own hum of activity.

Mrs Jones might have had the grace to laugh about the affair, but she had the bad manners never to forget it. From then on she called into Hall's at least once a week to ask for such nonsense as a yard of Paris.

I walked home that evening, even though my feet were aching from standing all day. I didn't feel confident enough to face a tram, and the proximity of all those people who knew the magical rules of life, including the names of nuances of colour. But I did feel hungry enough to brave the rough masculine noise of a fish-and-chip shop. I bought myself a twist of chips, wrapped in newspaper, and raced on, so as to be home with them still hot.

Chips proved to be a foolish choice when trying to smuggle food into a room. I should have known that the smell of them would bring Mrs Benson running the moment I opened the hall door.

'Miss Moore, perhaps you have not yet had the time to sufficiently study the set of house rules I furnished you with. In case you need reminding, let me refresh your memory. They clearly state that non-alcoholic liquid refreshment is all that is permitted in the rooms.'

She took a step back and, curling her lip slightly, looked me up and down before adding, 'You will of course appreciate that there is an ever-present threat of vermin infestation in an establishment such as this.'

She would have continued but I had had enough. I was hungry and tired and she was a drunk. So, instead of replying, I sang the chorus of one of her late-night songs. She looked momentarily confused and then walked away, tight-lipped, with what seemed to be anger but what I know now to have been shame. Perhaps even the me of seventeen saw it as shame, because I knew I wouldn't tell Harrie what I had done. But I do remember that I enjoyed my tea enormously.

The rest of the evening hung heavy, though. I called to Mrs Boothe but the visit only lasted for about twenty minutes. She was sitting at the same table surrounded with the same mess as the previous evening. She seemed pleased to see me but I did notice the disappointment in her face when she saw that I was alone.

'So where's dear Harrie?'

'She went out.'

'Quite right too. A young girl should go out as often as possible and stay out as long as she can get away with it.'

I stood listening, a failure to popularity and a failure to youth. Eventually Fanny motioned me to sit. I sat where Harrie had sat and listened as Harrie had done. But the conversation didn't flow with Harrie ease. I had to mention the weather to start her off and I had to ask her what certain objects were to keep her going, and even then she limited her answers to just the bare facts.

'And this?' I would say, pointing to something.

'A hat.'

'And that?'

'An umbrella.'

Finally we both sank into the silence of her dusty old room. When I finally stood up to leave I knocked over a box cup, and I banged my head retrieving it, jostling Mrs Boothe's careful mess of wax and newspapers. She didn't seem sad to see me go.

I returned to my room but couldn't face the depths of its brownness, so I decided to take a walk. It was a pretty city. Even now it is a pretty city, but then it was almost beautiful. It had all a city should have, wide roads and tree-lined streets, glamorous family establishments and colourful crowded tenements. Back then it was still small enough to contain a breath of the country. The parks were loud with birds, the air was sweet with flowers and the river was still clear and clean.

I took care with the application of my lipstick and the angling of my hat. I still had some small hope in my dream of that handsome man and the upset handbag. But I didn't even have that after my evening's walk.

I expected people to be busy during the day. The force of the crowds had initially scared me, but I had got used to them quickly. I was even beginning to feel a sense of camaraderie with them, and that evening I discovered why.

The commuting crowds commuted alone. They stood in trams staring straight ahead, they walked singly *en masse* with their heads pushed forward and down, and they stood impatiently on the paths waiting to cross, their minds filled with their separate days.

But the evenings were different. The evenings were filled with friends. Groups of young men lounged at corners watching groups of young girls parade before them. Couples, linked in togetherness, wandered aimlessly. The cinema queues grew longer and louder. Older women walked with definition, lost in their familiar, definite conversations. A few single girls and boys waited nervously around landmarks. But none of them waited very long. They were always collected with enthusiasm.

There was nowhere for a single girl to lose herself, no place where her solitude wouldn't be seen as a mark of failure. I walked hurriedly on for a while, as if I was late for an appointment, and then I walked hurriedly home.

I spent the rest of the evening writing a letter to my parents. It had to be informative but not overly detailed, enthusiastic but not silly and, above all, grammatically correct. My father was very proper about the art of letter-writing. He saw it as a feminine art and one that should be cultivated.

'You can always tell breeding in a woman by two things,' he would say. 'In her style of expression and in the shape of her nose.'

He held my mother responsible for the slant and the bulge of my nose, and he admitted that he couldn't do anything about them. But he took my letter-writing personally. It was, after all, his time that had bullied me and his money that had educated me.

I spent a gruelling two hours composing a one-page letter that was diverting and respectful, informative but impersonal. I was exhausted when I finally crawled into bed so I may have slept immediately, but I could have sworn that I was awake after midnight and that Harrie still wasn't home.

Chapter 7

I don't think I saw Harrie again for a few days. Though it may have only been a couple. Days without Harrie always seemed to stretch. I've been without her so long now, no wonder I feel old. I wonder if we all of us have our voids that age us. Is age the loss of something more tangible than youth? And does age only come to the old, because the old, being around longer, have had greater opportunities to lose things?

I definitely didn't see Harrie the following day. I remember because I was so disappointed. I had expected details of her date. I went to the bandstand for lunch and she wasn't there. I waited for longer than I should have but she never came.

Gillian had asked me to lunch again and I had refused again. I had tried to do so politely, but I knew by her reaction that I had been as abrupt as ever. It was probably a foolish move on my part. I should have realised that the new girl, who didn't know what cerise was, couldn't afford to act aloof. I couldn't bring myself to care though. I couldn't conceive of eating lunch with Gillian when Harrie might be waiting at our bandstand.

And I definitely didn't see Harrie that night because I remember the length and emptiness of that evening. I didn't visit Mrs Boothe, I didn't go for a walk, I didn't write to my parents, I didn't eat fish and chips. I sat in my brown armchair drinking lemonade and watching the light fade behind my rows of chimney stacks.

That was life without Harrie. It's very much the same today, except I look out on gardens instead of chimneys, drink brandy instead of lemonade and have no horror of tomorrow. But, then again, I have no hope for tomorrow either. Back then my horror was Hall's Central Stores and my hope was all that life could offer. One well outweighed the other.

I think it must have been the following evening that I saw Harrie again. I remember I was sulky with her because she hadn't turned up for lunch that day either. It had always been my way to sulk. I was never confident enough to confront anyone with an emotion as healthy as anger, and so I always ended up nursing it. It was one of the many things that my parents found annoying about me. I bumped into Harrie when I returned from work.

She was looking through the letters on the hall table and Lord knows what I was doing. Probably walking backwards counting my toes because I did, literally, bump into her. She laughed and I greeted her formally, with what dignity I could muster, 'Good evening, and how are you.'

She laughed again.

'Lord, Em, did you just swallow a judge in full costume? You sound so terribly serious.'

It was always that way with Harrie, she had no respect for any mood that did not reflect her own at the time.

I was angry then. I was young enough to be possessive about my humours and I had no intention of surrendering such a worthy sulk.

'I am no more serious than usual. I was merely enquiring after your health.'

Harrie opened her mouth wide to answer, she was surprised at my tone and may even have been angry. We might have argued, but we were disturbed by Miss Charter Thomas.

She shuffled past us on her way to the dining-room, lost in her private world of delusion and medication. She was dressed in an ancient, sumptuous, scarlet velvet gown and her hair was wrapped tight into a green bath towel. We stood silent as she passed us and strained to hear what she was saying. I said that she was muttering 'The duck will spoil.' But Harrie said it was 'Muck and toil.'

I don't know about Harrie, but I certainly didn't have the

vocabulary then to understand what she was really saying. During my entire stay at Benson's I only ever heard Miss Charter Thomas say this one phrase and it was years after I left before I translated it as 'Fuck yis all'.

But it didn't matter that we didn't understand what she said. It was enough that she was dressed so oddly and that she lumbered as she walked, knocking against the wall and rebounding against the furniture. Harrie grabbed me and pulled me to safety, out of her staggered path.

'Careful there, Em,' she whispered. 'I know from experience that one knock from that lady can leave a dent in you for a week.'

I laughed in response, a cosy, hand-over-my-mouth, shared laugh.

Everything was all right again. All that mattered was that we were together, a unit against an outsider. It was the joy of this, more than the peculiar spectacle of Miss Charter Thomas, that made me laugh.

Harrie linked me and we walked up to her room. She went in first and left the door open, assuming that I would follow her. I was delighted by such familiarity. In only a few short days we had attained the level of intimacy that negates formalities. I shut the door behind me and was fool enough, or confident enough, to remember my sulk.

'Where have you been?' I asked. 'You've been out late the past two nights and you never turned up at our bandstand today or yesterday.'

She turned suddenly. Her body snapped around. It was almost as if I had hit her. I immediately recognised the flaws in my question. I had said 'our bandstand', I had assumed that she had no-one else to meet for lunch and I had demanded information about her evenings that she had never thought to volunteer. I backed away from my mistake as agilely as I could.

'I thought you said that you had lunch at that bandstand every day. It's just that I passed it the last two afternoons hoping to see you. I was hoping to pay you back for last Sunday's treat. Remember, you said I owed you a date?'

Harrie listened to me in silence and left a slight pause before answering.

'I only go there sometimes.'

She wasn't going to tell me where she had been and she wasn't going to tell me the details of her dates. I knew that by her clipped, guarded reply and I felt a rush of panic. I had allowed her see to the depths of my need and there is nothing less attractive than need. Even the me of seventeen was wise enough to know that.

'Of course, well, I'm a little tired. I think I'll go and put my feet up for a bit. Later, I was thinking of going out for something to eat. If you're not busy perhaps you would let me treat you, and if you are could you recommend somewhere. I'm still awfully lost.'

I must have hit the right note of casual lack of interest, because Harrie responded well.

'If you're paying, I'm going,' she said. 'Give me a while to cement my beauty and I'll meet you in the hall. You rest your feet while I do my face and we'll probably be ready at the same time. Your feet cannot be more tired than my face is ravaged.'

We both laughed and I smiled all the way to my room where I spent a frantic few minutes tearing through my wardrobe in the hope of finding something comparable to Harrie's style of haphazard charm.

It was almost impossible. My mother believed in the seemliness of perfect co-ordination. I finally settled on a green skirt with a cream blouse from another ensemble. I loaded the pockets of my new belted jacket with the contents of my dainty handbag and then, just for good measure, I put on my jacket, sat in my chair and wriggled some creases into it.

If Harrie noticed anything when she met me she never said, though she did raise an eyebrow when I asked to borrow her lipstick. Perhaps she knew that scarlet would never suit me or perhaps she thought that the act of sharing a lipstick was too intimate, but either way she hesitated. Again I was sensible enough to sound uninterested.

'Unless you think I look all right without any. It's just that I can't find mine anywhere.'

'By all means use mine.' She obviously saw that my flesh-coloured lips needed something. She handed me her lipstick in its gold brocade case and I stood in front of the hall mirror and slowly kissed my mouth with the colour of Harrie's lips.

I must have looked ridiculous walking along beside Harrie, a gangly length of imitation, but I didn't mind. It was another magic evening. The beauty of the city that I had noticed and envied when I was alone enveloped me when I was with Harrie. She walked me deep into that pit of excitement that youth finds at night, in urban areas. It was all new and wild to me, and with Harrie I was involved but safe.

She showed me the famous pubs where the famous men drank. She mentioned politicians, actors and writers with ease, pointing out their birth places. I nodded, impressed but ignorant. I didn't recognise any of the names. She walked me by the river and we leaned over the wall to watch the trees and ourselves reflected in the twilight of the water, and, beyond those superficial images, we watched the dark and strange movements of the occasional fish.

She showed me the houses where famous people lived and landmarks where famous people died. One of these was a lamp-post where a revolutionary had been hanged a hundred years previously.

'And his hanging corpse is said to appear every year on his anniversary to give his murderers a chance to cut him down. There's not much chance of that happening now. If his murderers didn't take the trouble to do it during their lifetime they're hardly going to go to all the bother of getting out of their graves to do it now.'

And we laughed and I hurried past the post and we turned into the brightness of the shopping district. She loitered me past the store windows where famous people shopped, and pointed out the restaurants where they ate. She finally stopped outside a cheap, loud café and looked to me for approval. I nodded. It looked wonderful to me.

The place was crowded, so we sat in the back. The table was sticky with a day's use and the waitress was worn with a day's work, but I can still taste their omelettes and I can still sense the excitement of those surroundings.

It was a dingy and easy café, and Harrie and I made it ours over that summer. It was called Martine's and it was run by hard-faced, fast-talking women who spent their lives running with plates of food and shouting orders and insults at hidden cooks.

I loved it. To the me of seventeen it was young and cinematic. It was always full and it was always loud, if not with conversation then with the roar of music that was belted out of the wireless. We used to eat our food in time to the tunes, and laugh hysterically when it came to the chorus and we would have to eat frantically.

We never bothered with the other diners and they rarely bothered with us. Once or twice some men would make subtle advances, but we never encouraged them. I didn't, because, in my innocence, I didn't believe girls did such things unless they were thinking of getting married and Harrie didn't, because Harrie was in love. She told me all about him during that first meal at Martine's.

I began the evening with questions. I knew nothing about Harrie before then, but she knew everything about me. She had wormed my life out of me with casual questioning and flattering attention. It was always that way with Harrie. She gave you time, but took your confidences and left you feeling indebted.

I flatter myself that I played her at her own game. But that's not strictly true. My motivation was too selfish. Harrie was always interested in the person she was dealing with. I was only interested in my involvement with one specific person. But selfishness is a great motivator. I teased and probed with an enthusiasm that couldn't be deflected, and finally Harrie gave in. She began answering, rather than asking questions.

I began with her family.

'Your parents?' I asked.

'My parents what?'

'Well, anything. What do they do?'

'I would hope that they do as they please.'

'And where do they live?'

'Unfortunately, where they always have, a dreary little place.'

'Do you see much of them?'

'There was a time that I couldn't open my eyes without seeing one of them. But that wasn't my fault, I was in a cradle. And even then I didn't see that much of them. They were always very proper. I probably only ever saw their extremities, you know, their heads and hands.'

I laughed as long as politeness demanded and then I continued.

'But now? Now do you see much of them?'

'Well the 'them' bit would be a little hard. One of them died.'

I gasped. I hadn't expected such an answer and was shocked at the tone.

'Oh don't worry, it was only a father and it was a long time ago, before I was born. I never really missed him. A girl can always find herself another father or at least another daddy.'

I didn't ask what she meant. 'Well what did your father do? How did he die? I mean, if you don't mind talking about it.'

Harrie laughed.

'He did what most men do. That's why I'm here. I'm only joking.'

I had tried to hide my expression, but she must have seen it. I suppose she had fun shocking me, I was so shockable.

'You're right not to laugh – it's a bad joke. No, he died in the war, the Great War, in the first month of it, I think. I have my suspicions that he died from a fever rather than from a fit of bravery. Well, even a fever would be noble enough, I only hope that he didn't die from a court martial, they're usually fatal you know. My mother has always avoided giving me the details. Not that I deserve them, he's not really any of my business. I was barely conceived when he enlisted.'

'But he is your father.'

'No, he could have been my father, but all he ever was was a memory of my mother's, and not an entirely pleasant memory at that. And he has no-one to blame but himself. He insisted on volunteering to fight for king and country when he should have been happy enough to volunteer to bring home a salary.

'But I am being mean. Maybe he did volunteer to fight for a cause he believed in. And if he did, I should be proud of him, and I'm sure I would be if he hadn't left us so badly off.'

I had struck oil. With only a little encouragement, and, eventually, with only the encouragement of my silence, she told me it all. And it all was as far from my provincial upbringing as I could have wished for, and I believed every word.

She said that her parents had been wealthy, but that her father had speculated unwisely and had left his affairs in disorder and his family in debt. She told me that she suspected her father of running to war as a coward, and that that suspicion hounded and shamed her. He died a proud death, but left his wife and child to live dependent on charity.

They were taken in by her father's brother and Harrie was sent away to school when she was very young. She didn't see much of her mother from then on and formed no real attachment for her.

Though she was proud of her mother's beauty and wit, Harrie was, fundamentally, ashamed of her. She told me that she had reason to suspect that her mother and uncle lived as man and wife, and though her uncle wasn't married, he would never marry her mother. It wasn't so much that he didn't respect her, though that was part of it. It was because Harrie was a girl and her mother was unable to have any more children.

'And if you ask her, that's the excuse she would give for the gin, but that's a whole other story...' and Harrie laughed and moved on with her tale.

After her schooldays, her life seemed to have descended into a jumble of anecdotes. She told me that as she had no real home other than school, her graduation literally launched her into the world. She moved straight into the unskilled job market and the seedy lodgings that went with menial wages.

'But luckily, I didn't have to put up with either for long.' She brushed aside what must have been a traumatic experience with typical Harrie lightness.

'I trained at night and worked by day and regretted nothing except the thrill of coming out. I do so love the colour white and one can only get away with wearing it when one is seventeen, and even then, at times, it sits uneasy with the morals of some.

'I trained as a secretary and halfway through the course I met with the marvellous opportunity to travel, get paid and mingle with the best of European society and all I had to do was mind the occasional child. So I dropped out of my training, unfortunately before I had really mastered anything, and hot-footed it to Paris.'

She told me that she had lived in Paris for quite a while, minding children for an aristocratic family that travelled very properly, spending each season where each season should be spent, and she had delightful stories of roguish men and upper-class eccentricities to prove it. But perhaps all she had was a delightful imagination and a gullible audience. I even believed the story of the grandfather and the actress.

'They were a lovely family, Em. A lovely old family and old in such tight circles usually means inbred. It is cruel to say, but I had suspected as much when I first met them, they all looked so alike and they all looked so like pigeons, so the behaviour of the grandparents didn't come as so much of a surprise. The children's grandfather lived with them. He was kept in shame in a suite of rooms on the top floor and was never mentioned to guests, or indeed to me, until I started asking questions about things that I definitely heard go bump in the night.

'My employers finally admitted that they were minding their mad old penniless relative because his sane old penniless wife would have nothing to do with him. She had pronounced him dead and had buried an empty coffin in her garden to mark the occasion. She felt that she had no choice after he had embarrassed and bankrupted the family.

'He had chased after an actress, following her through France and out into the wilds of Europe. Eventually he caught up with her in a restaurant in Austria. The story has it that she loudly refused to drink with him and he had bowed his head and replied. "Madam I do not wish to keep company with you, I merely wish to offer you my all. I realise that being old I can no longer offer you strength, being a Dubois I could never offer you beauty and being dim I could never offer you wit. But I am a lawyer and so I can offer you my fortune, and this I do if you would be kind enough to accept it."

'And she did but she still refused to drink with him.'

I listened with my eyes wide and my mouth gaping. Once again, I had no conception that I was expected to laugh, so Harrie laughed for me. Her breadth of experience and her nonchalant way of mentioning people and places had rendered me incapable. I couldn't even finish my meal, I was too full of wonder.

Harrie had a hundred such stories that overlapped and contradicted each other, but were all too thrilling to question, even if I had thought to do so. Questions, I am sure, would only have revealed exaggerations. When I had time to think about her stories I deduced that there was a core of truth behind them all.

She must have known Paris well, she was so enthusiastic about its beauty and her French was definitely confident and sounded fluent to me. But then the phrases she dropped, on my request, might have been anything from a nursery rhyme to a menu.

She must have had some secretarial training because even if her typing was appalling she knew shorthand.

She must have travelled a lot, because she confidently mentioned small towns all over Europe, and families and jobs in towns all over the country, and she must have been in her mid-twenties though she looked almost as young as I was.

But, despite her prettiness, her age, her diverse jobs and the many friends that she mentioned, she was alone. Nothing and nobody in her life ever seemed to have got close enough to stick. Nobody except Mr James Hamilton that is, and he didn't have much choice because Harrie had made up her mind to stick close to him.

'He's a dream,' she told me. 'He's my dream and he just walked into the office one day. Straight out of my head and into my heart, because you know, up until then, I had always been careful not to fall for dreams, they're so forgetful and so untrustworthy.'

I had laughed, but Harrie was serious.

'Can you be sure that he won't turn into a nightmare?' I asked. I was still laughing, but Harrie took the question seriously.

'Oh yes! He's not handsome enough. Villains are always too goodlooking, and James is, well, intelligent-looking.'

She told me all about him with pathetic enthusiasm. Of course the me of seventeen didn't appreciate the pathos. I only saw the romance and felt the chill of exclusion.

Mr James Hamilton was from good middle-class stock. He was well educated and was finishing a law degree. He was going to be a solicitor, just like his father, and he was learning the ropes in the same firm where Harrie worked as a French-speaking secretary.

He was tall and slight with a large nose and thinning hair. He was very serious, though sometimes he told funny, inoffensive stories. He read Greek stories in Greek and Italian stories in Latin and all of two newspapers a day. He wore glasses when he read.

He had quite a lot of money and a healthy appetite for good food and fine wine. He constantly complained that neither could be found outside France. He smoked a pipe in the evenings, even though he obviously hated tobacco. He did it so that his tweeds would smell as tweeds should.

He had no fondness for animals or children though he did always assume that he would leave an heir. He was proud of his family and dismissive of everyone else's. He was satisfied with his own company and resented social intrusions.

I could go on, but all this is inconsequential and is not a part of Harrie's story. She never described James as anything other than wonderful. She was limited to the description of a boy and I am confused by my knowledge of the man.

We stayed late in Martine's drinking tea and talking. I drank tea and Harrie talked. I sat silent and alone watching the image of Harrie's dream man materialise between us. She finally noticed the time and my silence and laughed.

'You're so good, Em dear. A perfect friend, too polite to throw something at me.'

On the walk home, Harrie linked me and centred the conversation on me and the availability of eligible men for me. I described my dream man, the man who would pick up the contents of my dainty handbag and who would eventually break through my reserve, but I was embarrassed talking about him. With my hands curled into the pockets of my dirty jacket I seemed to have grown beyond him.

'And what would you have in your handbag? Not a dirty handkerchief, I hope.'

'Oh no, nothing but the best.'

'And how would he open the conversation.'

'With a shy compliment.'

'And would he take you dancing?'

'Yes.'

'And would he buy you a rose?'

'Yes.'

'And would he serenade you to sleep?'

'Yes.'

'And would he kiss you in the moonlight?'

'Yes.'

'And would he protect you against the world?'

'Yes.'

'And would he speak in verse?'

'Yes.'

We were running and laughing, and Harrie was shouting her questions and I was shouting my answers. Everything was all right again. It was us two again. Us two against the dream men.

Chapter 8

It was exactly three weeks after he was first mentioned that I finally got to meet Mr James Hamilton. I remember because we were in Martine's waiting for him and Harrie drew my attention to the fact that we were sitting at the same table we'd sat at on that first night. It was not our usual table – we usually managed to sit by the window.

'It's right we should sit here,' she said. 'Here is where you heard of him and here is where you'll meet him.'

I just nodded. I had been counting back the weeks and was shocked that three had passed. It wasn't that time had passed quickly. It was that time had distorted.

I could remember details of conversations and walks that stretched the hours they filled. But I felt that those magic hours had no relation to real time. They were precious moments in the afternoon of my friendship with Harrie and should not have been translated into the mundane passage of weeks.

But they had been, and they had brought with them the change that even the most uneventful passage of time brings. I was three weeks older and I was three weeks closer to Harrie.

We had developed an unspoken routine. I clung to it but knew not to mention it. I knew that if Harrie was aware of it she would destroy it.

Harrie saw James three times a week and on Sunday afternoon. During her absences, I sat at home, alone. Sometimes I walked, sometimes I visited Mrs Boothe and sometimes I wrote letters, but mostly I just waited. I had won a small victory in the fight for Harrie's trust. I had weaned her into the habit of calling for me when she came home from her nights with James.

I was proud of this. It sent Harrie to bed with my words in her ears and my face under her eyelids. I hoped that it would remind her of the solidarity of friendship and of the transience of love.

The first time she invited me into her room to chat while she changed for bed was the night that I had stood for hours in my nightdress, trusting to the effort and the cold to keep me awake. I had tried before to keep awake in bed or even sitting up in my armchair, but a day on my feet was always enough to send me straight to sleep. So, that night, I stood and waited until Harrie came in.

I heard her key and timed her on the stairs, and then I raced down to the bathroom. It was perfectly judged, she was just opening her door.

She was sparkling from her evening and I was good at pretending drowsiness. I let her persuade me to climb into her bed for a bit. She said she needed someone to talk to.

She twirled out of her clothes, dancing around the room and flinging them from her. They lay in gay little tired heaps. She brushed her hair into a shine and she smeared cream on her face lovingly. She was seeing herself as he had seen her.

Every gesture of hers reassured me that she was aware and approving of her audience. It is no fun to dance unobserved or twinkle unobserved or whisper quotes unobserved or to be in love unobserved.

I lay curled in her bed thawing into its warmth. I listened to her endless repetition of James's conversation and made the occasional envious coo. It was important to be seen to be envious. I knew I was becoming indispensable. But it was an effort to muster up sufficient enthusiasm. I was tired and James's conversation didn't match Harrie's for sparkle.

'...and then we went for coffee and he insisted on choosing a cake for me, even though I didn't really want one. He said my sweetness needed feeding... and when we were walking home he said that it didn't matter that the night was cloudy, that he had his very own star that he was keeping here on earth. He said that he felt a bit guilty because if he was unselfish enough to let me go, everyone else in the city would have at least one star to look at tonight.'

When Harrie finally collapsed into the bed, I stayed just long enough to warm her feet before I got out. She kissed my cheek and rolled sleepily into the hollow my body had left. She could dream of James but I was the taste on her lips and it was my heat that she was sleeping in.

After that first night Harrie would always call to my room on her way to bed. She always assumed that I was awake, because she could see my light from the street. I learned to sleep with it on and I trained myself to wake when she knocked. Then, I would follow her to her room and tumble into her bed. While she undressed, and danced, and trilled over her evening, I would lie quiet, and listen and wait to warm her feet.

It was a very happy time. Those were the bad nights. Those were the nights spent waiting, but waiting is so enjoyable when one is confident of an end result. The other nights, the nights with Harrie were glorious.

They started with the heavy heat of late afternoon and stretched into the light warmth of long summer evenings. Then, they softened into that purple twilight that passes for night in the city, in the summer time.

We would spend the late afternoon in a neighbouring park reading books that we discussed and swapped and enthused over. It wasn't so much that Harrie introduced me to literature – my father had seen to it that I had read what he perceived to be the classics, and as a result I was well versed in Dickens – it was more that she introduced me to her critical method.

Books were judged good or bad by how much one enjoyed them. I no longer had to consider how well written they were. And characters were judged good or bad by the effect that they had on one. A good character was one that you either wanted to meet or wanted to hate, a bad character left no impression. The ultimate compliment to a book was to dream about it. Harrie claimed to have dreamt of Darcy three times and I lied and described a nightmare based on *The Woman in White*.

Another activity Harrie introduced me to was sketching. She taught me the basic shapes of form that could be magically combined to produce still lives or even recognisable faces. We drew in a large pad that Harrie had produced from under her bed. It came with a dirty tin of charcoal and, eventually, Harrie taught me how to extend and detail those basic shapes with soft shadows in shades of grey. I think I was quite good. We never tore out the pages. We wanted to make a book of the summer.

I suppose I must still have that book somewhere, it would be interesting to see if I was as good as I remembered and it might be easeful to be able to look at Harrie's face again, even a clumsy caricature of it.

But I suppose it would be mean to send little Miss Kelly into the attic to look for it. Or maybe not. It depends on what she produces for dinner tonight. I have grown fonder of food. Now that I loathe the company I am forced to tolerate, I have to depend on the quality of the food.

With Harrie it was different – it was her company that mattered. I fasted alone and feasted with her. On the nights when she didn't meet James we would go to Martine's and eat great plates of fried bread and fried eggs or heaped servings of mashed potatoes and cold cuts of roast beef. Then we would walk home, slowly, by the river, trying to digest the mountain of food we had forced inside ourselves. It took me a while to get used to eating so late. I had been brought up to eat my main meal at mid-day and only to take light refreshment in the evenings. Needless to say, I never complained about this reversal. I considered it as further proof of my growing sophistication.

Once we got home, we would spend the rest of those nights sitting in Harrie's room listening to the garden, and talking in our deepening, intimate language, a language based on a network of shared jokes, allusions and abbreviations.

We pretended that my dream man was a reality and Harrie would ask me about fictional dates I had with him. My answering descriptions were always wildly romantic. I described evenings on yachts, days in gondolas and picnics on remote desert islands. And she would sigh and lament the fact that James was not a millionaire. We joked that my only romantic problem was that my dream man was called Fred. We did try to think of a suitably dreamy name for him, but Fred he stubbornly remained.

Another of our games was that we were both terribly famous and we would swap anecdotes of our days spent in exclusive shops, or being interviewed by the Pathé news reporters, or being spotted and chased by adoring fans.

I preferred those nights that we spent alone, curled together in armchairs, telling each other stories, but sometimes Harrie insisted on change.

'Come on, Em dear,' she would say. 'Let's do something.' And I would follow.

Usually all we did was visit Mrs Boothe. Sometimes we would knock on Miss Charter Thomas's door, but she rarely answered and when she did it was usually to peer out at us from her barely opened door and mutter her phrase once or twice, before slamming us out of her evening. Only once she appeared more lucid, and, when Harrie asked her polite usual question, 'Can we get you anything this evening?' she smiled quite warmly before muttering her curse. I never did manage to see past her to catch a glimpse of the dreaded watercolours and Harrie joked that I was lucky, that they had the ability to blind the sensitive. I swelled with pride then, delighted that Harrie considered me sensitive.

We only called on Mrs Benson once and she wouldn't even let us past her parlour door. She assumed that we had come to complain and was obviously dying to get back to her drink. All we said was hello and she drew herself up into her straightest, strictest pose.

'You may think that an establishment such as this is lucrative, but I can assure you it is not. If needs be I can show you the written proof in my account books. It is my accountant that is to be blamed for the recent rationing of butter. He has told me to serve margarine or serve my tenants with writs to vacate. I, however, agree with you. It is important to maintain standards, so I am willing to reinstate your butter rations at the expense of my livelihood.'

And she shut her door. We never called again but we did notice that for a short while afterwards we were given the choice of butter with our breakfast.

Although most of that time is blurred by repetition, a few evenings stand out as memorable. But now that I am thinking of that time the days are beginning to separate. With a little more concentration the hours will separate. Because the truth is that every hour, every minute, with Harrie was memorable.

Like the picnic. It was just a Tuesday, an average day for everyone else, but even at the time it was a golden memory for me. As each second of that evening drifted into my past I knew to cherish it.

The picnic was my idea. I was feeling worn by the city. Summer at home had always been an open, sandy, barefoot season and I was beginning to itch for a taste of the sea. I had only been home once and then only for a stiff-collared Sunday, and that didn't count. So I decided on a picnic.

I chose a particularly hot day and spent my lunch hour buying a selection of tasty, portable foodstuffs. I chose carefully and extravagantly and returned to work with a bag laden with the best I could find. There were two different types of cheeses, sliced ham and some cold beef, a couple of tomatoes and a loaf of warm, crusty bread.

It was the first lunchtime I hadn't spent at the bandstand. I was delighted when I heard that Harrie had turned up – she didn't always – and I was thrilled that she was put out. I met her that evening back at Benson's and noted that I had won another victory in my silent fight for her.

'Where were you?' She asked, but unlike me she didn't whine, she confronted me with her questioning if not with her anger. 'I was waiting for you at our bandstand. You said you would be there. I remember asking you last night.'

Her displeasure was beautifully reassuring. I gave nothing

away, though. I never pointed out her use of 'our'. I just apologised and showed her the food and I was forgiven.

Harrie was delighted with the idea and immediately leapt into action as I knew she would. I knew I could trust her to glamorise my idea with her charm.

'Well, we have the food,' she said, 'and such a lot of it. All we need now is a blanket, our books and notebook, some cushions, candles, matches, something to drink...'

I followed her upstairs and into her room and obediently packed what she told me to pack. We were ready within half an hour.

Harrie took me out of the city on a tram. We sat on top, at the front, and watched the city spread into suburbs, and the suburbs spread into single, glamorous houses. Harrie pointed a few of them out, associating them with some outrageous tales of upper-class decadence.

'See that house? The white one? There was a shooting there in the eighteen-forties. A duel between two women for the affections of a man. One woman died and the other was wounded and paralysed and the man went home to his wife. And that house! You can just see its chimneys. A respected society lady lived there all alone, she died in nought five and when they came for the body they found two beautiful young women in the house. They were her illegitimate children that no-one had ever heard of and because they had never been exposed to any society or any books they had developed their own language that no-one else could understand.'

Again I listened, wide-eyed, unquestioning, and when she was finished talking, Harrie, inexplicably, started to laugh. We got off at the end of the line and had to walk the rest of the way.

Harrie led and I followed her through a small seaside town, stopping to buy some chocolate and lemonade, and through the hordes of evening strollers that cluttered its streets. Harrie walked on, passing them all by, and I followed, weighed down with my bag of food. I had insisted on carrying the heavy bag.

Harrie was marching ahead swinging her load of cushions and candles.

I smelled the sea before I saw it, but still, it was a surprise when it loomed large in front of us. The sea near my home was confined within a small bay; the city, on the other hand, opened on to the ocean. We climbed over a wall, clambered down some rocks and had to walk some more, but I didn't mind. I trusted to Harrie and I was right to. We finally settled in the shelter of a quiet, almost hidden cove. We were hemmed in on three sides by black, heavy cliffs and the water lapped gently before us.

I took my shoes off, unclipped and unrolled my stockings and ran. I ran on the still-warm sand and on the cold foam of the gentle waves. I felt my city-softened body harden and stretch. My skirt rode high over my knees and I was aware of flashes of naked thigh and Harrie's eyes.

I ran back to her and she looked up from her cheese sandwich. She handed me one and I sat beside her. We watched the sea and the clouds and the sun and ate the bread and the cheese and the meat. And Harrie told me about a man she had met in France who was convinced that the sea had a language of its own.

'He thought that all the oceans and all the seas were separate beasts, but of the same species, and that the movements of their waves was their way of communicating. He wrote reams and reams of material on the subject, but no-one would ever publish it. In the end, he claimed that he had broken the code and was freely communicating with the seas, but that they didn't have much to say except that fish tickled them and anchors hurt them. He died soon after, a disappointed man.'

And I waited for Harrie before I laughed.

Later on, we lay on our backs waiting for the multitude of stars that never showed in the city. Even though it was still quite bright, we lit the two candles that we had brought with us and bolstered them upright with stones. Surrounded by their flickering light, lulled by the lap of the sea, we tossed our heads back to drink lemonade from the bottle and bit chunks of chocolate straight off the bar.

Later still, we lay side by side staring straight ahead and I told Harrie how my mother grieved for the loss of her beauty.

'She wanted a daughter so that her looks would live after her, but one look at me and she knew she was taking all she had with her to her grave.'

Harrie sat up and turned to stare at me.

'Poor Em! Don't you know that a pretty face isn't even half the battle? Your nose is a little odd and your mouth is a little wonky, but you have the figure of a film star. You're so slim and tall, you should flaunt it. Let your face hide behind your body not the other way around.'

And that's what I did. It's what I still do – it's what makes the little Miss Kellys of this world think of me as beautiful.

We lay quiet again after that. The night air was as dense and as warm as a blanket and I think I may have slept for a bit. I remember that I missed the beginning of Harrie's story. She was telling me about her uncle and her mother and her lack of home.

'I have looked long and hard for a little house where everything is mine and everything is right. But I was looking at buildings – that's where I went wrong. I should have been looking at people. I think James is my little cottage. He could well be my home.'

I didn't answer her, she didn't expect me to. Instead I stood up and brushed myself down. I packed all our rubbish into one bag and I clipped my stockings back on. I did that slowly. I flattered myself with the fancy that Harrie was jealous of my legs.

When I was ready I picked up the bag and held a hand out to Harrie. She took it and allowed me to pull her up. She stood standing small by my side and I resisted the urge to shake her. How could she not see that she was home already?

We went back to Benson's, tired but close, and even though it was late, Harrie asked me into her room.

'I have a feeling of that black mood – please stay with me, Em.'

We sat in Harrie's comforting armchairs, in silence for the most part. We were both tired from the sea air and the long walk from the tram. Downstairs we could hear the thump of Mrs Benson's singing and outside we could hear the rustle of creatures settling for the night. And out of the shifting silence Harrie told me about a German she had met somewhere in Europe.

'He always wore dark sun-glasses, even indoors, even at night. You see, he had undergone an operation and he was convinced that they had cut the top of his head open like an egg, and that they had filled him up with a blue gas, the same colour as his eyes. He wore the glasses because he said that now, whenever he changed his mind, everyone could see him doing it.'

And we stayed up a little longer discussing the demerits of such a condition.

'You would always have to be honest,' said Harrie. 'And honesty is one of the more dangerous traits.'

That night, after I warmed her feet, she held my hand and kept me by her side.

'I wish I was young, little Em,' she said. 'I'm so much older than my years, and I'm so very tired. It's about time that I went home. Wouldn't it be lovely to just go home and close your own hall door on the world?'

I didn't answer. I didn't want to pursue the conversation. I had a feeling that perhaps Harrie included me in her definition of 'the world'.

'But that's not life, Em. Life is like being thrown out of your house blindfolded and made to walk across town. The only thing you can be sure of is that at some stage you are going to fall down a hole or walk into a wall or walk under a tram, and the longer you are walking the closer you are to your end. Knowing that, it's a wonder we are not all gibbering idiots. But then,' and she pulled an exaggerated Charter Thomas face, 'maybe we are.'

I laughed, more with relief at the fact of her joke than the joke itself, but Harrie barely smiled.

She slept soon after, still holding my hand, her body curled around it. I didn't have the heart to remove it. I stayed awake for most of the night delighting in the numbness that was spreading up my arm. I had never been so close to anyone before. I had never been offered a sleeping body's trust.

Chapter 9

When we woke the next morning Harrie was obviously embarrassed. Maybe she was aware that she had shown me the depths of her need. Her embarrassment didn't last long, though. There was no room for it in our relationship. By that evening it was completely forgotten. By that evening we were busy with birthday celebrations.

Life with Harrie was like that, it was filled with its present and heedless of its past. It was I who collected its memories.

Mrs Boothe had told us the date and the time of her birthday party again and again, but still, on the day, she slipped a note under our doors in case we forgot. I suppose she was excited by the occasion. She was a woman who saw everything in terms of a potential celebration, even her growing proximity to death.

I read my note and ran down to Harrie. She was home and was wrapping the box of candles that we had bought as a present.

'What on earth does she mean by formal wear essential? Is she serious?'

'At her age, I would say that she was deadly serious.'

'But formal! I don't have anything formal. Anyway, formal for a walk down the hall!'

'No, Em, it's formal for respect and recognition of a friend's life.'

'Well, even if it was formal to meet the Prince of Arabia, I can't go. I have no formal frock.'

My lack of formal wear was an intentional omission on my parents' part. My mother thought it unseemly that I attend any formal function unchaperoned and my father thought it unlikely that I would be asked to any. That being the case, he ruled evening wear as unnecessary expenditure. It was an embarrassing admission to have to make but, as usual, Harrie faced the minor tragedy of the situation with the humour it deserved.

'But you shall, Em dear. You shall go to the ball.' She produced a dress with a flourish. 'It has always been too long on me, even when I wear it with heels.'

It was a heavy, olive-green satin dress with a dramatically scooped neck. I slipped it on and it settled on my suggestion of a bust and on the curve that should have been my hips. I looked at myself in Harrie's full-length mirror and realised what she had meant about giving precedence to my figure. Harrie stood behind me and clapped.

'Now all we have to do is hide your hair.'

We tied it up in a tight bun, scraping every straggling strand away from my face. I still wear it like that, and even now people comment on the length and elegance of my neck.

Harrie dressed herself in an ankle-length frothy blue affair of lace and frills, and decorated her neck and arms with loops of gold. We both wore her lipstick, the scarlet one, and I pinched some colour into my cheeks. For the first time in my life I saw myself as something other than ugly and I was suddenly disappointed that my new looks were going to get such a secluded debut.

Harrie carried the present and I carried the card we had made. It was a charcoal drawing of what was supposed to be Mrs Boothe, making what was supposed to be a wax cake. We were fashionably late. Mrs Benson and Miss Charter Thomas were there already.

They were sitting on stiff kitchen chairs on either side of Mrs Boothe's centre table. She had cleared it and polished it for the occasion, and it shone strangely in her jumble of dust. She opened the door to us, kissed us both and showed us to our seats – Harrie beside Miss Charter Thomas and me opposite her, beside Mrs Benson.

Mrs Benson said good evening and Miss Charter Thomas muttered what she usually muttered. She was dressed in her scarlet velvet, but her hair hung wild and free, a grey mess of tangles that she was continually pulling at. Mrs Benson had made only a slight concession to the occasion. Her usual combination of wool and cotton was extended to ankle length and was more than usually sombre in tone and, around her long neck, she had tied a pearl choker.

Mrs Boothe, as befitted the hostess, outdid us all. She sat at the head of her table, swamped in layers of purple taffeta and black lace, with her hair elaborately arranged around a glass tiara.

She took full advantage of her day and the attention due to her. Without pausing for comment from the floor, she spoke at length about whatever she wanted.

She told us, in detail, about the age-old customs of decorum and etiquette. She told us about debutantes who lost their futures through bad dress sense, and immoral girls who knew how to fool the eye. She told us of acquaintances who were rude in the wrong circles, and friends who proved themselves as gentlefolk wherever they went. We sat silent, listening as she lectured and politely waiting for refreshments.

And there we sat for nearly an hour. Five women of assorted ages, dressed to the best of their abilities, sitting on hard kitchen chairs, in a dingy bedroom, in a dingy back street, listening to an old woman tell old stories about old scandals.

Mrs Benson was the first to crack. It may have been that she noticed that Fanny was beginning to wander, but it was probably because she was missing valuable drinking time. She interrupted a fabulously complicated tale of arranged marriages with 'Mine's a sherry.'

'…and Richard would have been the youngest but he had the brains of that family as well as the looks, not that it took much to outsmart that lot, they were a low-domed, dim crew…'

'Or anything at all. It's the weather – it dries the larynx. Would you agree, Miss Elliott?'

'Indeed, though I prefer tea.'

'...but it took a woman of breeding to tame him. His father knew that much. He knew that it was smart to stick with breeding. Even if the girl in question did look very much like a horse and had the unfortunate name of Winifred. I came out the same year as she did but I never joined in on the name-calling...'

'A glass of beer in the summer is most refreshing, though a little crude, but I believe in Germany it is considered chic and some swear by its iron content.'

'...and white never suited her colouring or indeed her character. She was an ugly deb, but she was an absolute fright of a bride...'

'My father was a demon for the drink and my mother was a devil for it so I tend to stick to tea. Some day, I'm bound to go wild with a tipple of sherry, blood will out they say, but for now tea is as far as I am prepared to go.'

Then Miss Charter Thomas woke up and started muttering her phrase.

'Perhaps, Mrs Boothe dear, it would be wise not to offer Miss Charter Thomas a drink. It may mix badly with her medication.'

'...and the child was terrible handsome with hair as black as coal and a high domed forehead, so there could be no doubt but...'

'And not only my father and mother, my grandmother has been known to pawn for gin...'

The noise level rose to terrifying heights and I took the plunge and joined in.

'My mother's mother was a Hall, but she married badly, they say, and so here I am on the haberdashery counter.'

It was tremendous fun – everyone was talking and no-one was listening. I could have sworn that I heard Mrs Benson call Mrs Boothe 'a senile, tight-fisted cow,' and Harrie told me later that she spent the whole evening talking about her mother's ability to accessorise her men. I played it safe, however, and stuck to a detailed account of the contents of a haberdashery counter.

'...and hairnets and ribbons and some beads though not the

best selection and of course gloves, though the kid ones are on the ground floor...'

Eventually, Fanny Boothe realised that our attention had slipped and she rose to her feet slowly and majestically. She placed her two hands in front of her, palm down on the table, and levered herself upright. Then, once standing, she raised her hands and slammed them back down. We all hopped back from our monologues and into silence.

'Howard was always a gentleman and that is why he refused the invitation.' She continued her story still standing and we had no choice but to sit and listen. 'And that woman, who would never earn the title of lady, could not understand his scruples, the invitations kept coming...'

We were forced to stay quite late and left thirsty and hungry. We were never offered refreshments of any sort.

It was Miss Charter Thomas who broke the spell. With one last, loud mutter she got up and left. Although I still hadn't deciphered what she was saying, the coarseness of her tone was enough to dispel the air of parlour elegance that Fanny had tried so hard to sustain. The rest of us fell silent for a moment and then, as a body, bade each other good night.

Harrie and I sat curled in Harrie's room until late that night. Still in all our splendour, we stayed laughing hysterically at the absurdity of the evening. I fuelled the joke and lengthened the night with detailed impersonations of everyone. I screwed my face into tight primness and demanded alcohol.

'Oh, if you have nothing else, then white spirits with a dash of soda water will do...'

I puffed my cheeks into pleasant plumpness and rambled amiably,

'...and he married her and she married him and they married each other and I married the father...'

I finally shook my hair free and ran my hands through it, back-combing it into a nest of tangles, and then, muttering and lumbering, I knocked around Harrie's room, bumping into every piece of furniture I could reach.

Harrie began by joining in, then she just sat and laughed and finally she shooed me back to my own room. I left her confident that the next day would be as lovely, and I suppose it was. All the days before I met James were lovely and all the nights were fun, like the night we got locked into the park.

As usual it was Harrie's idea to do something. Her presence, her conversation was enough for me, but I understood that she needed more than I could offer. We were sitting in her room as usual, complaining about our public, as usual, when she dragged me out into the dusk.

'Come on, Em, we need a walk and if we wear our wigs no-one will recognise us.'

I agreed as usual, and followed as usual. The park closed at dusk, but we just managed to slip in by a side gate and Harrie pulled me off the path and deep into some shrubbery until she saw the park-keeper pass. He locked the gate we had got in by and moved off. I looked to Harrie in panic, it was getting dark and the railings were very high, but she just smiled.

'But Harrie!' I hissed. 'We could be stuck here all night and you don't know what kind of people could be locked in with us.'

'Oh, people much like us I should imagine – no more than two eyes, no less than four limbs, a head, a torso. They can't be very different or else they wouldn't be able to function at all. Goodness, cheer up, Em. We're here for a reason. Follow me.'

She led me over to the far side of the park, the side that opened on to a dangerously unfashionable area of town. I was growing more uneasy but I trusted Harrie. She stopped abruptly in the middle of a path and I braced myself for flight, thinking that she had spotted something that my darting eyes had missed.

'We're here,' she whispered, and I relaxed slightly.

'Where?'

'Here.'

She pointed upwards. I raised my head and then bent it backwards. I was looking up at what must have been the tallest tree in the park.

'And it's so easy to climb.' She kicked off her shoes and hid them behind a bush. I did the same and we both tucked our skirts into our knickers.

'I'll go first – I know the easiest way,' she said as she swung herself onto the lowest branch and disappeared into the first frill of greenery.

I followed quickly. Dangerous activity with Harrie was far preferable to the unknown waiting on my own. I clambered after her, using my hands, arms, knees and feet to cling to each branch. I hadn't the confidence or the agility Harrie had, but even so I soon forgot about how I might get stuck, and how I might fall, and I started appreciating the experience.

It was a very easy tree to climb and it was well worth the risk. Ten minutes later Harrie and I clung, breathless, to two of its higher branches and, enveloped in its perfume and fanned by its leaves, we surveyed the lights and the movements of the city spread beneath us.

'There's Hall's,' I shouted, over the rustle of the leaves and the call of the wind, but mainly over the rush of my excitement.

'There's the cathedral,' Harrie answered.

'The river.'

'The bus depot.'

'The Savoy.'

'The stone bridge.'

'A drunk with a dog.'

'A lady in a sin of a dress.'

We were both shouting loud with laughter at this stage and Harrie swung herself almost horizontal, across two branches.

'And there's the night sky,' she said softly. 'Em, we've almost climbed as high as the night. Do you think if we could manage to go just a bit higher, we'd break through the darkness of the night and find the day behind it?'

I didn't know what she meant, but then she went on: 'When I was a child, I was forced to knit, but I never could. My knitting was always clumsy and full of holes. When I was six, I was given some old black wool and ordered to make a scarf. Of course I couldn't, but that lumpy, holey scarf gave me the idea that God had knitted the night sky, and that every night he wrapped us up in his holey blanket. But behind the blanket the sun was still shining and that that was what the stars were, the sun shining through the holes in God's knitting.'

We both laughed.

'But seriously,' she continued. 'Doesn't it give you hope, that idea? Don't you think that it's good to have proof that the day will follow the night?'

I agreed, even though I couldn't understand her dissatisfaction with the night.

I very carefully manoeuvred myself into a similar position to Harrie and I stared up with her, in silence, staring at the sky we were so close to, breathing in big, deep breaths of green, living air. Eventually I relaxed fully and trusted myself to the strong, wooden arms that held me and seemed to offer me up to the drifting clouds and glittering stars.

We stayed there, two wild city urchins, until our limbs gave in to the cold and then we climbed stiffly down. My stockings were ripped and my dress was smeared with resin and madly crushed from being bunched so tight around my waist. Harrie looked almost as bad as me if not worse because the thickness of her hair had attracted a variety of stray leaves and twigs.

Once we arrived back on the ground we fell together in hysterics, partly because of the way we looked, partly with the relief of being in one piece and partly because of the thrill of being out so late and so illegally.

Harrie was the first to recover herself and she hushed me quiet and led me through a broken gap in the railings. Once out on the street, we raced home, keeping close to the side of the path away from the street lights. We were terrified of being seen in so bedraggled a state.

We parted company on the stairs. I didn't want to go into Harrie's room. I didn't want to talk about the experience. To analyse anything so perfect would be to deny it.

Things *were* perfect.

And then I met James.

Chapter 10

I was very nervous about meeting the famed Mr James Hamilton, but I knew it was an honour to be asked, and so I accepted with a show of enthusiasm. Harrie had invited me only the previous evening when we were sitting in the park. She was reading and I was drawing her reading. She looked up suddenly and threw her book aside, ruining the pose I had just captured.

'I'm meeting James tomorrow in Martine's and I warned him that I was bringing along a friend to judge him. Will you be that friend?'

I was very touched and very scared, but I answered casually.

'I can't promise anything, my public may need me, but I think I'm free.'

Harrie laughed.

'They expect too much, Em dear. Can't you leave them for one night?'

'I expect so. I'll tell Fred that I cannot make Errol Flynn's birthday celebrations.'

Satisfied, Harrie returned to her book. She linked me on the way home and when we were safe in her room she insisted that I repeat my earlier impersonation of Miss Walsh serving the lecherous old man and I did with pleasure. I drew my face up into the pinched expression that resembled Miss Walsh's and spat out the words: 'If Sir is not interested in ribbons could he please refrain from handling them and if Sir refuses to stay on his side of the counter I will be forced to call security and if Sir insists on knowing, the lingerie department is on the second floor.'

It was a night like all the others, but I was on edge. I had a feeling that I wasn't being called on to judge, I was being brought out to be judged.

The next day at work was a bad day. Well, every day at work was a bad day, but I was beginning to get used to it. I learnt how to humour the customers, tolerate the staff and avoid Miss Walsh as much as possible. But that day was a bad day.

I was nervous and damp and awkward all day long. I dropped everything I touched and offended everyone I served. It was a long, long day and it left me shattered and demoralised. I was not in the mood for giving first impressions, but I had no choice. There was never any choice where Harrie was concerned.

Harrie was home before me and was looking out for me. She was ready for my nerves and my doubts.

It was always that way with Harrie. She only ever expected you to do the best you could. She encouraged you to reach your potential and never demanded more, but she was aware of your capabilities and she never allowed you to deny them. She knew I was nervous and needed soothing but she knew that I was equal to the challenge. I just had to be told.

'Wear your brown,' was how she greeted me. She was in my room and was leaning out my window as I turned down the lane. She shouted down, 'Wear your brown,' and I laughed and laughed and didn't bother about the strange looks I was getting. Harrie had ducked her head back into my room and my fellow commuters could no longer connect my outburst of gaiety with anything or anybody, but I didn't mind.

Hall's Central Stores disappeared along with my tired feet. I ran up to and through the friendly, smiling door. Harrie was waiting for me with another whole evening.

I dressed in my brown with my new two-tone shoes and I wore my new scarlet lipstick. I put on my new gold bangle and my slightly grubby white jacket. I packed my pockets with money, keys, comb and lipstick and was ready.

Harrie wore her green dress that was a little short and a little tight but complemented her colouring beautifully. She borrowed my lipstick and straightened her stockings under my direction and we were off. She linked me as we swung out of the lane and I was surprised to note that she seemed nervous. I didn't know whether she was unsure of how I would be received or if she was unsure of herself.

'You look wonderful, Em dear.' She squeezed my arm tight in hers, emphasising the compliment.

I suppose I did in my own way. The brown dress was new. It had been bought with my first fortnightly pay packet and was my first truly adult frock. My uniform brown had given me the idea for the dress, but this brown was different. It was softer and lighter. I felt it complemented the slender height of my figure as well as my new position of independence.

I thanked Harrie and returned the compliment with a sincerity that obviously pleased her.

'Oh, Em dear,' she said. 'You'll turn my head so thoroughly I'll be forced to walk backwards.'

We were early, but we waited to order, and Harrie said, 'It's right that we should sit here. Here is where you heard of him and here is where you'll meet him.'

'Do you come here with him a lot?' I tried to keep the hurt out of my voice. I had always thought of Martine's as our special place.

'Oh yes, it was James who brought me here first. Why?'

'I just thought that if he didn't know the place he might get delayed, get lost you know,' I muttered. I had noted the sharpness of Harrie's question.

'Oh, he'll be here all right,' she said confidently, and he was. He arrived perfectly on time. Mr James Hamilton always prided himself on his punctuality and reliability, he considered them both masculine attributes.

Harrie saw him almost as soon as he had opened the door, and she sparkled. I had been describing my day and she had been listening when her head suddenly drew away from me and her eyes sparkled for him. She stood up and waved him over and I turned to see if I could see what she saw. I saw the mediocrity of Mr James Hamilton and I watched him as he came towards us, deliberately, slowly, at his own pace. Even the me of seventeen could see that Harrie was showing too much enthusiasm. I was shocked. I had never seen her try before.

He shook my hand before he sat down. He sat opposite me, beside Harrie. He hitched his herring-bone trousers up as he lowered himself into the seat and revealed a pair of chocolate-brown socks.

I glimpsed the socks and looked away quickly. I knew instinctively that Mr James Hamilton was the sort of man who would classify socks as underwear. He would not want to be reminded, that due to the necessity of preserving a crease in one's trousers, they had to be on view, and he would not wish to be in the company of a woman who was vulgar enough to interest herself in them.

But perhaps I am giving myself too much credit for intuition. Perhaps I am grafting my later knowledge of the man on to these early impressions. It is difficult, though. Linear narratives are not compatible with reminiscences.

However, I do definitely remember that his physical appearance did shock me. Or at least it surprised me. He was tall and angular. His face was closed and formal. I had expected glamour and charm and adult wit and I was more confused than disappointed. None of Harrie's descriptions of manly perfection, and none of her quotes, which dripped with romance or were chiselled with sense, seemed to have any connection with this man. I shook his hand in silence and looked for Harrie's eye. I wanted some kind of explanation, but when she did finally look over, all I saw was pride.

After shaking my hand and after sitting himself carefully down, Mr James Hamilton turned to Harrie and placed his hand over hers. She slapped hers over his and gave him a kiss on the cheek. He looked over at me and then glanced around. He was easily embarrassed.

'Let's eat,' said Harrie. 'It's so hot and I'm so tired, I feel like a big cat in need of prey, and the civilised approach to such a humour is to order the beef.'

She stretched as she spoke, arching her back and thrusting her breasts forward. Mr James Hamilton looked around him again. His eyes settled on me.

'So you work in Hall's, Miss Moore?'

My previous approach to men had been to hunch my shoulders, mutter and blush, but I couldn't do that with Harrie watching, and, with Harrie's smile waiting for my answer, I didn't even want to. I answered in my new cinematic drawl. It was an adaptation of Harrie's and I was quite proud of it.

'Oh do call me Em,' I said. 'I have a darling aunt called Miss Moore who has the most horrific facial hair, so her name won't do and the only other alternative is Mary and I think that's far too old for me. I'm sure to grow into it, but for the moment I prefer Em.'

It worked. James laughed and said, 'Em it is then,' and Harrie smiled one of her special smiles at me.

The waitress came and we all ordered the beef. While we were waiting for it, I obeyed all Harrie's orders to perform. I did my impersonation of Miss Walsh and Mr Newby and spiced up the character sketches with some shockingly exaggerated incidents.

James seemed amused. He didn't quite laugh, but his mouth did curve upwards and split open occasionally and Harrie seemed genuinely pleased, more by his reaction than by my stories – she was hardly listening to them. When they ran dry, she asked James about his day and he told her about it at length.

I sat large and forgotten, only half listening to their conversation. It seemed to be mostly about legal details and people I didn't know.

'Of course Ryan is going for the bar, but I don't suppose he'll get far with his attitude. And I ran into Justice Mooney today – he seemed confident about the nomination, but my father always claimed he would.'

The conversation, thankfully, stopped mid-anecdote with the arrival of the food. Harrie and James both ate with enthusiasm and I tried to, but my mother's fifth rule kept spinning in my head: 'It is unseemly for a girl to be seen to be hungry.' I couldn't shake it and I couldn't relax into my meal. Harrie noticed as Harrie would.

'What's wrong, Em? You're not sick are you?' She spoke between bites and blood-red lips and Mr James Hamilton looked away.

'I'm all right,' I answered. 'I just don't seem to have much of an appetite.'

Harrie out-ate us all. She cleared her plate, then cleared mine and then sat back patting the softness of her stomach. Mr James Hamilton watched, fascinated.

'I would hate to lose my lust for food,' she said. 'Don't you think that there is nothing more divine than the gratification of the senses? If one loses the urge to feed them, one loses the urge to live.'

I agreed whole-heartedly and Harrie laughed.

'I knew you would think so, Em.' She was looking at me and talking to me, but her words were obviously not meant for me.

'There's nothing like food when one is hungry, water when one is thirsty, bed when one is sleepy, but what about when you are fed and watered and rested? What would satisfy you then, Em?'

No-one expected me to answer. Mr James Hamilton did that – he grinned. He looked straight into Harrie's eyes and smiled a smile that could open wide and swallow her. She was touching up her lipstick, but she stopped for long enough to smile back at him. I felt sick. He clasped his hand over hers again and turned to me:

'I'm sure we need never worry about Harrie losing her appetite, need we?'

'No, we needn't,' I answered abruptly, and Harrie laughed as if something improper had been said.

Harrie seemed to grow in James's company. She was acting on a woman's instinct, posturing and pouting with a sexual maturity that wasn't compatible with what I knew of her position in life.

We left soon after that. James paid for the meal with the finality expected of a gentleman at that time. It would have been unthinkable to argue, even though I hated the feeling of being indebted to him.

We said goodbye on the footpath. They politely asked me to join them on their walk and I politely declined. I wasn't even tempted. I wanted to be back in the security of my brown room. I needed time to think.

I watched them walk out of view. They had barely left me before James snaked his arm around Harrie, pulling her close, pulling her in to him to be ingested, and she allowed it happen. She settled her curves along his length and she matched her step to his. She didn't think to look back to wave at me, though it was one of our jokes that we always, elaborately, waved each other out of view when parting.

I was awake that night when Harrie called in for me. I followed her down to her room as usual and I lay curled in her bed as usual. But I was listening to everything she said with a new intensity.

I was aware of a change in her way of talking, a slight shift of emphasis. It was nothing concrete, but it was definite. It was no longer us two against the dream men. Now that I had met James, I was a third party. I was a witness and a confidante and by definition an outsider.

'He thinks you're wonderful,' she said.

I thought, So those two were talking about me, the couple against the unit.

'He thinks you're so funny.'

And I saw it again, the couple deciding on the unit.

'He says that we seem to be so close. He said that I was lucky to find you.'

'Works both ways,' I smiled. But I knew that that was the ultimate insult. That was the couple deciding on my suitability. I had been right, I had been brought out to be judged. If Mr James Hamilton had found fault, Harrie would have rejected me as flawed.

I had sense enough not to betray my irritation. I just continued to smile and I agreed that Mr James Hamilton was all a man could be and all a girl could wish for.

'Why, he puts my Fred to shame,' I said, but Harrie didn't register my allusion to our shared story. She just continued with her backhanded compliments.

'He thinks you're very elegant.' I smiled and offered the opinion that I was far less elegant than him.

Harrie undressed, and danced, and dressed for bed as usual, but I watched with a new intensity, and I saw it again, that maturity of movement that I had noticed earlier.

I stayed in her bed as usual and I warmed her feet as usual and then, in the dark, I asked her: 'Do you think you love James?'

'I think I might,' she said. 'In a quiet way, in a fireside way. In the way that I want love to be.'

'And have you ever loved anyone else?'

There was a long silence. I was obviously right on track.

'No.'

'I'm scared of love,' I said. I was prepared to chase until the kill. 'My mother told me about, you know, marriage and all. It sounds horrible. It sounds like it's nothing to do with love. It can't have anything to do with kissing or holding hands or keeping each other safe. What do you think? Do you think you could do it with James?'

Harrie was quiet and stiff. I knew I was treading on thin ice. She could have closed her mind on me then and retreated for good, but I was willing to take a chance on my innocence, my closeness and the dark. It worked.

'It's got nothing to do with love.' She spoke very slowly and very quietly. She was speaking at a distance from herself.

Then she sat up and continued earnestly, leaning into her words as if trying to swallow them as soon as they were spoken. It was as if she regretted their honesty but she needed to be free of them.

'Oh, Em dear, I used to do it with men. I used to do it all the time. I thought it would be fun and then I thought it was expected and all the time I thought that one of them would give me that little house where everything was proper and everything was mine.'

'Did you?' I breathed.

I knew not to condemn and not to ask for details. It was important not to alienate her. My 'Did you?' was filled with admiration and tinged with envy. It was the right approach. In the role of experienced adviser, Harrie felt free to talk on.

She told me about them all, all four of them, including one married one. The married one was the first. He was a friend of her family's and his charms were too much for the Harrie of sixteen. He had lasted for a year and had given her a taste for it.

'It's like eating one strawberry,' she said. 'It always leads on to a yearning for the next one and up until now the next one was always a disappointment. I started too young. Secrets and furtiveness put an awful strain on youth.

'But with James it's different. With James I feel new again. I feel like a different, fresh person, one without any secrets. That's why I think my love for James is real. It's good and wholesome and I associate it with the stronger aspects of love, with bricks and mortar rather than with strawberries.'

'So does James know, then, about the others, about the strawberries?'

'Goodness no.'

'But you said that you had no secrets.'

'No I said that I *felt* like someone with no secrets and that will do for me, and that will do for James. It means that I act honestly towards him, and surely that's enough.'

I left her then. I felt that her feet were warm enough and I had heard all I needed to know.

Chapter 11

The me of seventeen was very prudish and would have been shocked by Harrie's confession if it had come from anyone other than Harrie. Sexual relations were bad enough but sexual relations with a married man – that was surely unforgivable!

It gave me a rush of power to know that I forgave Harrie when, perhaps, God wouldn't. My love was greater than His and, if that was true, how much greater than James's it must be. It was so obvious, and yet I knew that Harrie would need time before she could accept it.

Time was the problem. I was too eager. The me of seventeen had no concept that life would last as long as it has. I saw days without Harrie as stretches of eternity. I hadn't the imagination to visualise the reality of an eternity without her, and now, I don't need imagination. I'm living, and I have lived for years, in that place that used to be unbearable for an afternoon. But back then I didn't stop to think. I pushed events forward, and in doing so, I pushed my goal far out of reach.

After that first meeting with James, my life with Harrie never settled back into the seclusion it had once enjoyed. We were together more often, but in company or in discussion about company. Our quiet evenings in conversation with and about each other drifted away. It was as if she was bored with me or maybe it was just that she was sure of me and wanted my help to make sure of others. I had no intention of supplying such a service.

Together, through James, we were introduced to a variety of people. Other couples for Harrie and James and a selection of eligible young men for me, and this new social outlet seemed to be more than enough to occupy Harrie. She didn't have time for our jokes any more, or our games, or our dreams and I was foolish enough to resent this shift in our relationship instead of being wise enough to accept it. But then, as I have said, I was only seventeen.

All the young men – the eligible ones wheeled out for my benefit and the settled ones produced for James's gratification – had the look of James about them. They all spoke like him and dressed like him, and all the girls, who appeared on various arms looked very much like each other. They all dressed well and sweetly in floral prints, they all let their hair lie as God intended – and it was obvious that God had not intended much for them – and they all left their complexions bare and buried their lips under waxy layers of pink lipstick.

It was amongst these girls that I first realised my potential and began acting with the confidence of a beauty. So I suppose I have to thank them for that much, even if I still curse them for the hours of boredom they inflicted on me.

Groups of us would go out for evenings, and the young men would sit in elaborate, chin-stroking conversation, hedging at topics that were far too old for them – some of them even went as far as to smoke a pipe – and Harrie and I would chat to their partners, and accompany each other to the ladies' room to chat about them. There was still that much camaraderie between us.

After a film and a sufficiency of coffee, or a dance and a sufficiency of coffee, or a plate of food and a sufficiency of coffee, we would separate and walk home in pairs. If there was a man there for me, he would walk me to the top of the lane and if there wasn't, I would be foisted on one of the other couples. As time went on, I was gratified to see that the girls in these couples that were forced to walk me home began resenting me as a threat, and they were right to – their men were always too eager to do me the favour. That was a very new experience for me.

Harrie always came in much later than me, flushed and ruffled. As before, I always waited up for her, and I would amuse her by imitating the girls we had met or the man I had been offered.

Usually I was careful not to poke fun at James. I did not want to alienate Harrie, but sometimes my need to undermine the man grew out of control and I would hint at subtle defects of character.

But I'm being too eager again, and now I have no excuse. I have all the time in my world to remember every detail of my past.

Things didn't happen so quickly, nor did they happen so painlessly. The first young man James produced had a profound effect on me and deserves to be mentioned by name – if I could only remember it. I'm sure it began with R, so Robert will do very well.

It was about a week after my first meeting with James, maybe less. I turned into Marsh Lane with flat, sore feet and a slow, trailing walk. It had been one of the many very bad days at work. After a dizzy morning counting hat pins and thimbles, I had snapped at a customer. She had complained over the price of something and I had pointedly returned her potential purchase to stock, pretending that I didn't believe her to have sufficient money to pay for it. When she understood what I had done she was silenced and she did have the grace to leave, hopefully feeling suitably embarrassed.

Unfortunately, Miss Walsh had also seen what I had done. She hadn't seen enough to fully understand what had gone on, but she saw enough. By the time I arrived home that evening, my head was bowed low, beaten down by Miss Walsh's continued public ranting, and my mind was a blank. I expected Harrie to be out, but she was waiting for me.

She was hanging out of my window and started calling to me almost before I came into earshot. I looked up and saw her waving and mouthing and gesturing for me to hurry. I ran through her shouted words, catching only very few of them: '...late already... thought you were never coming... says he's the greatest...'

She continued her monologue when I arrived, panting, into the room. She shoved my new brown dress at me and hustled me on towards the bathroom talking all the time. She even continued talking through the closed bathroom door. I lost most of what she was saying, it came muffled through wood and was drowned in running water, but I understood her meaning and I washed myself slowly. I was terrified. I came out questioning, as calmly as I could.

'What are you talking about and what's the rush?'

'Oh Em, you're not doing anything tonight are you?'

I shook my head. We both knew there was no need to ask, but it was always that way with Harrie – she always made allowances for the impossible.

'It's James. I met him for lunch and am to meet him tonight, or *we* are to meet him tonight. He was so thrilled by your company that he told all his friends about you and one of them, Robert, is just dying to meet you. So say you'll come, Em dear. I know blind dates are torturous, but really Robert is supposed to be a catch, and if he's not, feel free to climb out the window in the ladies'. I solemnly swear that I will give you the necessary leverage to do so.'

We both laughed.

'But Harrie, what about Fred?'

'Fred? Oh yes. Well, hurry up – we're late already.'

'But really, is this Robert worth breaking a dream man's heart over?'

'Every bit of it. You will come won't you? Say you will.'

We were back in my room and I was putting on my new scarlet lipstick. Of course I would go. We both knew James was doing me the greatest favour. I laughed, dropped Fred from the equation, and went along with the charade of sophisticated boredom that comes with that one date too many, but my hand was shaking and I smeared my lipstick beyond my mouth. Harrie left then to get her coat. It was always that way with Harrie – she would always give you the time you needed to maintain your dignity.

We met in the hall and left in step. Both with scarlet lipstick and both in our shabby summer coats. Fanny Boothe passed us on her way to the dining-room and stopped to talk. For once I welcomed her meaningless chatter – anything that delayed the horror of a date was welcome. She was talking to Harrie about her bunions and her doctor and Harrie was listening graciously.

'...and the pain when I put on my shoes of a morning is something crippling and he said to me that he had never seen such bunions and...'

Harrie frowned in empathy and mentioned an aunt of hers who suffered a milder case far less stoically and I stood and waited. Eventually I ventured a comment. I looked at Fanny Boothe when I spoke, but as usual what I said was for Harrie's benefit. I had developed that approach to conversation almost subconsciously. It started with wanting to impress Harrie when I spoke to her; then it spread to wanting to impress Harrie when she was within earshot. Eventually it encompassed all my conversations. I ended up communicating with people in a way that would impress Harrie if she were to be hidden somewhere listening. I still do that: there's many a lecture I've given little Miss Kelly that Harrie would have been proud of.

I remember almost exactly what I said to Fanny Boothe that day because I remember her reaction being so queer.

'Bunions,' I drawled in my new Harrie voice. 'Don't they sound just too darling? They should be soft and smell slightly of cinnamon. Don't you think, Fanny dear?'

Harrie laughed, maybe a little uncomfortably, and moved away from me, towards the door. I stayed, waiting for an answer or an acknowledgement of sorts. Fanny Boothe looked long and hard at the length of me. Her usually silly face froze into an expression of shrewd awareness and she spoke without her usual lilt.

'You are obviously unaware of how painful my feet are.' She almost hissed, her mouth pushed high and pouting, close to my face. 'There's no warmth can come from stolen words.'

And then she stepped back, and called out to Harrie's back.

'Be careful.'

Harrie just waved in reply. She didn't notice the hard tone of voice. But I did and I went to meet my new horror in even more confusion than before.

The four of us went to dinner that night. A cheap dinner in a cheap restaurant that served a limited choice of bad cuts of meat, but did so with a certain amount of style. Waiters in starched shirts took your orders with a great show of solemnity and served your choices to you on china plates. The ketchup and salad cream were presented in glass dishes on silver trays and I thought I had died and gone to restaurant-glamorous heaven.

The boys were waiting for us looking as much like men as they could. In retrospect it was quite a sweet sight, but at the time it was terrifying.

Their squared, dark-suited backs were all we could see when we came into the restaurant, curved together, with elbows squarely on the table. The men had an air of solid, informed conversation about them. Their table was close to the door and Harrie called to James as she was handing her coat to an elderly, slightly dishevelled doorman. Both men – boys – turned and James waved and Robert stared.

Robert was tall, though not as tall as James, and slightly broader. He was sallow-skinned with thick, dark hair on his head, over his eyes, on the backs of his hands, dripping from under his cuffs and springing from under his collar. He was a large hunk of masculinity and I was expected to entertain him, and, if the films bore any resemblance to life, I was supposed to captivate him.

I let Harrie go ahead to greet the men and I went straight to the ladies' room. Harrie joined me there after a few minutes. I heard her coming and pretended to be washing my hands. I had been staring blindly at the mirror, willing my features into shape.

She pottered around me, fixing lipstick that had been perfect, patting her well-combed hair and wriggling smooth some non-existent wrinkles in her skirt. I watched her, drying my hands with elaborate care.

'Robert is terribly sweet,' she said. 'He's so nervous about meeting you, he splashed water all over himself, and I only mentioned your name. He said he saw you come in and he thought that you had taken just one look at him and gone home. He said that he wouldn't have blamed you if you had, because you look so outrageously out of his league.'

'He did?' I was obviously still inexperienced enough to believe anything.

'Would I lie?'

Harrie linked me and I left that toilet without further encouragement. I waltzed over to my date for the evening and greeted him effusively. I was driven by a deep sense of empathy and pity I believed it my duty, as a hostess of sorts, to put him at ease. If I had taken the time to observe the situation properly I would have noticed the flicker of disappointment in Robert's eyes as he rose to greet me and the firmness of his hand when he closed it over mine.

It should have been obvious to me that he had never as much as glimpsed me before and that his hand was perfectly steady and his suit was perfectly dry. But to have recognised that I would have had to question what Harrie told me, and the me of seventeen wasn't capable of such an action.

'Robert, I presume?' I drawled in my new Harrie voice, and the evening began.

'Yeah,' he answered, and he hunched his shoulders away from me to light a cigarette. I wasn't going to be so easily put off. After all, the poor man couldn't help being rude – he was shy-struck. I decided to be nice and to help him as much as I could.

'Well, Robert,' I began. I thought the use of his name would reassure him. 'Don't you think it's terribly warm for this time of year?'

There was no answer from the hunched shoulders. He was listening with complete absorption to one of Harrie's stories of gentrified eccentricities. I touched his hunch and repeated my question.

'Yeah,' he said and he half turned around. 'So you come from the country?'

'Oh yes,' I answered eagerly, and went into some detail about where exactly. He yawned.

'Must be awful quiet there. I'm a city man myself, need to have a lot of life around me.'

'Well, there is a lot of life in the country,' I answered. 'It's just that it is all horizontal rather than vertical.' There was a pause, I didn't quite know what I was saying. 'I mean a lot of animals live in the country,' I continued, a little too loudly. James and Harrie paused their conversation to listen.

'I mean,' I was fast losing my drawl. 'There are lots of cows and pigs and things in the country, so even if there aren't so many humans there's probably the same amount of living things as in the cities, except it doesn't seem that way because they – pigs and everything – don't all need separate houses.'

No-one laughed, not even Harrie. It was supposed to have been a droll point, but no-one laughed. Harrie smiled and Robert said, 'I see what you mean.'

Then Harrie said, 'I knew a woman once who had hair down to her knees, almost. It started off black, but the ends were snow white. She said that it aged as it grew. I absolutely loathe long hair on me. I had it once, you know, and I looked completely out of proportion. I swear that's why I'm small – the weight of it anchored me to the ground.'

And the evening was put back on track with Robert's and my laughter.

'It's a generation choice,' said James. 'Our mothers rebelled to have theirs cut, so I am surprised that you girls aren't fighting to grow it long. It's an age-old problem. Was it Socrates that lamented the youth of his day. calling them the equivalent of layabouts? Every generation thinks its children debauched. I would think that it is a healthy sign of growth, of Darwinianism, if you will...'

We sat silent listening. I was to find out that this was one of James's favourite speeches, and one that he managed to introduce into almost every conversation. He had a few that I now know by heart. There is the generation speech, the Indian speech, the colonisation speech, even listing them turns me cold with boredom. But that night I didn't mind. That night I was happy just to listen, and that's what I did. I stayed quiet for most of the evening.

I laughed when the others did and limited my conversation as much as possible. But even so I felt as if I was just barely surviving. By the time the trifle arrived, Robert was ignoring me completely. I decided to make one last effort and so, with a deep gulp, I asked him which film star he preferred.

'So who's your favourite movie star?' I asked with 'character' in my voice. The trashy women's literature of the day had assured me that 'guys' liked girls with 'character'. Unfortunately, I realised, too late, that that had been a schoolgirl's question and Robert treated it as such. He had just shrugged and said, 'Dunno.'

Luckily James took hold of the conversation before Robert's rudeness had the time to be fully appreciated. 'The dangerous power of the movies' was another of his favourite speeches.

'The movies as a cultural phenomenon are quite terrifying in the impact they are having on the social habits of the western world...'

I had failed. I hadn't captivated my man. I excused myself and Harrie followed me to the ladies'.

'I don't think he likes me,' I said. I didn't want to admit defeat. I wanted to be reassured and reassurance was Harrie's forte.

'Of course he does. Honestly, he is quite a rude man, and if he wasn't interested in you he would have gone by now. Honestly, that's what James says of him. James thought you might like him because he is so handsome but frankly, if I were you, I wouldn't bother with him at all. I don't think he's much of a gentleman.'

We laughed. I could see her point – it was all right if one failed in captivating a cad. To succeed in such a venture would probably be deemed unseemly by my mother.

I followed Harrie out of the powder-room with confidence. It was always that way with Harrie – she could empower you by just shifting your viewpoint. We went back to the table and our trifles, and Harrie, in her goodness, directed the conversation in my favour.

'Did you know, Robert, that Em works in Hall's? She has the most funny stories. Oh, you should hear the way she mimics the staff. Do Miss Walsh, Em, go on.'

I did and I shouldn't have.

'Miss Moore,' I said in much the same voice as I had used all night. 'You are precisely three minutes late. Do you understand the concept of employment? Do you understand that three minutes late is nothing short of three minutes theft?'

Before Harrie could laugh her encouragement Robert asked, 'Are you a Moore? My mother's family are Moore.'

I answered and returned to my trifle.

The real disaster came during the coffee course. The main course had been only lukewarm and the vegetables were water-laden and inedible. The trifle had been stale and, though the men had eaten theirs, Harrie and I had left ours largely untouched. I was still hungry and Harrie announced that she was starving.

'I demand cake,' she said. A waiter heard her and wheeled the sweet trolley over to us.

I never see elaborate sweet trolleys today. Back then they were a necessity in even the most basic establishment. I remember this one being especially mouth-watering. It was tiered and coloured and fragrant. We none of us could resist a choice. I picked a creamy strawberry flan and was served first.

I knew etiquette demanded that I had to wait for the others to be ready before I could start, but they were taking so long deliberating and the smell of those strawberries was driving me wild. I restrained myself for as long as I could and then I reasoned that the others would hardly notice just a nibble, let alone mind.

I picked up my slice of strawberry flan and took a large bite out of it. My fingers sank into the soft sponge and cream oozed out, over my hand. Two strawberries fell on to my plate and one on to my lap. Still holding the moist mess that had been a structured slice of cake, I began searching for a napkin. I could feel the coldness of cream on my chin, my cheeks and the tip of my nose. I could see the sugary mess soaking into the cuff of my new brown dress.

It was then that the waiter handed me my pastry fork. I carefully lowered the cake and looked up to see six eyes staring at me in bewilderment. There was a moment's horrible silence before everyone picked up their forks and Harrie launched into a story about a girl she had known who had insisted that her food be washed before she ate it.

'Imagine stew washed in cold water!'

The boys laughed and James added, 'Imagine porridge cleaned with soap!'

And Robert added, 'Cream cakes wouldn't survive the process. They'd disintegrate.'

And Harrie moved the conversation on.

I cleaned my face and hand as well as I could and drank my coffee. I couldn't bring myself to finish the cake.

We left after that. James helped Harrie into her coat, so Robert helped me into mine. Harrie and James walked ahead of us out of the restaurant, so Robert and I walked behind. James linked Harrie as they walked down the steps onto the street, so Robert clumsily held on to my elbow for the length of the three steps.

The four of us stood facing each other on the path, uncertain of how to end the evening. James and Harrie were eager to be on their own, but they both felt responsible for our awkwardness. There was a long moment's silence and then Harrie said, 'Em, you never told Robert your story about the drunken tramp in the women's lingerie department. Robert, you just have to hear this. It's a scream. And, Em dear, I'll see you later.'

Then she snuggled closer to James and walked him away. She had done her bit. She had left us with an opening for conversation. But it was only an anecdote and we both knew that after the anecdote we would have nothing more to say to each other.

We turned and walked in the opposite direction from Harrie and James. Luckily it was also the direction to Marsh Lane. We walked as quickly as we could and I told my anecdote as slowly as I could. I concentrated on the telling, forcing myself to forget the cake incident.

It was a good story with plenty of colourful language and I had the time to tell it well. When I finished, Robert laughed a little and matched it with a story of his about an uncle and a wedding.

'And I swear it's true, though it's hard to believe, but when the happy couple finally drove off for the night he was asleep in the back seat. They say he didn't wake up until the next morning and he was in the garage of the Grande. Well the poor man, there was nothing for it, but he had to walk home and him still in his underpants.'

I laughed rather too much at his story, even though I found it quite distasteful and hardly seemly. But I kept the conversation going by relating an imaginary incident concerning an imaginary aunt of mine who was fond of gin. By then we had reached the top of Marsh Lane.

It might have been the shading of the dusk or it might have been the flattering ring of my laughter, but, instead of saying goodnight, Robert said, 'Let's walk down by the river for a bit.'

The me of seventeen thought Just fancy! I've captivated him. And I said, 'All right.'

We walked down to the river in silence, both of us rather surprised by the turn of events. We walked past the park where Harrie and I spent our evenings and ended up by the same stretch of river that Harrie had shown me on our first evening walk together. We sat opposite the low stone wall on a slightly damp, slightly rotten seat.

It wasn't at all what I had expected. I don't know what I did expect. I suppose somewhere in the back of my mind I was hoping for the grace and charm of Fred Astaire. Robert didn't offer to wipe the seat for me, nor did he take my hand and place me gently sitting, nor did he offer me his jacket in case I was cold. I no longer felt that I had captivated him. I no longer felt cinematic. I was beginning to feel uneasy.

I looked up at him. I was going to ask him to see me home, but I didn't get a chance. His face was surprisingly close to mine and I got a brief glimpse of a smile that could open wide and swallow me, before his face was on mine.

His mouth was on mine. It had all happened so quickly, his mouth had closed over mine that had been opened for speech. Now, my unspoken words were forced back with his teeth and his tongue and his pressing gums. His threatening, musty smell was forced up my nose and his hair was in my hair, on my cheek and in my eyes. I pushed him off and ran home.

Well, I ran away from him. I only ran a short distance, because I was confident that he wouldn't follow me. I walked the rest of the way alone, enjoying the adult freedom of the night air and occasionally running my hand over my lips, trying to wipe them clean.

The closer I got to Marsh Lane, the slower I walked. I was unsure of how to present the case to Harrie. I didn't want to seem too prudish, especially in the light of her experiences, but I knew that my side of the story would have to be told, because Robert was sure to tell his.

I got ready for bed as usual and waited for Harrie as usual and when she came to call for me, I followed her down to her room as usual. She was tousled and tired but awake in the hope of shared confidences.

'Well,' she started. 'Tell me everything. What did you really think of him? He was a bit of a bore wasn't he? You can say – I won't tell James. But what's wrong, Em? What happened? Did he not bring you straight home?'

I don't think it was artifice on my part. I think I was over-whelmed by the emotion of the evening, but whatever the reason, I burst out crying.

Harrie ran to me and softly held my head, absorbing all my tears. She rocked me gently and stayed perfectly quiet. The room was bathed with the sound of my sobs and I wallowed, trance-like, in the comfort of them.

It is a cliché to say that I don't know how long we stayed like that, me in her bed and her kneeling by her pillow holding my head, and I refuse to use clichés. They are nothing but another prop for the aged. So, I will say that we stayed like that for approximately three minutes, which is a long time for uninterrupted tears in company. I think it was I who broke the silence.

'Oh, Harrie, it was awful.'

I hadn't meant to say that. I had intended to brush the whole affair off with a casual, sophisticated joke. But my tears had put me beyond that.

'He took me down to the river and he...'

'Hush, hush,' said Harrie and I never had to say more.

I didn't try very hard to explain. I would have felt foolish describing a mere kiss after such a show of emotion.

Harrie helped me back to my room and stayed with me until I slept. I don't know what she thought, I don't know what she told James and I don't know what James told Robert, but I think at some stage there was talk of fisticuffs and charges being brought.

It was a memorable first kiss.

Chapter 12

The next morning I woke with a clean spirit and a slight headache, but as the morning progressed, my spirit dampened and my headache grew. I sorted threads and remembered Harrie's face when she looked at James. I served customers and heard her lowered tone when she was in conversation with him. By lunchtime I was almost frozen with the chill of exclusion, and that was back then. That was mid-summer, when I was still a child. Imagine how cold I am today.

There is one cliché that is very much associated with age. I often hear it spat through the perfection of false teeth whenever two or more of my peers are gathered. 'Oh,' they say to each other, nodding their heads in pre-agreement – people of my age never expect to meet with a conversation they haven't had before – 'Oh, youth is wasted on the young.'

I've never bothered, but I've often thought of contradicting them. To me it seems obvious that the converse holds more truth – that age is wasted on the old. What good is wisdom to me now? What good is patience? What good is a lifetime's acquired wealth? If the me of seventeen had even one of those attributes my later life might have been very different.

But 'what ifs' are dangerous. I refuse to fall into that trap. The past is set in stone and the past is my story.

I still met Harrie for lunch most days. We still sat in the shade of the bandstand when it was sunny and in its shelter when it rained. On that day it was sunny and we sat on its steps eating our ice-creams.

There was no direct reference made to the previous evening. That was Harrie's way – she never saw the need to root about the effect searching for the cause, or to study the action in the hope of finding the character. She had a freer approach to past events and passing acquaintances – they just were, and they were to be tolerated or enjoyed. But that didn't mean that they weren't to be understood, or that they couldn't be cosseted.

'Let's do something lovely tonight,' Harrie said. 'Let's do something lazy, just us two. I have to meet James after work, but only for half an hour. Then, I would like to formally invite you to tea in my room. Even though today is Thursday I think I shall serve my cure for Monday.'

'Why Miss Elliott,' I answered in my best Miss Walsh voice. 'A shipshape life is dependent on everything being accounted for and everything in its place. A cure for Monday served on a Thursday is sure to give indigestion.'

We both fell back on to the boards of the bandstand in laughter. We lay there for a bit in silence, finishing our ice-creams. I stared at the underside of the old roof trying to contain the moment.

Harrie had never before made such a precise arrangement with me. I felt that perhaps, despite her uninvolved approach to life, she felt a little responsible for my trauma of the previous evening. It seemed that whatever she felt, she felt it strongly enough to break a date with James.

The moment lasted for as long as Harrie allowed and then she pointed with her ice-cream at the dark, rotted boards above us. They were pitted with holes.

'Don't you think, Em, that maybe God knitted this roof as well?'

I laughed and agreed. The dangerous-looking holes had suddenly become stars. I left the bandstand, secure in the knowledge that I was important and cared for, and returned to work in high spirits.

I greeted Miss Walsh with a smile and told Gillian that it was too hot outside for her cardigan and she should leave it in her locker. I sorted some ribbons without being asked to and I dusted down our display of gloves. I even faced Mrs Jones with humour. She came puffing towards me and started her booming questioning while she was still in soft furnishings.

Gillian, just returned from her lunch-hour, took up her duster and moved closer to haberdashery, ready for the fun. Miss Walsh hovered by my shoulder in case of trouble, and I fancied that even the customers themselves shuffled in and hushed their conversations.

'Ho-ho-ho, there she is! Can I have a yard of your finest ha-ha-ha Barcelona? Or do you have anything in a Moscow now? Do you think Moscow is my colour?'

I smiled through the tedium of her wit and waited for her to bore of her joke. Eventually she did. She took her newest creation out of her shopping bag. It was a large, ugly, over-trimmed hat and she plonked it in front of me.

'Now, what do you think of that? I think it needs a little something more. Maybe a dash of Luxembourg, eh? Ha ha ha. Or should we try the Balkan states?'

I smiled.

'No,' I answered slowly, as if lost in thought. 'No, I think it needs the bin.'

'What!'

'I think beads and ribbon.' I repeated calmly.

And the sale went on. Gillian choked slightly and one or two customers turned in surprise and Miss Walsh overheard, and, though she decided against reporting me to Mr Hall, she insisted on lecturing me for the rest of the afternoon.

'The customers, Miss Moore, are our duty and our livelihood. We should be ever grateful for their custom and we should delight in their humour. To think that I have lived to see such rudeness, and at my counter!'

I listened to it all carefully and didn't mind a bit of it. I had a marvellous night ahead of me and a marvellous story to tell Harrie.

It was a marvellous night. Just like old times, of a week previous. I clung to every minute of that night and watched them all speed by. I suppose something in me knew it would be the last night of its kind.

I arrived home before Harrie and met Fanny Boothe escorting Miss Charter Thomas down to the dining-room. Well, in context, escorting is maybe a bit of a euphemism. To be precise, and I pride myself on my precision, Fanny Boothe was physically supporting Miss Charter Thomas across the hall. Miss Charter Thomas was obviously having one of her bad days. It showed in the way she shuffled and in the wildness of her hair.

Dressed in her finest velvet, she was lumbering against the wall and rebounding on poor Fanny Boothe who was staggering badly with every blow.

'Slowly now,' Fanny was saying. 'If you just hold on to me.' And she was trying to link her companion's arm. But with every step, Miss Charter Thomas shook her off and with the same movement hurled herself in to the wall.

Filled with the expected joys of my evening, I stepped into their path and, addressing Fanny, offered my help. With enormous effort she brought herself and her companion to a halt. She had to hold tight to Miss Charter Thomas's shoulders as she spoke,

'It's not me that needs the help,' she answered, her face close to mine and her words hissing out.

'Oh goodness me, Fanny dear,' I drawled. 'Please don't take offence. Of course I was offering to help Miss C. T. here.'

'Where are you from?' demanded Fanny, and then, not waiting for an answer continued. 'I know well where you're from and I know well what kind of accent you had when you first came here. And I know that your jacket is long past needing a wash and I know that there's them that are incapable of good and they're the same ones that want it, and steal it, and ruin it.'

I stood shaken by her fury. Surprise fixed me to the spot. I was blocking their path. I only moved when Miss Charter Thomas clawed a hand out towards my hair and whispered her saying close to my face. I stepped aside and the two old ladies continued their painful shuffle. I may have been collected enough to step out of their way, but it took until they had disappeared behind the panelled door to the basement before the force of Mrs Boothe's venom dissipated.

I waited until the door was closed before I shrugged and continued upstairs. I forced myself to smile at the eccentricities of the old, but, although I tried my best, I couldn't fashion the encounter into an amusing story for Harrie. By the time she came in I knew that I wouldn't mention it at all.

I waited in my room until I heard her light step on the stairs. She called to me as she ran up to her room: 'Em, it's me. I'm home. Come and help me. Sorry I'm late.'

I flew down to her.

Together we unpacked our meal – white rolls with sardine paste, chocolate cake and strong tea. We sat on either side of Harrie's low table, curled into her large armchairs and ate and talked. Well, I talked and she ate.

'...and I said, calm as you like, I said "beads and ribbon".'

Harrie laughed and laughed.

'And Miss Walsh heard.'

'No! Oh do Miss Walsh! Go on, what did she say?'

'It is Hall's policy to treat our customers with respect. Perhaps no-one has made that clear to you. As we have always employed ladies, we presumed our staff would be aware of the common rules of politeness.'

We laughed and laughed and I repeated the whole incident, throwing in a fictional wink from a male customer and a fictional reprimand from Mr Newby: 'You can make a mistake with money, but it's no mistake when you short-change people with words.'

Afterwards we sat curled in our armchairs and Harrie talked and I toyed with her mermaid perfume bottle, stared into the dense greenery of the back garden and listened. Harrie proposed a walk in the park and I declined. Later, she proposed a visit to Fanny Boothe and I vehemently declined. So, instead, we just sat and Harrie talked.

Usually Harrie dismissed my refusals and usually I didn't offer much resistance to her suggestions, but we both of us knew that that night was my night and so we just sat and talked. It was quiet talk, though – the hilarity of our shared pretences no longer seemed apt.

Harrie told me more about herself than she had for a while. She told me about a holiday she had in Switzerland. A holiday that seemed to have stretched over seasons.

'You wouldn't believe the snow in spring,' she said. 'It looks like clouds fallen from the sky. Great big fluffy white clouds that might just take off and fly back to where they belong and you always hope that they will take you with them. The whole place was dominated by the sky. I suppose it was because we were so high up, but a blue sky meant a blue world and you could bear that, but a grey sky was horribly depressing, especially if it lasted a while, and when I was there it lasted all winter. For one whole winter I lived in a rain cloud.'

She lapsed into silence and I glanced over at her. She looked old and scared, but I put that down to a trick of the light. The me of seventeen couldn't register a vulnerable Harrie.

'Was that before or after Paris?' I asked cheerfully.

'Paris? Oh yes, Paris. No it was after. Although some of it was during.' She answered slowly and hesitantly, but regained her composure almost immediately.

'Paris was so different, Em. Paris in the summer wilts, positively dies, but Paris in the winter is the complete reverse of Switzerland. Paris in the winter is the sky and if Paris is lit up, the heavens are blue. I can imagine angels swooping and diving on Paris, to taste and remind themselves of paradise on earth.'

Harrie was in a strange mood that night, but I felt closer to her than before. I felt that I was being allowed close to confidences, but not quite into them. At times I had the uneasy feeling that she was almost talking to herself. I would ask her questions and she would ignore them or be confused by them, thrown by them, as if I had disturbed some deep, hidden workings of her mind.

I asked her more about the family she had au-paired for, more stories about the disgraced grandfather and she ignored me.

Later on, I interrupted her reminiscences about school to ask about the chronology of her first lover. She had told me that she first met him when she was only sixteen and I couldn't understand how a married man would be allowed access to a girl who was no relation to him. Especially when that girl was surrounded by guardian nuns.

'Oh, he managed,' she explained. 'We met during holidays and the affair continued because I missed quite a bit of school that year. I was sick. He was a doctor and nuns just adore doctors.'

And she was reminded of Paris.

'French doctors are beautiful things,' she said. 'They treat women with such respect. They allow us to keep the dignity of our depths and they just insult our façades with their probing. And they are so handsome. Every one I met was dark with large, worker's hands that were worn smooth with the handling of bodies. Not like here – doctors' hands here are soft with disuse and they use those soft hands to strip you down to your essentials and leave you to take care of yourself.'

'And did you know many doctors? French doctors I mean.'

'Oh yes, quite a few.' There was a short pause before she continued hurriedly. 'The man I worked for, he was a doctor and he used to entertain his doctor friends frequently. I was sent to his family because my father was a doctor and they knew each other. My mother would never have trusted me in a strange man's house. But enough of this,' and she shook herself free of her disjointed memories.

'I need a walk before bed. Come on, keep me company around the park and tell me again, from the start, about Mrs Jones. No, don't start now, wait until we're outside.'

This time I agreed with the necessity of a walk. Harrie's melancholy mood was contagious and I was tired and perhaps a little scared of trying to pin her stories down with questions. We flung on our coats, twirling the atmosphere of the room into something brighter, linked each other's arms and walked smartly out on to the street, relieved by the night air and the comfort of motion.

Once we had settled into our stride, I told my story again, from the beginning, and Harrie laughed as much as if not more than she did on first hearing. This time, third time around, I threw in a cameo appearance by Mr Hall himself, complete with umbrella and cumbersome watch. By the time I was finished with it, it was a very funny story.

We walked once around the park, around the outside. It was past dusk, so the gates were locked. We contemplated breaking in through the gap in the railings and climbing our tree again and maybe staying there till dawn.

'Or we could live there,' said Harrie. 'Two mad park girls that no-one quite believes in but everyone is terribly scared of.'

'The abominable park girls.' I loved the idea, I loved the we-ness of it.

'Yes, but eventually we would get too tired, fall asleep and fall out of our tree.'

'Oh we wouldn't be so stupid,' I said. 'By then we would have a tree house, a wood burner, two carved chairs and a store of nuts for the winter.'

We both laughed.

It was getting late and we were tired, but we both returned to Harrie's room and curled back into our armchairs. It was as if Harrie had as much need for me then as I had for her always.

We sat silent for a while listening to the vague echo of Mrs Benson's rebel song. And then Harrie spoilt it all and began talking softly of James.

'I trust him to mind me,' she said. 'I trust him when he holds me and when he thinks of me and when he bosses me. I trust that he knows what is best and that he will make sure that I do what is best. Because you know, Em dear, I very rarely know what to do and I often do the wrong thing.'

I laughed and I shouldn't have. Harrie was leaning forward into her argument, trying to catch the words as they escaped. She was deadly serious.

'No, Em, I don't even think that I truly know my right from my wrong. I have done so many wrong things with so many wrong people. I think James is the one man that I will trust to decide for me. He is the one man that I will trust to love me. With him I won't be thinking of the next one, because he will be my all.'

'You haven't... I mean you and James haven't...'

'No.' She shook herself slightly and answered a little coldly. 'No we haven't, and we won't until we can do it properly, legally.'

'So do you think that you'll marry him?'

'Oh yes.' She was definite. 'And I think he may be beginning to agree with me. Not that it has been discussed, but I can see it in his eyes.'

I had to agree with her, though I didn't do so out loud. I knew what Harrie was talking about. James's eyes took on a depth when they were focused on Harrie. I could see that for him the rest of the world was two-dimensional.

I left soon after that. I didn't stay to watch Harrie undress and get ready for bed. I wanted to be alone and I wanted to be somewhere beyond the echo of James's name.

I left with a sour taste in my chest that kept me awake late into the night. It may have been the sardines, but I doubt it – they have always agreed with me.

Chapter 13

Harrie's intention to marry blocked my reason. I had so much then, but I couldn't appreciate it. I was young and I wanted it all. I saw no joy in half measures and perhaps I was right – compromise is nothing more than an admission of failure, a way to live with mistakes and mediocrity. And I should know: I was married for the best part of half a century.

That was my last night of calm before I was launched into a society of sorts. I look back on that time and feel the warmth of that summer. It warms me still, it warms the old bones, deep in my body. The bones that the sun can no longer reach. I look back on that time and I see colours and patches of vivid memories. I can smell the food I ate and I can touch the fabrics I wore, and, through it all, I can sense the sadness I felt. It was the birth of the sadness that is heavy in me now, after a lifetime's growth. Harrie and I were together, we linked arms and faced the world together, but her world was James, and I was left looking at her, looking at James.

I think it was just the next day that I was plunged into my second date. Back then things changed from day to day, even the weather seemed to be more adventurous. It seems impossible to me now to imagine that one day I was an innocent, virgin, free of male contact, and within a week I was to be confused by which man had said what and whether he had a moustache. Of course, again, I am speaking with that superior knowledge of hindsight we old people are so proud of. The transition was, I remember, rather fraught.

Harrie insisted that I came out again with her and James. She had obviously been in consultation with him about me, and they had concluded that I needed diverting and entertaining to get over the trauma of Robert. Harrie had no need to insist: I was willing to do as I was told. But it was always that way with Harrie – she would never take the responsibility of your decision-making away from you.

We met for lunch that day as usual, but for a change she was there first. She waved her ice-cream at me from a distance and I broke into a run.

'Em, darling,' she drawled, when I finally reached her. 'Garbo is back in the Savoy and rumour has it that she is only there to see us. It would be rude to keep her waiting too long.'

I was delighted, it had been one of our jokes that we were the actresses and our world the film. Every now and then we would pop into the cinema to give our fans on the big screen a treat. It was Harrie who decreed it should only be every now and then – she didn't care much for the cinema really – claiming that if we went more frequently we would lose our mystique.

'But she's such a bore, don't you think? So clingy, so adoring.' I was in heaven – two whole nights with Harrie!

'I know what you mean, dear, but she is so loyal. I do think we owe her the occasional appearance. And if she does get a little over-enthusiastic, at least we will have the protection of our escorts.'

She turned to see my reaction and I, anticipating her move, kept my disappointment well hidden under curiosity.

'Protection? Escorts? Why, Harrie dear, you have me intrigued.'

'James has another friend.' She caught my eye and laughed, and a split second later I joined her. She continued almost immediately. 'He's nothing like Robert – he is a very nice man. Terribly well spoken and shockingly well dressed. I know this for sure because I met him and was struck by how much he looked like every mother's dream.'

'And would you say that he looks like my dream? Anything Fredish about him?'

'There's a definite Fredishness about the hair.'

We both laughed, but Harrie dropped the shared joke

immediately. It was as if she was scared of the intimacy it implied. She continued for a while, alternating praise of the man with quoted reviews of the film. As I have said, there was no need – the me of seventeen always did as I was told. Especially when I was told by Harrie.

I returned to work bundled in nervous energy and suffered another afternoon of awkward fumbling. It seemed as if everything I touched bounced off the rawness of my nerves, and everything I dropped was witnessed by Miss Walsh, who insisted on helping matters by positioning herself close to my shoulder and sucking air through her pursed mouth whenever I as much as moved.

I returned to Marsh Lane slowly, dragging my feet through every step. I had had a whole afternoon alone with my thoughts, imagining every social disaster and every physical variation of Robert. I was almost immobilised with the horror of it all.

I told myself that it was a film. Conversation would not be necessary for most of the evening, and, when it was necessary the film should provide ample material. But I knew that conversation wasn't what scared me. These men didn't bother with conversation. I had hardly spoken to Robert and he had....

I still don't like thinking about the physical proximity of such men. Or indeed any man, but some do seem far more masculine than others. James must have understood this and his initial mistake, because my film date turned out to be absolutely nothing to worry about, hardly masculine at all.

This is where I do truly get confused. James always had a supply of interchangeable male friends. They were all small and slender, usually with sandy colouring. They all worked in the legal profession, carefully tucked away from sunlight. They all kept their nails and hair very clean and they usually smelled rather nice. Just to add an extra dimension of confusion they all had chummy, monosyllabic names such as Tom or Jim. God only knows where James had found Robert.

So, on that first night of many, I went to the cinema with Harrie and James, and Dan or Bill and I enjoyed myself. I had arrived home late, due to my reluctant feet, and so I had to wash, dress and smear my face with sophistication at great speed, with Harrie beside me urging me on. I may have looked harassed and wild by the time we arrived at the cinema but I felt more composed. I hadn't had the time to fret. And once I took one look at Dan or Bill I didn't have the inclination.

I relaxed, watched the film, ate the chocolates Jack or Tim gave me, and when it was over, and I was being helped into my jacket, I was confident enough to give the boy a smile comparable to a pat on the head.

Afterwards we went to Martine's for coffee. Harrie and James walked ahead and myself and whoever walked behind. James linked Harrie and my little friend blushed. I saw his confusion and relaxed even more. I was even able to take control of his embarrassment and help ease him out of it.

'So are you in the same line of work as James?' I asked.

'Yes, yes, well, sometimes. And you? Do you work with Harrie?'

'Goodness, no.' My drawl was heavily influenced by the recent film. 'I doubt I have a brain cell to spare once I have decided what to wear for the day.' And he smiled. 'No, I think thought is wasted on work, so I work in a shop.' And he laughed.

'I'm sure it takes brains to work in a shop, all that money and everything.' It may sound patronising now, but it was meant as a shy kind of compliment.

'Believe me, it doesn't. Not if you're smart enough to get out of the way of the customers.'

After a moment's confusion, he laughed. It was lovely. I was captivating. Harrie glanced back to smile at me – she had heard the laughter. I felt her absolution for the fiasco that was Robert and I knew I would never agonise over that evening again.

We walked on in conversation, a conversation that I dominated. The poor boy walked in obedient silence, laughing when I paused on a high note and nodding whenever I made a point. He looked happy just to be with a girl, especially one of such impressive height and with such taste in lipstick. He was, they all were, the kind of man that rarely came into contact with scarlet lipstick.

We walked to Martine's and the four of us sat around a table for about an hour. Harrie and I talked together and James and his little friend spoke of histories and wars loudly, probably for our and the restaurant's benefit. The film, a simple, tragic love story, had somehow reminded James of the American civil war, and it just so happened that he had only that evening finished a book on that very topic.

Later, we were joined by another friend of James's and his little girlfriend in pink, with baby pink lips. He dazzled the boys with insider knowledge of the track. His claim to authenticity was a five-pound note that was said to have come from a twenty-to-one outsider. He hadn't won anything in a year, but he was still considered an expert.

Harrie and I kept our faces straight, but kicked each other under the table when we found this out. Harrie had politely listened to his story about the five-pound note and then had innocently asked, 'Do you have it with you?'

'Oh no, it's long spent. I won it last Christmas.'

Even so, the boys were still willing to take his advice, if not act on it, and they left us girls behind as they waded deeper into the mysterious world of form. Again, it was a conversation much too old for them. Harrie and I were left with the girlfriend and her tedious details about her sister's baby.

Still later another couple stopped by, but there was nowhere for them to sit, so they just stopped to say hello. Another sandy-haired boy and another curly-haired girl, with lips of unkissable pink.

We ate chips and drank coffee and Harrie and I nudged each other and laughed and laughed at jokes that were told, or jokes that we winked at each other about over our companion's descriptions of christening robes.

It was late when we left. I had hoped that Harrie would come with me, she had seemed to take so little notice of James over the evening. But she didn't. We four stood on the path while James said goodbye to his friend. Then his arm snaked around Harrie, and even in the darkness I could see the glint of that smile of his. That smile that could open wide and swallow her. She curled into him and waved at me and I turned away.

Jim or Jack or Tom or Tim or whoever he was walked me home. He walked me home with great deliberation and with a grave quietness suitable to his position of responsibility. He had a mission to take me safely to my door. He took care to walk on the outside, protecting me from the horrors of the road, and he took care to keep the conversation as impersonal as a conversation could be between people of the same age and race.

'They say that the tram system is to be overhauled.'

'Do they?'

I was thinking of Harrie. It had dawned on me that her good humour in Martine's probably had nothing to do with my presence. She had sparkled because of the proximity of James and because she knew that she would be spending time, later on, alone with him.

'Yes, they say that the average working man loses one hundred working hours a year due to delays brought about by the trams breaking down.'

'Do they?'

She was alone with him now and she was probably happier than she had ever been with me.

'They say that it was the fault of the initial engineering. Back-handers were involved.'

'Do they?'

Harrie would have in-jokes and shared pretences with James, just as she used to have with me. They had a language I didn't even know about.

My date droned on and I smiled and listened, as I had been brought up to do when a man spoke. I had no fear of unwanted kisses from this man, and, if I had been a different woman, I would have had no hope of wished-for kisses.

He walked with me to the smiling, gummy door of 26 Marsh Lane, and insisted on standing outside until the door was safely shut behind me. We shook hands and I thanked him for my evening and he waited while I got my key.

I did try and get rid of him – I knew he would be upset by what he was bound to hear, and he was. I opened the door and we were both hit by a blast of one of Mrs Benson's rowdy, happy-drunk ditties.

> *A girl in the park*
> *With no face in the dark*
> *And I kissed her for the lark.*
> *Well my God she said*
> *But he's sick in bed*
> *I'd swear you were me Fred.*

I shouted my last goodnight over the shocking chorus and closed the door on the young man's surprise. I kept my laughter until Harrie came home and then we shared it.

I was dressed for bed when I heard Harrie on the stairs but I wasn't yet in it. I ran out to meet her halfway, eager to reclaim the last hour I had lost to James. We ran giggling into her room and I jumped into her bed and moved my legs rigorously under the covers to warm the sheets.

'Well, Em dear, have you found love?'

It didn't cross my mind that she might have expected a declaration of enthusiasm from me. I took the question in the spirit of a joke and laughed. A split second later Harrie joined me. When I had sobered myself, I jumped out of the bed and began walking up and down the room with my shoulders hunched and one foot turned in slightly, as if in an agony of embarrassment.

'My name is Jim,' I said in the monotone that James's friends considered sophisticated. 'I think girls are nice and if you are a girl I like you. I'm sure you will like me because I am terribly interesting and to prove this to you I am prepared to tell you all I know about the history of this, our great and good country, and when I'm finished I will tell you all I know about the history of that great and good country and, if that's not enough for you, I'll throw in the history of the other great and good country.'

It was a parody of Jim or Sam, and a good one I had his intonation down to a tee, but it was a parody of a friend of James's, and, it was a parody of James's choice of conversation. Harrie took a moment to laugh and she didn't laugh happily. I moved swiftly on. I sat on the bed with my knees tucked safely in my arms and my head resting on them. I pouted and fluttered my eyelashes and spoke as sweetly as I could.

'Oh, you must be Harrie. I'm Rose. Well,' giggle, 'Rosie actually, amn't I, Bob? Oooh Bob do stop. Oooh not now. Oooh what'll they think? And my sister, she's Daisy and her baby is Violet, but because she's still such a baby we all call her Petal, now isn't that too darling? It's just like me when I was a baby, my Daddy, he always called me Rosebud.'

And Harrie laughed for real, but I knew that she was just laughing at the performance. Her laughter never went beyond that, to laugh at my inspiration.

When I had finished with Rosie, I told her about my walk home and poor Tim's face when he heard Mrs Benson at her best. I think I did a very good impersonation of it, complete with jug ears and flared nostrils.

Harrie laughed and laughed. She sat on one of her armchairs with one stocking on and one off, her legs kicking with the laughter, and I repeated the whole story and added an elderly couple, who happened along the opposite side of the road just as I opened the door.

I left Harrie sleepy and smiling. I stayed in her bed long enough to warm her feet and then I left, hoping that her smiles had more to do with my jokes than James's kisses.

And that was how things went for the next six or seven weeks.

Chapter 14

Over the next weeks my work suffered, even by my standards. I came bleary-eyed on to the floor in the morning, and by mid-afternoon I was slumped in apathy and exhaustion.

My relationship with my parents suffered. I missed my father's birthday weekend, because it clashed with a dance to celebrate James's birthday. At the time I felt that it would be dangerous to leave Harrie and James unattended to toast each other in the warmth of a summer night. Such occasions were made for propositions.

My wardrobe improved considerably. I ate a lot less and spent a lot more on clothes and discreet cosmetics. It was money well spent – I still have one evening dress from that summer. It is an ivory satin with outrageous green flowers flung all over it. It was very spectacular in its day, especially when worn with a long neck. I wore it to my eighteenth-birthday celebrations.

My friendship with James also improved considerably. I made sure that it did. I made sure that Harrie and James were not left alone to form the social core of our set. I made sure that I never missed an evening out and that I was ever-present in any decision-making. I made sure that our set had a social core of three, and James helped in this.

He provided me with escorts and I provided him with excuses as to why I couldn't pursue a relationship with any of them. His continuous search for my new men ensured that I was always on his mind, and my continual rejection of them ensured that we continued to be linked by the camaraderie of a single purpose. We were also linked by Harrie.

There is a tedium about couples that I could never tolerate. I think their inherent boredom is what drives most couples to procreate. When a third party is introduced, they bring with them a whole host of power struggles, potential intrigues and alliances. Even the most disinterested third party does that, and I was far from disinterested.

Initially, and for as long as I could, I clung fast to Harrie, trying to link her to my concerns, trying to distance her from James. It never worked. She held on to James with all her heart. She was so sure of him, she never needed reassurances from me, and so she never felt the need to confide in me.

Oh, she told me about him all right. She told me about his behaviour and his ambitions, she even told me about her hopes for him, but she wasn't really confiding in me. She wasn't looking for my approval or even my opinion. She was only using my ear as an extension of her thoughts. I tried to shake her resolve, but it never worked.

I took to asking probing questions, questions phrased in the negative language of concern. We would sit in the shade of our bandstand away from the heat of August and I would always steer the conversation around to James. That much was easy, Harrie was always willing to talk about him. We would talk about the night before or the night ahead or the night planned for the weekend and I would relate as much negativity as I could specifically to James, asking questions like, 'Rosie is so irritating. Is she a close friend of James?' Or 'Do you think James will ever ask you to meet his family?' Or 'Can James dance? I can't imagine him dancing can you?' Or 'Don't you find westerns so boring and violent. Does James really like them?' Harrie answered all my questions at face value. It never seemed as if she considered them for long enough to let their tone or their content settle in her mind.

I was more direct at night. When we came home from our evenings out, and when I was curled in her bed telling her stories and laughing at our companions and making her laugh at my impersonations of them, I allowed myself the occasional dig at

James. Some she laughed at, some she ignored and some she listened to tight-lipped.

I was very good at sitting as James. I would carefully hitch my dress or nightgown as high as my knee and, after checking my seat for visible dirt, would lower myself into it. Harrie always laughed at that.

I also did a very good impersonation of James's drone. It was slightly nasal and seemed to fly from the depth of his epiglottis – it was usually flecked with saliva. It was, as I say, a good impersonation and one that I perfected over the years, much to the delight of many a dinner party, but Harrie never acknowledged it. She would carry the conversation over my silliness and on to more general topics. It was always that way with Harrie – she could display her displeasure in the subtlest ways.

She was even subtle about heartfelt anger or hurt. I saw that the time I took a chance and put my soul behind a parody of the complete pomposity of James in his youth. It was about a week into my new life of glamour on a shopgirl's wage. As usual, I was home first and as usual, I followed Harrie down to her room once I heard her on the stairs. I hardly waited to greet her before I launched into my attack. We had spent the evening in the cinema and later in Martine's. The film had been a tedious western – not that I have ever seen another kind of western – and my date was a tedious solicitor, another waste of a good adjective. It had been a dull night with just the four of us. No Rosie or Sally or Jane to cheer us. No extra Tom, Dick or Hal to divert us. We four sat for an hour and half over eight cups of coffee and James spoke. He told us about the responsibility Hollywood had to document the demise of the Indians as honestly as possible.

'The white man took their culture and as such it is incumbent on him to document and catalogue what he has taken. He obviously has no intention of giving it back, but it would indeed be a greater evil if he replaced it with nothing more substantial than falsehood and self-serving fabrication.'

He pointed out several inconsistencies in the film we had just seen and then went on to tell us, at length, how he would have managed the entire affair.

'I would employ Indian actors and Indian researchers and insist on getting the details right, such as the correct war paint on each tribe. Authenticity may cost a little more, but quality will always end by paying its own way.'

It was an evening of James at his worst and I did expect Harrie to appreciate that.

She opened her bedroom door to me that night with much the same expression of good humour as usual. She greeted me and returned to her armchair and her hairbrush. I walked into the room as James. I seated myself carefully on her bed, after first hitching my nightgown as high as my knee, and proceeded to drone as wetly as I could, 'It was the extinction of the buffalo that did the most damage. Not the railroad and not the armies, though of course the former was largely responsible for the slaughtering of the herds. Now if I were to have managed the growth of the railroad I would have insisted on employing buffalo drivers and buffalo conductors, thereby ensuring the preservation of buffalo culture…'

'I'm tired tonight.' Harrie interrupted me. She had started to unbutton her dress and had stopped midway. She was holding it closed, tight across her chest. 'I'd much rather be alone. Close the door tight behind you.'

I left without another word.

It was the closest we had ever come to an argument, and I spent the most part of the night crying with the terror of having committed an irreparable harm. Well, I like to think that I cried for the best part of the night, but youth doesn't really have the physical make-up for drama. Young bodies are always healing themselves. They are always being betrayed by sleep and hunger and the will to survive. I'd say, in honesty, that I cried for a bit and then slept soundly, but I woke up worried, and was tempted to call on Harrie before I left for work.

An unusual flash of common-sense stopped me. Somewhere I

got the wisdom to know that the best course of action to take was one of ignorance. I would leave it to Harrie to broach the subject, and, if she did, she would have to admit that James was, at times, deeply boring. She didn't. She met me for lunch and was just as she always was. She spent our entire forty minutes telling me about a Belgian woman she had met in Paris.

'A wonderful woman in all things except in her treatment of cats. She hated the poor creatures. Towards the end she had herself convinced they were messengers from hell. And that would have been all right in its way, except she was convinced that all hats were made out of cat-skin. And even that would have been all right in its way except she worked in a hat shop. She was advised to get another job, but she insisted on staying put. I think she felt safer keeping an eye on the enemy.'

It was a very funny story, especially Harrie's descriptions of the elaborate lengths the lady went to to avoid touching the hats while serving customers, and I did enjoy it, even if I was slightly disappointed. I had hoped for the opportunity to denounce James, but I was relieved that Harrie had forgiven me, or, better still, understood that there was nothing to forgive. I left James and his foibles alone after that.

But James and I were destined to become close. It was the emotion we both felt for Harrie that bonded us and that was enough. We two lived to prove that we had nothing else in common. When we first met, Harrie had been like a bridge linking us. We stood on opposites sides, facing each other, and she ran between us. But, as that summer progressed, Harrie seemed to move more into herself and more into the world in general. She was funnier, louder, wilder in company, but she was sadder in private. By the end of the summer James and I were standing side by side, facing our world together, and our world was Harrie.

I never discussed this time with James, so I don't know for sure how he felt, but I can guess that he felt as confused as I did. Perhaps more so, but then any additional confusion he suffered would have been my intentional fault

The first night I noticed this change in Harrie was the night of James's birthday celebrations. But now that I think of it, she had been changing since I first met her.

James's birthday fell on a Wednesday I think, and he spent it with his parents. I remember being relieved that Harrie wasn't asked to join him, and I remember Harrie making excuses for the slight.

'He says it will be too tedious an affair. A dinner full of aged relatives that are nosy enough without encouragement. He says that his mother asked me, but he put her off. I'm to take tea with them soon instead. He is so considerate. Tea is such a more manageable meal, don't you think?'

I answered with one of my questions phrased in the negative language of concern: 'And did he fix a date for this tea?'

'Soon,' was all she could say for sure.

But to give James his due, I think he was planning a meeting. He had begun mentioning his parents more and more, dropping hints as to what they expected from young people, how they expected young ladies to dress, that sort of thing. I took the time to notice these comments, but Harrie made it her business to memorise them. It was around this time that she bought her first high-collared floral frock. She never went as far as to wear it, but she kept it fresh and aired, ready to be worn to tea.

James's birthday celebrations were held on the Saturday following his birthday. My father's birthday was on the Sunday. I hadn't seen my parents for weeks. I'm sure they felt that such a length between visits could only be interpreted as unseemly by the neighbours, and they were, initially, very put out by my refusing to wish my father well in person. Eventually, however, they accepted that an evening with a solicitor friend was more important than an evening with them. And, when it came to facing the neighbours, the excuse of a solicitor was far preferable to the presence of a daughter.

Well, at least my mother saw it this way, but my father, who had less faith in my honesty and in my ability to marry, took the time not to write to me for two whole weeks. His letters were usually frequent – I got at least two a week. I think he saw them as furthering my education, or else he visualised them published after his death. They were very peculiar letters, very didactic and totally impersonal. I remember one being solely about the feeding habits of polar bears. But all this is dangerously sliding into a tangent, and I refuse to humour such an aged tendency.

The use of James as an excuse didn't come as a complete surprise to my parents. I had mentioned James in most of my letters. I had told them all about my new social life. I must have still been innocent enough to be proud of the fact that I had one, and I had mentioned James as my constant companion. I don't think I intentionally meant to mislead them. It was just that I couldn't bring myself to share Harrie with them. So, James's name kept cropping up on its own.

My new social crowd decided to go dancing as James's birthday treat. It was an option that James would never have chosen himself, but then we knew that and so he wasn't given a choice.

Back then it was the fashion for hotels to hold monthly dinner dances that were relatively expensive but beautifully luxurious. James's birthday weekend coincided with one of the best of these dances. It was too good an opportunity to miss – the cost of the tickets demanded an occasion and, until then, we could never come up with one.

Harrie and Rosie and Sally and Jane and Tim and Tom and Bert and I and all the rest of us were thrown into a flap of excitement. James looked on in silence. It wasn't so much that he wasn't fond of dancing – though that was true – it was more that he was never fond of spending money, though that became more pronounced in later years.

Finally the waited-for Saturday came and Harrie and I spent the afternoon shut away in her room with an array of beautifying equipment. It started off as a lovely afternoon. We were both excited and a bit giddy, but that was all. Harrie seemed as calm as usual.

I remember her then as I always want to remember her. She

sat curled in her armchair, wrapped in her silk kimono, intently concentrating on the cake she was eating. Her hair was wild about her face with thick curls bouncing off her shoulders. She had tied it in rags the night before, and the sun, beaming through the open window, danced off every strand. I sat opposite her in my corset – a contraption that was completely superfluous in my case but one that my mother had convinced me was absolutely necessary – and bathrobe and I think, even then, I appreciated a deep sense of home.

We painted our nails, toes and fingers. We put egg-white on our faces and tried not to make each other laugh. We rubbed tonics and lotions into our skin and tweezed hair from our eyebrows, shaping them into permanent arches of sophistication.

We were finished way too early. There were still hours to go before we could put on our dresses, and so we just sat. I told Harrie about my six-week-assessment conversation with Mr Hall, which had gone remarkably well. He had shaken my hand and had complimented me on the flurry of activity he had noticed around the haberdashery counter since I had started. Afterwards I analysed every nuance of his tone and every flicker of his expression, but I couldn't detect any note of irony. Miss Walsh, contrary to her threats, must have kept her misgivings about me to herself.

'See,' said Harrie, 'you are just as brilliant at your job as I always suspected.'

'Oh, I wish I wasn't quite so brilliant,' I answered. 'If I was just average perhaps the fans would give me some rest.'

Harrie ignored my allusion to our shared joke, as I knew she would. She was silent for a moment and then she told me about a girl she had known in Switzerland who was terribly beautiful and terribly vague. Her mood changed as her story progressed, and what started off as a cheerful anecdote ended up by dragging Harrie low.

'One day, Em, she just disappeared. She left us her beautiful, breathing, body but she took her soul with her, and she disappeared somewhere deep inside herself, somewhere far away from us. They say you can see a person's life in their eyes, and hers were always so bright. They were beautiful, but their light was always the light of sadness. You know it can dazzle brighter than the deepest joy.

'That was it, she was just dazzled by sadness. And then she disappeared, and the light of grief left her eyes and you could see nothing except repose, the deep death of complete repose.

'I've always envied her, Em. She always looked so perfectly content. She had placed herself where no-one could hurt her.'

It was not a happy story but it didn't merit the terrible heaviness with which it was told. When Harrie had finished, she sat still and sad, and I remembered one of the first things she ever told me about herself.

'Em,' she had said. 'I have black moods. They're darker than those blues that people sing about. Much darker.'

Once before, she had tried to describe her black moods in more detail and I agreed with her, they did sound darker than most depressions. That afternoon, sitting waiting to go to a dance, I got the feeling that I was witnessing her blackness.

I remember I was scared and confused. Her story and her humour had come from nowhere. There was nothing in my comic impersonation of Mr Hall that could have triggered such sadness. But the sadness was there and I was scared.

I left then to wash my hair. I placed a hand on Harrie's shoulder when I passed her and she held it a bit too tightly. I remember the glow of happiness that welled up in me. If Harrie needed me as much as the tightness of her grip seemed to suggest, then perhaps there was hope for us. I somehow felt that James had never seen her so vulnerable.

I stayed for a long time in the bathroom. I wanted to give Harrie enough time to recover herself, and if she didn't, I wanted to work out how best to comfort her without frightening her with intimacy.

I stayed there far too long for a communal bathroom and finally was shouted out by a frustrated Fanny Boothe. It was

Saturday afternoon, and it was fifteen minutes passed her bath time when she finally banged on the door. I collected myself and my possessions as quickly as I could and bundled myself through the narrow door and around the waiting Fanny Boothe. I think her features must have been set to greet someone else because, when I opened the door, she was smiling apologetically. All that stopped when she saw who it was. She looked me and my housecoat up and down and said, 'So you haven't invested in a silk kimono yet, eh?'

I didn't answer her. I just stepped away from the power of dislike in her eyes.

'If you were a real friend,' she said, 'you would leave the girl alone. She may be making a mistake, but it's her mistake, and I've known her long enough to know that she knows what she is doing.'

I fumbled some answer and I fumbled past her. I was nearly clear when I dropped my hairbrush. She bent with surprising agility to pick it up and return it to me, but before she did, she raked her fingers through it collecting a ball of wet hair.

'I leave it out for the birds,' she explained. 'Young girls' hair is the softest thing for lining nests.' And she closed the bathroom door.

Chapter 15

I walked slowly down the hall, back to Harrie's room, and knocked on her door. It was the first time I had ever felt the need to be so formal, but I wasn't sure what I would walk in on, she had seemed so strange. I needn't have worried about depression. Harrie swung the door open and laughingly reached out for my arm.

She grabbed me and pulled me towards her, and then, with my arms still full of a damp towel and hair accessories, she tried to waltz me around the room. She was laughing and laughing and my whole being melted with relief. I dropped what I was carrying, and holding tight to Harrie, chased after her humour. I never caught it.

'One, two, three,' she was shouting. 'One, two, three and back two, three and to the side two, three and shuffle two, three...'

She led me, literally, a merry dance, and I followed as best I could, always a step behind and always perilously close to tripping her up.

I was too delighted by the change in her mood to question it. The me of seventeen took everything that Harrie gave me without ever thinking that she might be just giving me everything that I wanted. That evening I took Harrie's good humour and never thought to thank her for the effort she put into the production of it.

We finally stopped dancing. We parted and twirled breathless into our armchairs. Harrie didn't rest long, though. I was still catching my breath when she was tearing dresses out of her wardrobe and flinging them behind her onto her bed.

'Em dear, what shall I wear?'

'Your blue, of course your blue. Remember, you decided, you tried all those before.'

I was nothing more than puzzled by the waste of energy involved in going through the process again.

'Blue? Do you think? Isn't blue just slightly dull? Oh, I wish I had a scarlet dress. A dress bright enough to light up the darkest night. But you're right, blue it is, sky blue. There's something dazzlingly bright about sky blue don't you think? It reminds me of Switzerland in the spring, but red reminds me of Paris in the winter. Oh, I suppose either will do, blue will do as well as anything else. It is only a dress, it is only a dance.

'Oh, Em, do Miss Walsh for me. Do Miss Walsh talking to Mr Hall. Or do Mrs Jones – you haven't done Mrs Jones for ever so long. Do you remember "I think beads and ribbon"? I don't know when I have laughed so much. Go on, tell it again.'

And I did, again and again. Finally, bored with the repetition, I invented a later incident when Mrs Jones asked for a remnant of Venice and I ran off and fetched her a glass of water. Harrie laughed even harder at the new story and I joined in as best I could. It was suddenly a very jolly occasion.

I wore Harrie's green dress, the one that she had lent me to wear to Fanny Boothe's party, and she wore her blue with all its trimmings of lace and frills. Just before we left, we stopped our bustle and our laughter to stand side by side facing Harrie's full length mirror.

I remember that picture as vividly as any framed photograph I have lived with. It is a picture that has never faded or been worn negligible by familiarity. It is a picture that has always been deeply personal. Its story has never had to be explained to anyone. Even on the days that I don't think of Harrie, on those long days that I train my mind to busy itself with the present, even on those days, that picture of us dressed and happy is before me. It is how I see myself and how I wish I could still see Harrie.

I stood beside Harrie and slightly behind her. She rested her body against my right leg and my right arm. Her head was supported by my right shoulder. Her blonde hair, unruly with curls, spread across my bare collar bone. I can still close my eyes and feel the light pressure of her body, the tickling of her hair and the mixed scent of her shampoo and her perfume.

She was an angel in that blue dress, a sky-blue angel of femininity, all softness and curves. By contrast, I was hard and angular. My neck and head were sleek and gracious. My hair was scraped into a tight bun and my neck was lengthened by the cut of my dress. It barely stopped where decency began.

But we were the same, Harrie and I. Our eyes shone in unison and our scarlet mouths were curled upwards at the same joke. Our left hands, which hung idly by our sides, were cuffed with the same gold bangle. We were the same. I saw it then, but Harrie just laughed and broke away..

'Come on, Em,' she said. 'Shake a leg and look shapely, we don't want to be late and we're heading that way.'

'But we've time yet.' I was annoyed at her for shattering the pose. 'We don't have to be there for at least another hour.'

'Ah yes, but I have organised a detour, and if we are late for that we will be late for our escorts and if we are late for them we will be late for our dance and if we are late for that… well, do you have any idea where it will all end? We will be late for our own funeral.'

I laughed as I eased my bare shoulders into the delicate jacket that came with my dress and I plagued Harrie with questions as I double-checked the contents of my delicate handbag. Harrie picked up her mac and stood watching me and smiling. She merely shook her head in answer to anything I asked and I left the room with her, still questioning. I followed her down the stairs with my stomach tingling with anticipation. I imagined all sorts of treats that Harrie could have arranged for just us two. I thought she was joking when she stopped and knocked on Mrs Benson's door.

'What are you doing?' I whispered. 'Come on, let's run before she answers.'

I pulled at her arm. I was eager to get to my treat. But Harrie just shook me off and straightened her finery before opening the door and sailing into Mrs Benson's parlour.

Fanny Boothe, freshly bathed, Mrs Benson and even Miss Charter Thomas, who was going through a fairly lucid phase at the time, were all gathered there. They were old, lonely women and they had heard about the dance. Seeing us in our finery was the closest any of them was ever going to get to socialising again. I can understand that now, but Harrie, in her goodness, could understand that then, and so she made sure to make the time to include them in our big event. It was the only time that I was ever invited into Mrs Benson's front parlour and even then I was only admitted on a 'with guest' ticket.

The three ladies were waiting for us, sitting primly on over-stuffed chairs, holding tight to the delicate stems of their sherry glasses. A silver tray on the large, ornate, sideboard was laid with a decanter of heavy amber liquid and a further two glasses. Mrs Benson was sitting within easy reaching distance of it.

The room was tense and silent and as dust-laden as I remembered it. Heavy prints frowned down from the walls and heavy blocks of furniture anchored the room solidly to its past. Harrie had the good grace to turn and grimace at me slightly before she gave the ladies the benefit of her smile and the full warmth of her charm.

The three women rose to her flattering attention and, in a cloud of age and dust, moved forward. Harrie laughed and twirled in front of them and all three sucked in their breath in admiration, and clasped their hands to their chests with the emotion of it all.

'Oh, Harrie dear.' Fanny Boothe was flushed with genuine pleasure. 'You're so pretty. Your skin is as pure and as white as your character. I think sins always show in the flesh, but yours is as innocent as it is beautiful.' And she flashed a sidelong glance at my one heavily powdered spot.

The sherry and the excitement were beginning to get to Miss Charter Thomas. She pushed her face into Harrie's and muttered her phrase. And, before Harrie could react, she shuffled off to the far end of the room where she continued to mutter and could be seen, in the gloom, turning in circles and pulling at her hair. At least she could be seen by me – the others sat with their backs to her.

Mrs Benson, aside from her initial gasp, had not commented on Harrie's appearance and, when Harrie stepped aside to push me into the limelight, she turned away.

'Such an occasion merits marking. So, even though it is against my better judgement, I have decided to ask you to join me in a sherry before you depart. Of course, feel free to decline the offer if you have any reservations.'

The latter part of her speech seemed to be directed at me, but I shook my head in affirmation of the drink, as did Harrie. Mrs Benson returned to her decanter and Harrie turned to me.

'Well, Fanny, hasn't Em done us proud? Have you ever seen such a length of glamour off the big screen?'

I could feel Harrie's confusion and I'm sure she could feel my embarrassment. She hadn't thought that Fanny would need prompting to compliment me.

Fanny finally responded, but she did so more to humour Harrie than to reassure me and her admiration was almost insulting in its brevity.

'Yes, she looks a picture. Just like one of those movie stars.'

We all sat down to our sherry. It was the first drink that I ever remember taking and I remember thinking that it was worth the wait. It was a cheap sherry – Mrs Benson drank too much to afford decent stuff – but it worked for me. It warmed me inside and out and it reddened my cheeks better than any rouge could.

I drank it rather too quickly. I wasn't being called on to talk so I had nothing else to do with my mouth. The others were chatting excitedly about the dance ahead and all that it might entail.

At least Harrie and Fanny were chatting excitedly. Mrs Benson was busy sipping her sherry and topping up her glass, but her body language included her in their general humour. She was bent towards them listening to every word.

swamped in a fuss of tulle. They held tight to the primness of their purity and to the arms of their selected examples of manhood. I felt sorry for their escorts, the two other boys, but I suppose it was pity misspent. They couldn't have known better, boys in men's suits, hired for the occasion, dripping with low expectations and their fathers' after-shave. They wouldn't expect anything more than a highly coloured cheek turned for a kiss, or a brief contact with the pursed hardness of young pink lips.

Harrie and I had no need of them. We waved to them and, linking our men, we walked two by two out of Martine's and down the road. Harrie and James walked ahead and John and I followed. I granted him a few words of greeting and then disentangled myself and ran the three steps to Harrie's side.

I had seen James's head bend to hers with ominous intent, but I caught her attention before he had a chance to speak. I drew her away, whispering, and let John entertain James. I think that the pain and awkwardness of a premature period was the excuse I used, but it couldn't be used for ever. There was a whole night of dancing and stolen moments to chaperon.

It was a challenge, which, I am proud to say, I rose to with style. It was the first night in my long social career, that I consciously used my all. I used my height, my new-found glamour, my wit, my solicitude, my all. I exhausted myself but I gained my advantage.

We arrived at the Central, still walking two by two, Harrie and I leading the way, and we were directed to the Hunter suite. Harrie wanted to wait in the foyer for our escorts, but I grabbed her hand and pulled her up the sweeping, marble staircase.

'Come on, Harrie dear,' I encouraged. 'Our public will be growing restless.' She smiled and allowed herself to be manoeuvred but didn't further the joke.

The Hunter suite faced us when we reached the top of the stairs. I had learnt a lot over the previous few weeks. I had learnt when to laugh in company and who to laugh at. I had learnt what to wear and how to accessorise it. I could speak about films, and mention books with as much confidence as someone who had read them. I fancied myself sophisticated, but I was constantly proving myself to be a child of seventeen. The rush of joy I experienced when I first entered the Hunter suite couldn't be described as anything other than innocently childish.

The dance was contained in only one room. It was on the first floor of the hotel and its six enormous windows, which stretched almost to the ground, looked out on the sleeping centre of the city. Lights from shop windows below, and street lights almost parallel, mingled with the twinkling fairy light of the room.

There was a chandelier sparkling with its own echoes and reflections, hanging low over a dance floor, at one end of which a small but noisy band were already hot with playing. Two men stood and sat and wielded brass instruments in unison, a woman with silver sleeves hitched up to her elbows was kneading away at a piano and a handsome, suited and sleek-haired crooner guided his crew with a baton and whispered introductory nothings into a mike. In my eyes he embodied all the romance of the movies and all the sophistication of adulthood.

Around the floor, away from the busy light of the chandelier, there were tens of tables all round and all discreetly lit by candles covered by coloured glass shades. Most tickets were sold at a group rate, so the tables were large. This wasn't a place people came to for intimacy – it was a place to be seen in.

I sighed with joy, but also with relief. I could sit by Harrie all night. I had prepared myself against the eventuality of cosy tables for two. Harrie heard the sigh and she reached for my hand.

'Is it too beautiful, Em? Can it be this beautiful for a whole night or should we just slip away now?'

I took her little hand, covered it with mine and nodded. I understood exactly and agreed with all my being. But I didn't have time to answer. James and John arrived behind us and began fiddling with our coats and a waiter appeared before us. James took charge, as he would, and we were escorted to our table, a suitably cramped one in keeping with our age and probably with James's tone. He was one of those men who disguised the awkwardness of their youth with rudeness, and it was a habit he never got out of. He spent his life barking orders at waiters.

The rest of our party arrived just as we were settling and immediately ruined the magic for me. The boys slapped their hands together, rubbed their palms noisily and blew inanely hearty comments out of nervous mouths.

'Boy, oh boy, but isn't this some show?' they asked each other, and their girls answered with enthusiasm, 'Oooh, isn't it lovely. Ooooh, you're right there, Jim.'

Harrie sat first and I sat beside her. John held my chair for me and James held Harrie's for her. Then they both went to take their places by our sides. I was busy with my bag and gloves, and with the smoothing of some wrinkles that tended to collect around my waist when I sat, so I was in no position to pre-empt Harrie's move.

She suddenly sprang up, squealing something about wanting a better view of the dance floor, and before I knew the reason behind her outburst she had swapped places with James. I was left sitting between him and John, facing a girl in pink and a boy with a ginger moustache. That was the end of any appreciation for the room that I had managed to retain.

I started work immediately. John was already leaning towards me with an expression that oozed romantic drivel. James and Harrie were smiling and talking into each other's eyes, and the rest of our party was following suit and fragmenting into couples. I had no intention of allowing such a situation to develop.

'Well, here we are.' I addressed the table in general and I addressed them loudly. It wasn't a very gripping remark but it got their attention and it removed the threat of John's conversation. His face retreated from my peripheral vision.

'Isn't it too marvellous and why didn't we do it before? James, I hold you responsible. Why did you delay your birthday for so long?'

He had to turn to me to reply, and he had to laugh at my joke, seeing as he was the good-humoured cause of it, and, being James, and being so mannerly, he had to do both at length.

'Ha ha ha, you know, I did it on purpose to annoy you. But I do think that I did choose a good month for my birthday. It breaks the year to have a birthday in the summer.'

By the time he had finished, Harrie was in conversation with one of the pink girls and I had my follow-up strategy ready. I asked him what star sign he was. That was a stroke of genius on my part. We spent at least half an hour examining different aspects of that same topic. Everyone had to tell everyone else their sign and then we all had to comment on whether that person exhibited the correct traits. There was some confusion about one of the boys and a cusp, but we got over that and went on to discuss the compatibility of the couples in zodiac terms.

It was a beautifully communal conversation, but it was finite. It was interrupted by the arrival of the waiter. Our ticket included a supper, but the waiter was just a formality – there was no choice of menu. He stood by our table with his pen poised over his pad and went through the whole charade of asking us what we wanted. We all did as we were told and ordered cutlets and fried potatoes, except for the ginger-haired boy who asked for a 'rare steak, and if you don't have that then a usual one will do'.

He seemed delighted with his joke and it took him some time before he could control himself sufficiently to own that he was only 'having a lark'. There was a polite silence while we all watched him laugh and then James rescued our dignity as a group by asking for the wine list. He studied it at length and then ordered a bottle of the house white. He always did have a tendency to splash out on his birthday.

After the waiter left there was a dangerous lull in conversation. I broke it before it had time to settle properly: 'I simply love this song.' The band had just hit the chorus of one of the more popular ditties of the day. 'Harrie, did you hear Mrs Benson last night? I'm sure she was singing this.'

I lent across James to ask Harrie directly and so she answered me directly. Then, as before, I drew the conversation into the public domain.

'Have we never told you about Mrs Benson?' I addressed one of the girls in pink. 'Harrie, how did we overlook Mrs Benson? Oh, you have no idea what a nut she is.'

I sat back and took the questions as they came, referring at least half to Harrie. And, as I had hoped, once she settled into the conversation, she began to enjoy it. Mrs Benson was good anecdote material, and the girls in pink and the boys in suits were a flatteringly attentive audience.

'And, Em, do you remember when the doctor came to Fanny? Not the last time, the time before?'

I remembered well. There was a pause when our food arrived, but I prompted Harrie back on course once the waiter left. I was delighted. I couldn't have hoped for a more improper story.

'You tell it, Harrie. You do it so much better than me.'

'All right then, but really Em is better at doing the voices. It was about six weeks ago, the doctor came to see Fanny. He came late because he always leaves Fanny to last because there never is anything wrong with her, and this night, I suppose there was a lot wrong with everyone else, because he came very late. He also had to stay very late, the poor man, because Fanny thought that there was more than usual wrong with her. So, as it was late, Mrs Benson was drunk...'

The girls in pink sucked in their cheeks and James looked guiltily at his – still full – bottle of wine. It didn't seem to be the right time to start offering it around.

'...and, as we have mentioned, when she gets drunk, she sings. I suppose she must have forgotten that the doctor was in, because she usually is very proper around professional men, but, whatever the reason, she started singing and when she starts singing everyone in the house, and probably in the street knows all about it. And what was worse she started singing one of her bawdier songs.

'Poor Fanny was in agonies of embarrassment. She kept

shouting louder and louder to try and drown out the words and Mrs Benson was drinking more and more and singing louder and louder so Fanny was forced to shout even louder. In the end the racket was something dramatic. Myself and Em sat outside Fanny's room and we were deafened, do you remember, Em?'

I laughed and agreed and then caught a glimpse of James's face. He was smiling, but with effort. Stories about drinking women and women's consultations with their doctors in bedrooms seemed to him to be stories in the worst possible taste. I could see that in his expression, but, when it came to James, Harrie could only see what she wanted to.

'Go on, Harrie,' I said, and she grinned at the memory of it. She knew what I was referring to and I nodded my encouragement. 'Go on, you haven't told them the best bit. The best bit is what everyone was shouting.'

'Oh, do tell us the best bit,' echoed all the little boys and girls and so Harrie did and she shouldn't have.

'Well, Fanny fancied that she was having a little bit of trouble with her digestion and she was describing her symptoms in detail, but because of Mrs Benson she was shouting her symptoms in detail. I won't tell you quite how much detail, but Em and I know now why she spends so much time in the toilet so late at night and we also know why she appears for breakfast with that peculiar pinched look, and all the time she is shouting these details, Mrs Benson is bellowing, how does the chorus go, Em?'

I shook my head and frowned in an effort to shake the memory to the fore.

'Something about a soldier?'

'Oh yes!' Flushed with the triumph of her powers of recollection, she didn't think to stop and censor her material. 'It went like this:

The girl she wore a cap and gown
The soldier wore his trousers down
And though his king had breathed his last
His flag was flying at full mast.'

Harrie's story finished on that triumphant note and was greeted with a moment's silence, a silence made all the more obvious because Harrie's voice had risen with the excitement of the telling. Her rendition of Mrs Benson's song had managed to silence the neighbouring tables as well as our own.

I was the first to laugh. The boys, except for James, followed enthusiastically, and their girls followed politely.

Harrie returned to her dinner and James pushed his away. He sat still, staring at his lap, while one of the pink girls tried to start a debate on the merits of contemporary crooners. I glanced at him from time to time and congratulated myself on at least postponing the proposal.

After that, things began working in my favour. Tom or Tim or Jim insisted that Harrie repeat as much of Mrs Benson's song as she could remember. His pleas distracted her from James. She hadn't time to notice his face tightening into a scowl of displeasure. I began to relax.

'You know that song of Mrs Benson's, it really reminds me of that story you told me the other night. You know, the one about the man in Switzerland.'

Again I leaned across James to talk to Harrie and only she heard what I said but the table heard her answer.

'Oh, yes, that man, that poor old man.' She laughed and we all leaned forward to listen, even James. I was watching him closely.

I was surprised at Harrie's willingness to talk. She usually just limited herself to short but apt comments, especially when faced with more than two listeners. I was surprised, but very pleased. I listened along with the others.

'He was a very old man when I met him, but he was still hell-bent on getting married. The reason he wasn't married already was because he insisted that his wife had to be a virgin when he walked her down the aisle. He didn't trust women at all, so he gave every potential wife he ever met an ultimatum, either you sleep with me before we get married to prove to me that you're a virgin or else you have something to hide.

'He was a handsome old man and I would say he was a very

handsome young man and his family had a lot of money, so it was probably true, what people said, that he got a lot of women willing to take him up on the offer. Unfortunately for him, he never thought it through properly. The ones that didn't sleep with him he discarded as wild women with pasts to hide, and the ones that did sleep with him he was forced to discard because they were no longer virgins. But there was the school of thought that believed him to be totally in control of the situation and very happy about it. Without ever having to commit himself to anyone, he got the best there was to get out of the purest he ever met.'

This story was greeted with a great show of shuffling and a hearty laugh from me and the boy with the orange moustache. James covered up the silence before it had a chance to melt into a polite show of amusement.

'So who would like some wine?'

Harrie thrust her glass high and I pulled John away from temptation and out on to the dance floor. I felt that we should leave the wine for those who needed it.

'Come on, Rosie, come on, Tim, don't send us out on our own.'

They followed, as I knew they would, leaving the wine behind them.

John and I danced for a while and then I danced with one of the other boys. Then I danced with a strange man and then I stood by an open window for a while, listening to John's praises. Then I returned to our table.

I had confidently left Harrie and James together for the best part of an hour. When I did finally return, James was there alone. He told me Harrie was in the powder room. What he actually said when I asked after her was, 'I don't know – the ladies' I suppose.'

It wasn't like him to be so rude. I could guess at what I had missed and it certainly wasn't a proposal.

I found her there. She was sitting in one of the large wicker chairs that the management considered stylish. Her head was down and she was staring fixedly at her opened lipstick that was being passed nervously from hand to hand. The bright, bustling clouds of women rustled past her in twos and threes, instinctively lowering their conversation and flicking their eyes over her as they drew close.

She sat amongst them, the brightest of the lot, but I could sense a part of what she was feeling. I could almost see the blackness she was so fond of mentioning. I cut across the scented, smoky room and knelt in front of her, my own hands reaching across her thighs to quieten the flutter of her little hands. She raised her head slowly and I could see that her mouth was already layered with lipstick. Her lips were swollen by its uneven lines and her expression leered drunkenly from under smeared blotches of scarlet.

'Oh, Em, it's you. How lovely you look. Is it cold tonight or is it just James? Or is it just me? We've been talking icicles at each other for the whole evening.'

'You're talking nonsense, Harrie dear. You are at a dance and you haven't been dancing. The talking comes later.'

'Yes, dancing, of course, words out of place are always wrong.'

She stood suddenly and I was left staring up at her, still on my knees. She left before I could stop her and I think I might have. Her mood change had been so worryingly swift. Yes, I'm sure I would have stopped her if only to tell her that her lipstick needed blotting and to remind her that James hated dancing.

I followed her as soon as I had got to my feet and had brushed my skirt free of wrinkles. I saw her fling her arms around James from behind. He gently but firmly disentangled himself and turned to face her. She had her back to me so I had no idea what she was saying, but James was facing me and I could see his confusion and it was only a veneer, a social covering of his disgust. He was emphatically rejecting whatever suggestion Harrie was making.

Finally Harrie removed her arms, stepped away, and reached out for John. He was the only other man at the table. She held her hand out to him and he politely took it and allowed himself to be led on to the dance floor. I waited until they were thick in the throng before I sat beside James.

'Where is John?' I asked as sweetly as I could.

'Dancing.' James didn't elaborate. Harrie had been right – he was talking icicles.

'And Harrie?'

'The same.'

'Oh, I see them,' and I pointed them out as they passed. 'Harrie does dance beautifully doesn't she? She must have had a lot of practice.'

We both sat in silence after that, watching Harrie shimmying around the floor. It was just her way of dancing, and I could see from her sideways glancing that she was dancing for James, but James couldn't approve. Even if he knew it was for his benefit, even if he enjoyed the spectacle, he couldn't approve of his maybe wife wriggling her heavy bottom, arching her curved back and splitting her scarlet lips. Harrie's experience with men was beginning to betray her. She was winning James back into good humour in a way that had obviously worked for her before.

'Will you dance?' I held my hand out to James. 'My partner seems to have abandoned me and I do love this tune.' I spoke lightly. There was not a trace of malice or jealousy in my voice, but there was enough wistfulness to remind James that Harrie was in my man's arms and that he had a duty to soothe any slight that I might be feeling about the situation. He took my hand and led me on to the floor where we danced in ever decreasing and ever more wooden circles.

The nature of dancing in those days demanded conversation. Unless one was in the arms of a loved one, and then you were supposed to melt, Hollywood-style, into each other's eyes. A silence, when one wasn't with a loved one, intimated that either partner might be contemplating 'a melt'. So, to avoid such complications, dancing demanded conversation. I started us off.

'Harrie is in marvellous form tonight isn't she?' She had just flitted passed us and had waved with one, high, stretched arm, loud with bangles.

'Yes.'

I stayed silent. I could see that James was deliberating whether to pursue the conversation. He finally continued.

'She may be in too good form. Have you noticed it?'

We both looked around automatically and caught her changing partners mid step. With one forward shuffle she had transferred herself into a stranger's arms and with a happy little wiggle she settled herself there.

'Well, you did give her wine didn't you?'

'A glass and that is all. That wouldn't leave an impression, especially as we have been eating.'

James's voice was rising high with indignation, although he was trying to control it. I had a brief wish to laugh. It was ludicrous to even vaguely hint that James might be capable of plying a girl with alcohol. But I didn't laugh and I continued.

'I thought she only had a taste, but a full glass on top of the sherry she had earlier might have had an effect.'

'Sherry! She was drinking earlier?'

'Well, yes. But don't get me wrong, it wasn't very much, no not very much, and she doesn't very often. She knows well enough not to, I mean she has the example of her mother.'

We stopped dancing. It may have been because of James's shock or merely because our circle had decreased to the diameter of our shoe sizes and could get no smaller, but, either way, we came to a sudden halt. The lighter dancers whirled past us, Harrie included. She was latched on to another man and her blotched, scarlet mouth was split open on a laugh.

'What about her mother?'

'I am terribly sorry. I have obviously said more than I should have. Excuse me and please forget this conversation.'

I spoke in my best Miss Walsh voice and I do think it managed to morally clear me. I returned to John and our miscellaneous companions who had tired of dancing. I left James on the floor, where he cut in on Harrie and gently danced her over to one of the long, cool windows. Once there, their heads fell together in close conversation.

This was not what I had intended. I had obviously done wrong in providing Harrie with an excuse. It seemed that all James was waiting for was an excuse to forgive her. I felt all the ground I had gained slip quickly from beneath me.

I did not want night-time confidences about disagreeable parents. I did not want James to feel the need to protect. I did not want to leave them alone in the soft darkness of a summer's night with both of them warmed by a deeper realisation of their need for each other. I sat beside John with my mouth clenched tight in anger. He placed his hand on my arm and I shook it off.

'So, you have decided to come back to me,' I hissed. 'And what makes you think I want you now?'

I went on to accuse him of preferring Harrie to me, of being low enough to try and cause trouble between her and James, not to mention between her and me. I told him that I never wanted to see him again and that I was going home that minute and I was going alone.

I got quite worked up with the force of my hurt and by the time I ran up to Harrie to tell her that I had broken with John and was going home that minute and was going home alone, I was crying enormous, generous tears. Harrie of course couldn't leave me in such a state, though she did try. Her first idea was to take me to the comfort of the ladies' room, and when I wouldn't, she proposed a quick breath of fresh air, but I insisted on going home and so she finally offered to take me.

'It's all right, Em dear,' she said. 'Don't you worry, I'll mind you home and I'll mind you to sleep.'

I allowed my sobbings to abate once I got her promise and I overcame the powerful temptation to laugh at the incongruity of such sober empathy coming from her over-painted, leering clown lips.

As soon as it was arranged that Harrie was to go with me, James dutifully left us to fetch our coats and call a taxi. I must have succeeded in looking dramatically upset, as this was an unprecedented extravagance. Then, under Harrie's direction, James kept our curious friends at arm's length until the taxi arrived. I took his place beside Harrie in front of the long cool window. Harrie tried, gently, to ease the details of my upset out of me, but I gave her nothing except my repeated promise that I never wanted to see John again. I had nothing else to give her.

When the taxi did finally arrive, James informed us and suggested that he should go and collect get his coat, but my tears and my constant whisperings in Harrie's ear finally dissuaded him from accompanying us.

The night ended then and it ended abruptly. I could tell from the two of them that I had interrupted Harrie and James in the middle of some sort of heart-deep discussion, either an argument or a reconciliation. Whatever it was, it was passionate and potentially dangerous. I sank into that taxi weak with relief. I had been right. I couldn't have trusted them alone in the night.

Harrie was embarrassingly solicitous. I did feel guilty, but only because it went against my nature to be dishonest. I was confident in my superior knowledge of her needs. She took me home in silence, except for the odd soothing murmur, and she insisted on tucking me into bed. It was only when I was safely there and securely comfortable that she mentioned John.

'Are you sure that it is totally over? He is a good man, you know, and terribly fond of you. He told me that while we were dancing.'

'Yes, it's totally over.'

'And do you want to tell me why?'

She laid heavy stress on the *you* of her question and I guessed that John had already given James his version of events. James must have whispered its essentials into Harrie's ear as they had exchanged their prolonged goodnights. Harrie was right. John was a good man but he was no-one's best friend, so I took the chance that my word would be believed before his.

'Promise you won't feel bad if I tell you, Harrie dear, but he told me that he had very strong feelings for you. I had always guessed as much – he was always comparing me to you – but tonight he told me how he felt and what made me so angry was not only that he insulted me but by giving time to his feelings he insulted you and James. And James is so fond of him isn't he? So you do see, don't you, that I couldn't stay with him and have him see me home, not even for politeness' sake? And I am so sorry that I ruined your night, especially as it was James's birthday and...'

'You didn't ruin a thing and you are not to worry about James. He – we – had a lovely night and it was all the more precious for being that bit shorter.'

Harrie sat with me for a while after that, but she didn't say another word. She just hugged me before she left, and I deduced from the strength of that hug that once again I was morally clear.

Chapter 17

After that night, Harrie's behaviour got stranger and stranger. She was loud in company, forever talking. She used to just sit quiet and wait for that perfect moment that suited her perfect comment, but now she talked, and talked loosely.

She was constantly referring to the past – it didn't matter that it wasn't always hers. She had always been so private. Now we all knew, every Jim, Tom and Tim of us, about her travels and her parents, though the latter did seem quite nebulous and the version she had given me all those weeks ago had never been repeated. I fancied that I had been privileged with the truth.

Her manner changed as well. She still drawled when she spoke and she still dragged her limbs when she walked, but now she was constantly drawling and constantly moving. She seemed suddenly scared of the dark, staying up late into the night talking and then sleeping with her light on and she seemed scared of silence. She took to singing to fill the threat of every social void. Eventually she took to singing continuously. She would sit in Martine's humming to herself and beating out the tempo of her song on the table.

She ruined music for me. The me of seventeen was passionate about songs and singers, as I suppose all seventeen-year-olds are, but I was more discerning.

My tastes were educated beyond my years by my father's choice of evening entertainments. As a child I had been sat in front of our wireless night after night and been subjected to an hour of classical music. Eventually the beauty of the music cut through the resentment of the constraint and I grew to love Mozart and the lighter works of Beethoven. I also learnt chunks of lyrics from Gilbert and Sullivan and, when called upon, sang them to visiting relatives. And of course I had my favourites amongst the smooth-singing crooners of the day. If Harrie hadn't taken up the habit of continuously singing, I am sure that I would have grown to be passionate about the more complicated movements of Rachmaninov.

But Harrie ruined music for me. The songs she chose to hum or sing were the ones we had shared a love for. They included the best of the popular croons and the pick of Mozart, Beethoven and Gilbert and Sullivan. When Harrie left, I didn't know a scrap of music that didn't hurt and so I gave up listening. I resent it now. I equate television with junk food and I find it hard to concentrate my eyes on print. Life gets very tedious when one is dependent on the likes of little Miss Kelly to stimulate one's brain.

This new Harrie scared me slightly. On one level she seemed to need me more than before. She looked to me to lead the laughter at her jokes and she looked to me to supply her with new jokes and fresh laughter. She also looked to me to mind her to sleep at night, to talk her through the longer, colder dusks, but this need was superficial. Harrie's soul was retreating, alienating itself behind the gloss of laughter or the drama of sadness. I could fight against her love for James but I was powerless against this new fight for personal independence.

After James's dance and for a few weeks, our social life continued much as before. We would meet and go to the pictures – something Harrie by now professed to enjoy – or we would meet and go to Martine's. We spent our Saturday afternoons by the sea eating ice-creams and we spent our Sunday afternoons walking, following the river, out past the train station, and into the countryside.

When I say 'we' I mean me and Harrie and James and a variety of cute little girls and boys with strong, adult names. After John, I was taking a break from the pretence of looking for a boyfriend. I pleaded the excuse of a broken heart and I was enjoying the soft treatment that came as a result. Harrie made sure that even in company solely made up of couples, I never felt an outsider. She would often leave James's side for mine or link me and place me between the two of them. Her vanity obviously believed my story about John and felt responsible for his slight.

As a result, our outings were always very communal. James would talk to Tom, or Bert, or whichever boy was there and I would talk to Harrie and Harrie would talk to me and then more and more frequently she would talk to everyone. She was almost reaching celebrity status in popularity. Our friends were getting used to her risqué stories and the boys, except for James, were beginning to call for them.

I remember snippets of Harrie's behaviour during that time. I remember that she took to visiting Fanny Boothe frequently and alone. I used to know where she was at every moment of the day, but I didn't any more. I would knock on her locked door some evenings and she wouldn't answer, even though I knew that she was there. Later, on those same evenings, she would call for me and demand that I amuse her until she finally fell asleep.

She stopped meeting me for lunch most days. Now our meetings were limited to one or two a week, and once I saw her as I returned from our bandstand. She was in the park, sitting alone on a bench, staring at the ground in front of her. I was scared to disturb her. Again I was afraid that our friendship wasn't strong enough to withstand her reason for not going as far as the bandstand.

But mostly I remember her wild and bubbling good humour, like the time she appeared in Hall's. I heard her before I saw her and I dismissed the thought that it could be her. She was supposed to be at work – it was a Tuesday afternoon – but I turned anyway, curious as to who could sound so like Harrie. She was slowly walking the length of the floor, dragging her limbs and swaying her hips. She was bearing down on the haberdashery counter and drawling complaints about every display she passed.

'Goodness, after the trauma of the lift I was looking forward to *terra firma* and I am greeted with a billowing scarf display. Can you not get realistic mannequins? Do you suppose that I want to look like an emaciated giraffe? Soft furnishings! Surely this concrete cushion belies the term?'

And she walked past the staring Gillian and on towards Miss Walsh and me.

'Oh, this is so much better,' Harrie continued. 'Here is a department of order. One can see it immediately in the straightness of that young assistant's collar.'

She pointed at me and glanced away, careful not to betray herself by catching my eye. I tried to hold on to my bland shopgirl expression and I didn't say a word. I was deeply flattered that Harrie would go to such lengths for me, but I was very scared for the same reason.

Harrie stayed for a long five minutes and eventually bought a hairnet, but not before she had raked her approval over my every responsibility.

'Those threads! Well, if ever I need thread I am coming straight here. The artistry in the juxtaposition of the colours leaves me breathless, but even they pale into insignificance when likened to the majesty of your ribbon display. And as for thimbles, it's enough to note how flushed I am now and believe me when I say that I was never excited by them before.'

Miss Walsh stood as silent as I and as silent as Gillian throughout. She took Harrie's money and parcelled her purchase without addressing her at all. It was only when Harrie and her hairnet were safely in the lift that she spoke.

'A friend of yours, Miss Moore?'

'No,' I muttered, my head low with the obvious falsehood.

'An acquaintance, then, I presume.' And she sailed by me.

I had the tact to give Harrie a different account of Miss Walsh's reaction. I rushed home from work and ran into her room. She was there waiting for me, eager to laugh about her trick.

'What on earth were you doing?' I asked, my face bright with smiles. 'Why weren't you at work?'

'Tummy-ache I told them. And I hinted that it might be monthly-inspired, so they shooed me out of the office with lots of uncomfortable ahem noises. But wasn't it worth it? Didn't I show them all how great you were?'

'Oh, you did, you should have heard Miss Walsh.' I drew my face up into a pinched expression of approval and in a new, slightly softer, Miss Walsh voice said, ' "You are looking remarkably presentable today, Miss Moore, and I have not perhaps taken the time to compliment you on the arrangement of colours that seemed to have taken that lady's fancy. I am not one to withhold praise and so I must tell you that I am pleased. Perhaps now you will learn the truth behind the maxim that the customer is always right." And it wasn't only Miss Walsh. Gillian changed her cushion display and they moved the scarves.'

Harrie laughed and laughed and the memory of the prank kept her happy for the whole evening. But it was getting harder and harder to keep her happy or to keep her entertained. She always had to be talking or doing or laughing.

Her energy carried her beyond us, James and me, and quite often we were left watching, side by side, our world filled with the movement of Harrie. And again, with all the wisdom of my youth, I knew to take my opportunities as they came, and Harrie's behaviour ensured that they kept coming.

There was one Sunday I remember in particular, when we were taking our usual pre-cinema stroll by the river. There were seven of us and we were walking slowly in twos and threes. It was a long walk and a hot day. Conversation was listless but companionable. At least, it seemed companionable to me, but Harrie, walking by my side, was finding it irritatingly quiet.

She hummed and sang and ran forward to James and the boys and back to Rosie and Nellie or whoever they were, but no-one could hold her interest for more than a few moments, though the boys, by James's side, did try very hard. Finally she ran ahead of our group and, putting two fingers in her mouth, let out a piercing whistle. We all stopped short, as she knew we would.

'All right then, everyone, shoulders back, chests out, stomachs in, chins up, noses to the wheel and shoulders to the grindstone. Forward march.'

The boys marched and the girls giggled and followed suit, tripping every now and then in their eagerness to keep up.

'Call yourself troops,' she continued. 'I've seen better examples of manhood in a skirt and better examples of womanhood in a pram and better examples of childhood in the womb.'

James and I fell to the rear. We both felt slightly too mature to join in, or maybe we both just felt slightly jealous of Harrie's divided attention.

'Harrie is a strong personality,' I said as much to myself as to my companion. I was speaking in a dreamy voice. I am sure that I was hardly aware that I was speaking out loud. James was such a quiet companion one usually forgot that he was there. 'I mean, it takes such strength to make a joke of one's greatest hurt.'

'What hurt?'

I started as if I was only then aware that someone was listening.

'Why, her father of course.'

'What about him?'

'The war. You know, how he died.'

'I didn't know that he was dead.'

I suppose that I would have known that poor James was ignorant of that fact. Harrie had mentioned her father often enough and always as a going concern.

'You must have. He died before she was born.'

'I tell you, I never knew. How can you be sure?'

'I was told, he died a war hero. But if Harrie didn't tell you herself, she must have her reasons and then I have said too much. I'm sorry, but I would have thought that you would have known. After all you are going to want to meet her mother soon.'

He didn't answer, and we both resumed our watch of Harrie. She was walking backwards, waving her arms in time with her steps and barking out orders.

'At the back, eyes ahead. No slouching in the ranks. No giggling when marching to something as serious as war.'

She was so engrossed in her role that she ignored our frantic warnings and walked straight into a post box. It must have hurt – she was momentarily winded – but she gathered herself immediately and joined in the laughter. I didn't laugh and James didn't laugh. He ran to her side and murmured in her ear. She looked at him as she always looked at him and he smiled with his eyes. I could tell that she was still, at heart, his Harrie. She held on to his hand but twirled around to face everyone again.

'Well, that just proves that I don't have eyes on the back of my head. But do you know that I was quite an age before I knew that for sure? My father was always telling me that I did. He would check under my hair and say, 'Yep, two eyes shut tight'. He would tell me to open them and I spent hours trying to find the right muscles. I'd say that I've exercised muscles in my body that most of you don't know that you have.'

She raised an eyebrow as she finished her story and the gang laughed, but James and I locked eyes in confusion.

I slowly grew to understand this new Harrie. I still got to spend at least an hour alone with her every night. I saw how she drooped when the crowds disappeared. I saw how she listened to my stories with her mind elsewhere. I knew how much she grew to hate the dark and solitude and so I had patience with her ever-growing need for diversion.

Unfortunately, she must have shown this vulnerability to James during their private moments because, although her behaviour obviously disturbed him, his patience stretched far beyond what I would have considered its limit. However, he no longer mentioned his family and the promised tea, and with the promised tea went the promise of a proposal. I was grateful for that much, but it worried me that James was willing to weather such erratic behaviour.

He sometimes showed his displeasure, but he never lowered himself to temper. I still laugh when I remember his face, that time by the sea, when Harrie, bored with our conversation and fed up with her second ice-cream, challenged James with it.

She stuck her cone out with her right hand and curved her left in the air like we had seen Errol Flynn do so many times. She advanced on James sideways thrusting her ice-cream at him and shouting the odd *touché* or *en garde*. The rest of the gang, and a few other day-trippers, gathered to watch. James continued to eat his cone and laughed a little, nervously, but as Harrie continued her game he addressed her quite seriously.

'Come on, Harrie. Leave me to eat in peace. If you don't want it, just throw it away.'

But Harrie didn't, she went for a kill and left a large ice-cream stain on James shirt, just where his heart should have been. She skipped off immediately, expecting a chase, and James looked after her, his face crumpled with displeasure that went deep enough to wound. He had been made fun of in a public place.

That night Harrie walked home with me. James had left us in Martine's. She clung tight to me during the walk and she insisted that I stay with her until she was asleep.

'Oh, Em dear,' she said, as we both waved goodbye to James. 'Don't you feel sometimes that there are worse things than death? Do you ever feel that the darkness of the coffin stalks us while we are still alive? I feel it now and I feel it close. It's a big, dark, cold nothing, and I can't seem to lighten it. I knew a man once, I think he was German, and he always professed to a fear of being buried alive and it wasn't just the earth he was scared of, he was scared of being buried by anything – by work, or by sentiment, or by true emotion. He felt the darkness like I feel the darkness. It is a loneliness that can isolate you even when you are enjoying the warmth of companionship and the heart of life.'

I didn't answer, I didn't know how to and she didn't expect me to. It had to be her that broke her melancholy. It was always that way with Harrie. The depths of her moods protected them against outside interference.

She cheered up before she slept. She lay in bed and told me about a man she knew in Paris who had looked exactly like her father.

'It was amazing, Em. He was just like a twin, except of course he only spoke French and he had a habit of thinking that he was a butterfly. He would lie cocooned in his bed for days and then would get dressed in his brightest waistcoat and run around the garden. The really sinister part of the likeness is that I remember a time when my father collected butterflies.'

It was a good story and I took it as such. There seemed no point in reminding her that her father had died long before she could have collected any memories of him.

When I left her that night – I'm sure it was that night because I was equating her father fixation with James in my head – I ran into Fanny Boothe. As usual she was as rude as she was strange.

'Why couldn't you have left her alone?' She asked as she walked passed me. She turned before she went down the stairs to her room and looked me up and down. 'You've taken so much from her. Did you have to take it all?'

I must have looked genuinely surprised because she continued in a slightly softer tone. 'Do you not know what you have done?'

I didn't answer. I turned and walked away, but, alone in my room, her words worried me. I undressed slowly. I hung my grubby belted jacket on the back of the door. I tossed my new, carefully battered dark green skull-cap on my armchair. I took off my new light blue dress carefully and hung it up beside my yellow one. I smoothed some cream on to my face and over my lips to remove my scarlet lipstick, and, once in bed, I slipped off my two gold bangles and left them on the chair beside me. I knew what Fanny meant. I had taken all I could.

That was a Saturday night. Harrie didn't see James again until the following Wednesday and by then he had fully recovered his usual mannerly good humour. It was a dull night out. Five of us sat in Martine's for the evening. We spoke about our news of the week and Harrie beat out a popular tune on the table.

I told them how I was due a pay increase on my birthday, which fell on the following Saturday. It was an old Hall's custom and one that Miss Walsh decided was inappropriate in my case. In my best Miss Walsh voice I repeated what she had said to me.

'Miss Moore, the birthday increment was established to reward a year's loyal work. As you have only been here a matter of weeks and in that time shown neither loyalty nor an ability to work, I have no option but to demand your increase be postponed.'

Everyone laughed and Harrie continued to beat out a tune on the table. James nudged her in an attempt to remind her of her manners and she started into awareness.

'Goodness, I almost had myself hypnotised there.'

She yawned, stretching her back and pushing her chest forward. 'I'm so bored. Wouldn't you love just once to get completely and foolishly drunk?'

She was addressing one of the pink little girls facing her and, understandably, didn't get a positive response. Then she turned to James and repeated her question.

'No, no, not at all. If one is bored sober one will be bored drunk and far more boring to others.'

'Oh, but I'm not talking about others, I'm talking about myself. I want to be interesting to myself. I want to run. Come on, Em, let's go to the park and run or climb. Remember when we climbed as high as the night?'

She started beating out a louder, more up-beat tempo. James and I looked at each other, and, finding no help in each other's eyes, we both looked back at Harrie.

'Hush, Harrie, you are making quite a noise.'

She was banging on the table and beginning to annoy the other diners. She stopped obediently and smiled up at James.

'Don't you ever need a noise? Don't you ever need a noise to drown out your thoughts?'

She spoke lightly, but she seemed to be seriously looking for information. The diners that had been drawn into our conversation by Harrie's tapping stayed, listening for an answer. It was James's nightmare – another social embarrassment – and this time he showed his displeasure.

'Not at all. Incessant noise reminds me of nothing except my susceptibility to headaches.'

Harrie stopped tapping after that. She just laughed as loudly as she could and she demanded a funny story from each of us as an excuse. Her continuous laughter filled every silence in the restaurant.

James walked her home that night, and, as usual, I joined her in her room once she came in. She undressed quickly and silently and then hopped into the bed beside me and I reached down to warm her feet.

'Do you feel the silence, Em?'

Her tone was surprisingly earnest and I could tell that she needed reassurance. Her behaviour in Martine's had obviously been discussed with James on their walk home and her preoccupation with the topic led me to believe that it had been discussed heatedly.

'I feel it, Harrie, but I like it.'

'Oh no, then it's not the same silence. No-one could like my silence. My silence is the silence that comes from being buried alive and it doesn't matter that I'm being buried by noise and activity and even a little bit of love. The silence still comes.'

Chapter 18

I was due home that Saturday to celebrate my eighteenth birthday with my parents. I got the day off work and was to take the morning train so that I would have the joy of two whole days with my family, as my train home didn't leave until Sunday evening. Needless to say, I was not looking forward to the affair.

My parents had a strange way of celebrating occasions. They always managed to include religion. Of course, some holidays come complete with a religious content, but birthdays and anniversaries surely deserve a secular element. However, my parents weren't ones to acknowledge that. As my mother would say, 'A party isn't a party unless God is on the guest list.'

The reason they told me to take the early train was that they wanted me to have time enough to polish and preen myself before confession in the evening. Confession on your birthday was cutely dubbed your 'gift from God'.

The night before I went home I spent in the cinema and later in Martine's with Harrie and James. We drank a toast of coffee to my birthday and I was disappointed that there were no presents and no surprise entry of our friends *en masse*. But I was pleased to note an obvious tension between Harrie and James. Harrie was quiet, almost back to her usual self, but James was over-watchful and over-critical. He was finding it hard to relax in her company, not a good sign for a maybe husband.

Twice he went so far as to snap her back into order when she threatened to raise her voice or lower the tone of the conversation and twice she just smiled up at him and lapsed back into silence. I could tell, though, that her heart wasn't in this demure show of obedience. Harrie's heart could never function under restraint.

I left them early and walked back to Benson's alone. I was beginning to relax about the threat of James and worry about the puzzle of this new and unapproachable Harrie. That was all I worried about over my weekend away. A month earlier and I would have expected a proposal in my absence.

I saw Harrie only briefly when she came in. She said that she was too tired to talk. She had come in a little later than I had expected and she seemed tousled and dreamy just as she used to be, but I think I just noted those signs in retrospect. At the time I was happy enough to leave her as I had to be ready and waiting for my train in town before nine.

I had hoped that Harrie would join me for breakfast, even though I was eating earlier than usual. It was, after all, my birthday and I was, after all, leaving for two whole days. She didn't appear, though, and I stopped myself from calling in on her.

I ate alone and left alone when I heard the bump and shuffle that could only be Fanny Boothe helping Miss Charter Thomas. I met them in the hall, but just put my head down and passed them. There was no longer any pretence of civility between me and Mrs Boothe. It had been a bad birthday morning and I left Benson's in quite a temper.

There's nothing much to be said about that weekend. I caught my train and sat on it for five hours as it jerked me around the countryside. I got off feeling nauseous and dirty and was greeted formally by my father. He was waiting to take me home on foot, although we lived almost two miles from the station, because, being a daughter and not a person that demanded impressing, I did not merit the 'unnecessary expenditure' of hiring a car.

He kissed the top of my head which was as affectionate as he had ever got in my youth and it was a sweet gesture then, but now, now that I was taller than him, it had turned into a ridiculous pantomime. I had to bend my head down to his lips.

His duty done, he walked swiftly on. He didn't offer to carry my case and I didn't expect him to, but I did expect him to walk at a conversational pace. He was striding ahead of me, and even though my case was light, the pull of it and the speed at which I had to walk dragged the air out of me. I was forced to limit my conversation to monosyllables.

After the first tense exchange of words – 'How are you?' 'Well.' 'Mother?' 'Well.' – he launched into his inevitable criticisms. I think, for the first time, I might have had the confidence to argue with his negative judgements, but I just didn't have the breath to. I had no choice but to lower my head and listen as I always had, and soon my still fragile confidence ebbed away.

It seemed that I was too thin and too pale, my lipstick, which I had foolishly worn out of habit, was vulgar, my skirts were too short and my hat was ridiculous. My hair aged me beyond the years God had given me and my shoulders tended to slouch. But aside from all that, he said that I was welcome home and that he wished me a very happy birthday.

My mother was even worse when we finally reached her. She held tight to my hand and bemoaned every aspect of my appearance before finally hugging me. I suppose I was a shock to them. I hadn't seen them for about two months and I had forgotten how much I had changed. I even forgot about my drawl and I found myself having to repeat my every comment before they understood me.

All difficulties were soon ironed out, though. I was sent upstairs to wash my face, and I did, and I put on my prettiest, lightest summer frock, the one I had first worn in the city. My mother freshened up my grubby jacket with a sponge and found me a sensible old hat of hers and I let down my mousy hair. That evening, walking to confession between my parents, I was, once again, mousy Mary Moore who chewed her Ss and slurred her Ts along with the best of them.

When we got home, my parents gave me an envelope with quite a substantial sum of money in it, and a long lecture on the benefits of savings bonds. Then we sat down to tea, in our mahogany-laden dining-room.

The meal was dragged out far longer than the ham, tomatoes and iced sponge cake merited, but that was always the way with my parents. They thought that the measure of a good meal was the length of time one took to eat it. They would spend hours eating mediocre food with the smugness of connoisseurs.

'So tell us about this James,' said my mother.

'I hear he's a solicitor,' said my father.

'Not a ... I hope.' My mother never liked the word Protestant.

'Have you met his parents?'

'Has Mrs Benson met him?'

'Are we going to meet him?'

'Could he have come with you this weekend?'

'The Grants fancy that they may have met his father.'

I answered every question as sweetly as I could and all the while I hugged my secret Harrie tight to my heart. It was right that they should never know her name, because if they knew even that much, they would try and own her or destroy her with their probing.

Their questioning about James continued for the whole evening. Just as I was going to bed my mother stopped me on the stairs, out of earshot of my father.

'That James, did he give you that lipstick that you were wearing today.'

'No.'

'Does he like that shade of lipstick?'

'I'm not sure. I think so.'

'Well, I'm sure he is a proper young man and I am sure you are a sensible young girl. But you are a very young girl so I am going to go against my God, but I'm going to go with my heart as a mother, and if that's a sin then God help me but I'm a sinner like all of us miserable creatures.'

She followed me up the stairs and beckoned me into her bedroom. I did as I was told in complete bewilderment.

'If your father knew that I was giving you this he would kill me and have God on his side. If he even knew I read such things myself he would have me before a priest,' she said with tears in her eyes, and handed me a pamphlet. 'The doctor gave this to me on the understanding that the information it held would only be used inside the sanctity of marriage and he only gave it to me because of my condition.' She patted her belly as she spoke, and mouthed the word condition.

'I'm giving it to you on the understanding that you will wait until you are married before you use the information in it, and even if you do use it in marriage you will have to take the responsibility of the sin. If you use it outside marriage it will be a great and terrible sin, but still an awful lot of bother might be avoided.'

I thanked her in some confusion and took myself and the pamphlet to bed where I read it transfixed, and more than slightly sickened. I was amazed by the effect a tight hairdo and some lipstick had had on my mother. The pamphlet was a detailed account of the natural method of contraception.

I spent the next day sitting in the garden greeting visiting friends of my parents with slurred Ts and chewed Ss. I received a few more sums of money and two dainty floral vases. I ate a heavy three-o'clock lunch that would have stretched into the night if I hadn't had a train to catch.

My parents were still lingering over their plates of tapioca pudding when I excused myself to pack, and they were still toying with cups of coffee and fingers of fruit cake when I returned to say goodbye.

My father did make a show of insisting that he walk me to the station but he was happy enough to be persuaded to stay at home. Actually, without much effort, I managed to persuade them both to stay at the table and so I didn't even get accompanied to the door. My mother kissed my cheek and my father kissed my head. She sent her love to James and my father offered him free access to the house. They couldn't have been more polite to him if he had been there.

On the train I re-applied my lipstick and I scratched my hair back, away from my face. I kept my white jacket on, even though the seat looked grubby, and every now and then I wriggled my back close against the grimy upholstery in an effort to crumple its new-sponged freshness.

I didn't arrive into the city until half-past ten and it was after eleven before I was back in Benson's. It seemed as if I had been away for ever. I pushed open the soft smiling door, ran through the noise of Mrs Benson's singing, and arrived panting at Harrie's door. I was desperate to see her. All weekend I had been studying and practising my parents and I thought that I had perfected quite a show.

I knocked and there was no answer, I called her name and there was no reply, I turned the handle and it was locked.

'She's out.'

I turned around, and there, as I had expected, was Fanny Boothe.

'She's out. She's been out all day and she was out late last night. I had breakfast with her this morning and she was as happy as I've seen her in a long while. No worries for her this weekend. No unwanted company. No soul-sucking vipers. Just herself and her man, as it should be.'

Fanny shuffled on and I waited until she was safely locked in the bathroom before I followed her. It had been a long time since I had spent any time in my room. I was tired from my journey but I needed to unwind before I could fall asleep. I sat in my brown chair, looked out on my view of parallel chimney stacks and worried about the lack of Harrie.

I was in bed and almost asleep when I heard her come in. For the first time in a long time she didn't call to collect me for a chat. I had no option but to believe that she thought I was staying another night with my parents. She must have got the days confused, I reasoned to myself, she must have forgotten to check my window for a light. I had no reason to believe that she would be anything but pleased to see me. I pulled myself awake and ran down the cold steps to Harrie's room.

'Oh, Em!' She sounded surprised when she opened the door to my knock, and not very happy. 'You're home! I had completely forgotten, and did you have a nice birthday?'

I followed her into the room and curled myself under her blankets refusing to confront the fact that she had 'forgotten' me.

'No.' And I began my impersonation of my father's greeting.

Harrie laughed, but I could tell that she was no longer desperate to be amused. I continued, but both of our minds were on the events of her evening.

She looked beautiful that night in the soft light of her bedside lamp. She swirled around the room like she used to, flinging her clothes off and leaving them in gay little piles. Her superior, secretive smile was back on her lips and behind her eyes, and her confidence moulded her body and features into an ideal of beauty.

I watched from the bed, tense and scared. It was obvious that I had missed something, and, though it hurt to ask, it was worse not to know.

'Here's me prattling on, what about you? How was your weekend? How is James?'

'He's the most loving and the kindest of men. You know I haven't been the happiest recently, and we were beginning to squabble a little. Nothing much, but any amount is too much, and now everything is sorted out and everything is wonderful. You know what the problem was, Em dear?' She paused, ominously, and I flushed though I tried not to. 'We weren't spending enough time alone.' She answered herself. 'All couples need time alone, time to rub their dreams together and make wishes.'

She was sitting on the bed when she was telling me this and she talked directly into my eyes. The words settled on my heart and spread their chill throughout my body.

I didn't know then if I had been discussed that weekend. I never knew for sure if notes had been compared, but I knew that I had missed something and I could guess at what had been decided in my absence. I only hoped that it had been Harrie's decision. I couldn't bear to contemplate James's part in my rejection, the couple against the unit.

'Speaking of couples, James has found you the most marvellous man.'

Again she spoke directly into my eyes, and I understood that this was the last man James was going to produce for me.

'James said he would bring him to Martine's on Wednesday, if you want to meet him. Now goodnight, dear. You must be tired and I am exhausted.'

She kissed me lightly on the forehead, a thing she never did before, and I got out of the bed before she got in, a thing I rarely did. I climbed the stairs to my room with her kiss burning on my forehead. It burnt like a kiss goodbye.

That was almost the end of my friendship with Harrie, but it was still only the beginning of my love for her. Over the years she has always been with me. She is the sparkle in my eye when I am diverted and the turn of my head when I am bored. She is my funniest anecdote and my wittiest retort. She is my singular style of dress and my husky, nasal voice. She is everything that I have created for myself and everything that I admire most about myself. But that is the end of my story and I am not there yet.

Chapter 19

The me of eighteen faced Hall's Central Stores the following morning alone. I got my pay rise and I got my annual handshake from Mr Hall, and, for the privilege, I suffered the full wrath of Miss Walsh. She took me aside as soon as I left Mr Hall's office.

'Mr Hall is no fool, but he is kinder than a businessman should be. Your insolent manner, your lack of initiative, your refusal to learn the simplest task, all these have been noticed by Mr Hall. Unfortunately, I presume that your family connections are also noted by him. But mark me well, girl, blood may be thicker than water, but nothing is thicker than money. If you continue to lose us customers, you will continue to lose us money, and eventually you will lose your position. Mr Hall and I are as one on that point.'

I had a brief mental image of Miss Walsh and Mr Hall joined at the hip, like a picture I had seen once of Siamese twins, and balancing on the point of a needle, but I wasn't even tempted to smile. Automatically, I had started to phrase the joke for Harrie's benefit, but then I realised with crushing certainty that Harrie would not be at our bandstand that lunchtime.

She wasn't and she wasn't at home that evening. I was losing, if I hadn't already lost. I spent that evening sitting in my brown room, staring out on the rows upon rows of chimney stacks and thinking.

It obviously didn't matter to James that Harrie was sometimes erratic in company. It didn't matter to him that her subject matter was frequently improper. It didn't matter that the stories she told about her past and her acquaintances were contradictory and often incredible. It didn't matter that her mother was a drunk. It didn't even matter that her clothes were cut tight across her chest, that she wore scarlet lipstick and that she could dance like a professional.

The me of eighteen was confused. I had been confident in my initial assessment of James and time did prove me right. He always was a narrow, conventional man. But with Harrie – and maybe it was a combination of Harrie and his youth – his oh-so-shallow waters momentarily ran deep. He was obviously prepared to run the risk of trusting her.

I found out, much later on and piece by piece, that I had been right. That James had decided to throw caution to the wind and place his trust in Harrie. They had spent that weekend, in my absence, in close conversation. A lot had been said and a lot had been explained, obviously not everything on Harrie's part, but enough to reassure James.

I don't know for sure, but I can say with some certainty, that James's questions proved to Harrie that her trust in me had been misplaced. James, for his part, reassured Harrie with the promise of a future, and, although marriage wasn't specifically mentioned, they both knew that they were just waiting for the right moment.

It must have been James's renewed confidence in her that soothed Harrie. That is why, on Sunday night, she had relaxed back into her old, confident self. But this was a Harrie with a difference. This Harrie had no time for me. This Harrie would leave Benson's on a bridal cloud. This Harrie would leave me behind as a discarded and soiled memory of her life before her life began.

I imagined children with blond hair and serious natures. I imagined a house filled with white and light and beautiful objects. I imagined a home and a fire and large Christmas dinners and always James. James with his thinning hair and his censorious eyebrows. I wanted much more for Harrie. She deserved so much better. I'm sure that was my motivation. It was basically selfless.

Of course if I had known then what I know now, I would have known that Harrie's relief could only be temporary. But I was young, with my life before me, and didn't feel that I had time to waste. As I have said before, age is wasted on the old.

If I had even waited a month longer, I could have been Harrie's comfort when her composure shattered again, as inevitably it would have. They said that the security of marriage would have helped her, but I'm sure that James wasn't the man, he hadn't the strength of character necessary to sustain her.

My security was what she needed. She could be here with me even still and I would have no need to depend on the likes of little Miss Kelly and this heavy brown house that people call my home would be filled with the lightness of Harrie's touch. Even old age and even our eventual death would be an adventure to be enjoyed.

Harrie came in late that night and didn't call for me. This time there was no excuse. She knew I was home and my light was on. Undeterred, I ran down to her. She seemed pleased to see me, but she was in such a happy humour, she would have been welcoming towards anyone. She swung the door open for me – I had taken the precaution of knocking – and she only hesitated for a second before stepping aside to let me in. I pretended not to notice the delay. She had already undressed and she was wrapped in her silk kimono.

'I had the most wonderful night, Em, and I am exhausted from it. Don't you think that happiness wears one out much more than the comfortable plodding we creatures are used to?'

She had returned to her hairbrush and her night creams and I had followed her over as far as her dressing-table. While I was listening to her, I picked up and toyed with her mermaid perfume bottle. It was a habit I had. I used to run my finger down its silver hair, around its silver tail and up again.

'Oh, Em, I missed your birthday didn't I? I meant well. I was doing unto others what I would have them do unto me – ignore the gathering of my years. But you probably haven't reached your ideal age yet and until you do that you still need birthdays, so I'll grant you this one. To mark the occasion please keep the bottle.'

'This one? Your mermaid one?'

'Unless you see a bottle you'd rather.'

'No, no I love it, you know I love it.'

Maybe it was a farewell token or maybe she forgave me a little or maybe she was just so full of happiness that she couldn't be discreet about who she shared it with, but in my heart I knew that there was a darker reason behind the gesture. There was no warmth in the giving, it was as if she no longer cared for her treasure. It was as if my constant pawing at it had tainted it for her. I thanked her as best I could, but the words stuck. I found it difficult to be grateful for such an insult.

'Oh, you don't have to thank me. Even one "thank you" takes all the good out of a gift. It makes one feel as if one has to grovel for the privilege of receiving something you probably don't want, from someone who feels smug enough already.'

We both laughed a little too loudly.

I didn't get into her bed that night, but I sat on it and worked hard. I was still hoping to win her back. I told her all about Miss Walsh and Mr Hall's handshake. I invented a meeting with Miss Charter Thomas and I was careful not to mention the bandstand or her evening out. I knew that I wouldn't be able to do either without sounding petulant.

Harrie laughed at the right moments, smiled throughout and even took the time to ask some pertinent questions, but she didn't need me to entertain her. She was all kindness and all empathy, but I felt that I was a burden on her time. I left before I had to face the indignity of being asked to. The Harrie that had pleaded with me to repeat my stories and the Harrie that had held tight to my hand and asked that I mind her to sleep was gone.

She stopped me at the door and my heart bounced with hope.

'Em dear, you won't forget Wednesday, will you? James is so sure that you will like this man. We will expect you at sevenish.'

I just nodded and left. Her parting words sank deep and hurt at every level. The inference was that she did not plan to see me before Wednesday and the strength of her commitment to James was obvious in the way in which she stressed that magical 'we'. She didn't even want to arrive at Martine's with me.

Before I got into bed that night I tucked the mermaid bottle out of sight, under some spare blankets, folded on the bottom of my wardrobe. I left it there when I left Benson's.

I didn't see Harrie until Wednesday. I spent Tuesday sorting trimmings. Feathers together and silk cherries together, various widths and colours of elastic together. Miss Walsh supervised and Gillian flashed her new engagement ring at every customer and every member of staff who took the time to climb the three flights to our floor to congratulate her. Miss Walsh gushed and cooed and gave advice on venues.

I said, 'Congratulations. It is a lovely ring.'

Gillian said, 'Thank you.'

Other than that I didn't talk to anyone else except customers and I think Mrs Jones appeared that day with her usual, loud wit. I cut her a length of Turkey on her request, and I offered to dip it in Greece to enable it to be fried in Japan. Mrs Jones had the good grace to scream with laughter and the stupidity to repeat my joke to Miss Walsh. I spent the rest of the afternoon being hounded by the familiar lecture on customer relations. This time there was no joy in memorising or scrutinising expressions. There was no Harrie waiting for my jokes. I bought an apple cake on my way home and I ate it in my room. I wasn't asleep when Harrie came in, but my light was off and my eyes were shut.

On Wednesday I was told to dust the threads that were already on display and to make a note of which shades needed re-ordering. I spent my lunchtime sitting alone on the steps of our bandstand and I spent my afternoon freshening the glove display. No staff members spoke to me and few customers approached me. I was weak with loneliness by the time I reached Martine's.

I was early in my eagerness. I sat at one of the larger tables and waited. I waited for half an hour before Harrie and James and my new man arrived.

'Em dear, can you forgive us?'

I nodded. I could forgive Harrie everything except her use of 'us'.

'James and I are only just back from the sea. We both took a half-day today and had the most wonderful picnic.'

She stopped to squeeze James's arm, they were obviously still filled with their lovely day. I kept smiling, even though I was visualising James usurping our picnic cove.

'Where did you go?' I asked, my voice light with disinterested politeness.

'I think it was where we went that time. Do you remember, Em? It was ages ago.'

I screwed my face tight for a moment and then nodded as if I had forced a memory.

'We were late for Bill as well. We had arranged to collect him on the way here. So already you two have a lot in common – you are both angry and you both hate the sight of me and James.'

She stepped aside as she spoke and sat opposite me, patting the seat beside her for James. Bill, who had been standing behind her, loomed into view. We nodded at each other and then we both turned to disagree with Harrie, but she wasn't listening. Her whole being had turned to James and there it stayed for the night. Even when we were joined by another two couples.

Initially we had planned to see a picture, but because Harrie and James had been late and because Bill was hungry and because we were joined by two other couples, we ended up staying in Martine's. Well, Bill and I stayed for the evening; Harrie and James stayed for about an hour.

It was a pleasant enough evening, and, in my state, pleasant was much more than I had hoped for. Bill was very handsome. That may have helped. And the couples that joined us were flatteringly enthusiastic about my birthday and the girls in pink looked flatteringly jealous of my companion. He was something bigger and better than James's usual friends. Perhaps James had decided that I had grown sufficiently to handle another Robert and perhaps he was right.

Bill was broad and musky, confident and ardent, and I was succeeding in captivating him. I was enjoying the thrill of success, but nothing really eased the pain I felt when I was forced to watch Harrie and James leave early and walk into the early autumn dusk alone.

Before they left it was decided that my birthday needed celebrating.

'Eighteen!' cooed Rosie, her eyes wide with the wonder of my maturity. Rosie, who, under her display of awed deference, was at least twenty at the time.

'Eighteen!' echoed Jim and Tim.

'Something should be done about a girl turning eighteen.'

'Eighteen!' said Bill and snuggled a little closer. I looked to Harrie, but she said nothing.

'I know,' said Rosie's little pink friend, 'we can have an evening at my house. My father has just got a new gramophone and my parents are both away this weekend. They won't mind, I'm sure of that, and we can have an evening. Us eight and maybe Ellen and Joe. They won't mind ten of us and with ten we can have dancing and we can have fruit punch and a light supper. I'm sure they won't mind. They're always asking me to invite my friends around, but I suppose this will be different because they won't get to meet you, but I'm sure they won't mind...'

And she talked on and on. The sophisticated me of eighteen longed to yawn in her face. She was always eager to please, little what's-her-name. I had difficulty remembering her name then and I certainly don't remember it now, but I do remember that she had a great line in frocks. And not only frocks. Her hats always matched her gloves and her shoes always matched her bag. She was the type of girl who bought outfits instead of clothes and even then she looked dull and dumpy. But she was offering me a party all of my very own, so I smiled at her over my yawn and thanked her effusively.

'Thank you, thank you. I don't know what to say. That would be just too wonderful. But are you sure that your parents won't mind?'

'Oh no, I am sure that they won't mind.'

'It's just that my parents tend to mind such things, especially when they are away from home.'

'No, I think they won't mind.'

'Perhaps you should ask them before we make any plans. They might mind.'

'No, I'm sure they won't mind.'

I looked to Harrie to see if she was following my joke but she was alone with James and so I dropped my teasing and it was decided, with no help from Harrie, that there was to be a party, subject to the consent of the parents involved. We were told the address and we all promised to be there the following Saturday at eight o'clock.

'And as it's just us and just fun, let's say semi-formal?'

We all agreed that semi-formal would be fine, but semi-formal or not, I decided to use my birthday money to buy the full-length ivory dress with the olive green flowers that I had been visiting on the second floor of Hall's.

Harrie and James left soon after that and the rest of the evening passed easily and flatly. The other couples drifted away and Bill and I went for a walk by the river. It was assumed, without any prior consultation, that our evening was just beginning. We walked, and talked about work and films and how I knew Harrie and how he knew James, and, once we had passed the brightness of the last shop window, Bill talked about me.

He told me that I was beautiful. He told me that my eyes were like stars and my skin was like alabaster. He told me that my lips were like rose petals and my teeth were like pearls. I listened and thought that he could have saved himself the effort. All he had to say was that he wanted a kiss and I wouldn't have minded. This was different from Robert. This didn't matter. That night, staring into the darkness of the river, I felt that nothing mattered any more, nothing mattered except my lack of Harrie.

I kissed Bill. I kissed him while he was still likening me to various ideals of beauty. I think he had got as far as my neck being like a swan's and he got no further. I closed my mouth over his and silenced the clichéd tedium of his speech. He walked me home eventually and for the first time I was home later than Harrie. I walked passed her door and saw the light under it and I continued noisily on.

Harrie heard, as I had hoped she would, and popped her head out.

'Goodness Em, you are a disgrace! Your hair has been ruffled, your lipstick is gone and it's one in the morning. Have you been with a man?'

She was delighted with the situation. She was interested and amused, but she wasn't worried or jealous – she was relieved and I was insulted.

'A man! Whatever gave you that impression?'

We both laughed and Harrie closed her door and I walked on alone.

I had been right. Nothing mattered, everything was over. And then it got that little bit worse.

Chapter 20

I know now why I ration my thoughts of Harrie. It's because they inevitably lead to the end, and the end still hurts. It hurt then, but it only smarted. Now it aches deep inside of me. It grew with time, that pain. And it grew strong because I allowed it to dictate my life's decisions.

I suppose I can't blame the me of eighteen. At that age one never expects one's decisions to have life-lasting consequences. But, with hindsight, one learns that even the most trivial choices can instigate an unbreakable chain of events, an example being my decision to accept the offer of a birthday dance.

That dance was the beginning of the pain that grew into my marriage, my life and my stiff old age. It wore me fragile over the years, draining me of joy. It left me nothing to give to my marriage, nothing to give to friendships and nothing to give to a child. I had nothing to give but pain and now I have no-one to give that to except little Miss Kelly, and where's the joy in that?

I don't think I saw Harrie again until the night of the dance. I may have caught a glimpse of her coming and going and I presume that we ate breakfast together on Saturday morning as usual, but I didn't really see her until that night. It was only a short time since James's birthday dance but everything had changed.

Bill called into Hall's on Friday to see me. He made quite a scene at the haberdashery counter, asking loudly for a selection of very feminine articles. Miss Walsh served him and, despite myself, I felt the urge to laugh, but I didn't. I avoided Bill's eye and listened as closely as I could. I was busy sorting needles at the far end of the counter, but I was doing so silently and so I overheard most of their conversation.

'So sir would like to see our summer range of ribbons?'

'Ribbons maybe, but I was more interested in elastic. Elastic is my vision, but it must be blue.'

'And may I ask what sir needs it for?'

'My hat. My panama is just too too dull. My, but are they rosebuds? I must have them.'

'Rosebuds! Sir wants rosebuds for his panama?'

'Do I not? I bow to your better judgement.'

'Perhaps sir would like to try our selection of hats in our gentlemen's department on the first floor.'

'I just did and they have nothing as cheerful as rosebuds, and I almost forgot, I need a hairnet.'

'A hairnet!'

'Do they come in colours?'

I almost felt sorry for Miss Walsh, she was so far out of her depth. She lived by the maxim that the customer is always right even if, as on this occasion, he is a little odd, so she tried valiantly to please Bill. She didn't suspect that he was anything other than he seemed. It was in keeping with her general opinion of me that it never dawned on her that a handsome gentleman could be in any way connected with me. Or perhaps it was because Bill was better than Harrie at playing cruel jokes on the deserving.

Either way, he kept Miss Walsh busy until I politely interrupted to announce that I was going on lunch. Miss Walsh smiled and said, 'Very well.'

Then she followed me to the end of the counter and hissed.

'How many times have I told you never to interrupt a sale? Now look, the gentleman has left without buying a thing.'

I looked back and Bill was gone. He was waiting for me outside, grinning madly. He was very handsome when he grinned. I smiled with him, I linked him and I had lunch with him, but I was aching for Harrie. Once, a week ago, I would have run to the bandstand and to Harrie, filled with the fun of Miss

Walsh's confusion, but that was a week ago and a world away. Bill was amusing company and an attentive escort but it wasn't enough. The meal he pampered me with that lunchtime was no match for a plain ice-cream and a rotten bandstand.

He delivered me back to Hall's when my break was over and asked, humbly, if he could collect me and take me to my party on Saturday night. He was very handsome when he was being modest. I said he could. I knew that Harrie would want to arrive with James.

And she did. She knocked on my door early on Saturday evening and told me that she was meeting James in Martine's before the party. She just told me – she didn't offer to include me in the arrangement, but I ignored the slight and said, 'That's perfect, because Bill is picking me up.'

With hindsight, it seems an obvious peculiarity that James never collected Harrie from Benson's, but at the time I never thought to question it.

Harrie smiled and relaxed and went as far as to come into my room and sit down. I told her about Bill's visit and she laughed. I showed her my new dress and she admired it, but as before, I felt that I was a burden on her time. She didn't stay long and didn't invite me to dress in her room. She just asked me to show myself when I was finished and even that was said half-heartedly. I think her exact words were, 'If you're ready before I leave, drop down, but anyway I'll see all your new glamour tonight.'

I smiled and managed a blasé retort, but I made sure to be ready early. I couldn't bear that Harrie would only see me as one in a crowd. It was bad enough that she already thought of me in that way.

I was beautiful that night. My colouring suited melancholy almost as well as my thin, drooping figure did. I wore my new dress of ivory satin and olive green, with its matching stole draped loosely around my shoulders. I wore my hair tied tight in a green velvet ribbon and I wore a slash of scarlet lipstick. I didn't need anything else. I saw myself in Harrie's mirror and I saw myself as beautiful, wistful and vulnerable with a dash of sophistication.

Harrie wore a silver dress that I had never seen before. It shimmered when she walked and sparkled when she stood still. It was a dress for a far bigger occasion than a mere birthday party. Harrie was dressed for a night that she planned to remember for the rest of her life. She was dressed for a proposal.

She barely showed me the dress before she covered it with her battered mac. It was as if she didn't want me associated with it. A week ago such an important purchase would not have been made without my approval. However, I did see enough of it to gush over it and despite herself, Harrie flushed with pleasure and in much her usual tone she gave her usual response to flattery, 'Enough of that, Em, or you'll turn my head so thoroughly I'll be forced to walk backwards.'

She left then and waited by her door until I followed her out. Obviously I was not to be trusted alone in her room.

I followed Harrie downstairs and waved her down the lane, though she only turned once, and then I waited in the hall for Bill. He arrived on time, beautifully dressed, in a shiny black taxi and I kissed him for his trouble. I knew that the taxi would be seen and admired from behind Mrs Benson's lace curtains and I hoped that the fact of my date would be seen and appreciated by Fanny Boothe. I was still young enough to aim for everyone's approval.

Bill took my kiss and linked my arm and held the car door open for me. I stepped in as I had seen the stars do in the newsreels and Bill joined me and just like the movies he barely stopped to give the driver his directions before he swept me into a kiss. It was a short journey, but it was long enough to ruffle my hair and smear my lipstick. I felt very adult sitting in a cab with a musky man watching as I snapped my powder compact open to re-apply my make-up. And then we were there.

I wasn't long enough in the city to know how its class structure related to its streets, so it was a shock to me when we arrived at little Miss Nobody's house. It was huge. A flight of ten granite steps swept onto the pavement and up to an imposing, heavy door, flanked with stained glass panels. Three storeys towered above it, a basement sank below it and four far-spaced windows framed it. I stood in awe and Bill pulled a metal lever that jangled a bell deep in the bowels of the house.

'Goodness!' I couldn't stop my exclamation. But Bill, older and more seasoned, purposely misinterpreted my meaning.

'Yeah, what a racket,' he agreed.

We were greeted by a uniformed maid who took our coats and showed us to the first floor. I followed our guide and took Bill's arm and tried my best not to give in to the temptation to stare. It is funny to think that here I am now, all these years later, sitting in and cursing a similar house.

We were a polite half an hour late, but we were the last people to arrive. The others were obviously more eager than polite. Our party was held in the library. An unusual choice, but when I was shown the grandeur and dimensions of the main reception rooms, I understood. A party of ten would be dwarfed by them. The library itself was almost too large. Its name was evidently more historic than descriptive. The only books it had all fitted in one average-sized case. The rest of the room was filled with an expensively aged suite of furniture, a long table spread with a cold supper and a huge fireplace that looked hollow and grey with summer disuse. The big, shiny gramophone took pride of place, centred between the two windows.

I got an enthusiastic welcome rather less enthusiastic than a cheer when I arrived, and, for the first few minutes, I was surrounded and kissed and generally fussed over. Then I was largely forgotten. My birthday was very much just an excuse for a party, not the real cause. I was, however, presented with a silver comb. I was told it was from 'us all', but I suspect that it was from little Miss Nobody. No-one else had that kind of money or that pathetic desire to be liked.

I laughed and smiled and kissed them and thanked them and then broke away and headed for Harrie. She had waved when I came in, and she had joined in the half-hearted applause when I opened my present, but other than that she had remained engrossed in James, who was so engrossed in her that he barely registered my arrival.

'Harrie, isn't it beautiful? Did you know about this?' And I turned to include James in my question – it wouldn't do to be rude – and James took it upon himself to answer for the two of them.

'Yes we saw it earlier and we knew that you would like it.'

Then Bill joined us and I was relieved to see that James seemed happy to talk to him. I stood by Harrie, and waited until the men had lost themselves in discussion before I tried talking to her. She would have to take notice, I reasoned to myself. She couldn't possibly pretend that she preferred to listen to the details of some sporting fixture than to listen to me.

'Isn't it divine, Harrie dear, how one's public never forgets one?'

She smiled absently, but she shifted further away from me. She was embarrassed by my allusion to our joke about our celebrity status and the old intimacy it referred to.

'Did you hear Mrs Benson last night? Is it me, or is her voice breaking?'

Again there was no response. Harrie was looking at James talking. I wouldn't be able to break her concentration alone. I decided to turn that gathering into the noisiest, liveliest, most frantic party ever. It was my only hope of postponing the inevitable. Party games and modern dances were not compatible with romantic declarations. They probably still aren't.

I broke away from Harrie's side and swung into the middle of the room and the clutch of guests that were huddled there. They were talking politely about the beauty of the house and little Miss Nobody was shyly taking credit for everything.

'I love your curtains, they're such a dreamy colour.'

'Thank you.'

'And the fireplace – what a lot of marble.'

'Thank you.'

'And you have so many paintings and they're all so good.'

'Thank you.'

It was my first realisation that the praise bestowed on the rich for their taste often far outweighs the praise granted to the artist for his work. I listened impatiently to the fawning of the girls in pink and then I broke them apart.

'Come on, guys,' I said, raising my arms, swaying my hips and sashaying through their huddled politeness. 'Where's the music? Let's get dancing.'

Little Miss Nobody obediently scurried over to the gramophone and I followed her. She chose a waltz, but I insisted on some jazz, and I insisted on some volume. Then I returned to centre-stage, stopping on the way to pick up Bill.

We started the dancing and I made sure everyone followed suit. Eventually, and awkwardly, they did, even James and Harrie. They didn't have much choice after I directed everyone to circle them and force them into movement.

We did look terribly silly, five couples shuffling around the blocks of furniture that were too old or too large to move. It didn't help that we were none of us very good at dancing, though I was graceful and Bill was confident. The others, except for Harrie, were embarrassing, and Harrie, that night, was being very proper about her moves.

We shuffled on, twittering at each other, and I tried to keep up a flow of general conversation. I talked to each couple as I passed them. I talked about the music and the room and the house and their appearance. There was a wealth of material for discussion in those girl's dresses, but I restrained myself. That night I was limiting myself to being charming.

'Hey, love your hair,' I shouted. 'Keep an eye on your hands there, Tom. If you two dance any closer we'll have to call the fire brigade in. Hey, everyone, take a look at James and Harrie dancing cheek-to-cheek from head to toe.'

It worked for a while. I was exhausting myself, but the room was busy with music and flying comments, and, even though Harrie wasn't joining in, even though I fancied that I saw her wince at my tactics, I knew that I was successfully destroying any opportunity for private conversation.

But people couldn't be trusted to dance and shout all evening and when I began to feel their enthusiasm wane, I broke free of Bill, kicked off my shoes and hopped on to a foot stool.

It was hard, and it probably sounded ridiculous, but over the jangled jazz beat, I began to bark out some dancing orders in that American square dance way that we were all so familiar with from the cowboy movies.

> *'Move your partner to the right*
> *And grab her waist with all your might*
> *And girls when you turn to face your boy*
> *Swing those hips and don't be coy...'*

It was a desperate attempt at fabricating some hilarity, and, though it worked for a while, it could only last so long. There are, after all, a finite number of rhymes for dance and partner, right and left, girl and boy. I did, however, get them all to change partners by stepping the boys to the right and the girls to the left. It was a relief to see Harrie free of James's enthusiastic arms.

The dancing finally broke down when the girls on the inside collided with the boys on the outside. I suppose it was too much to expect them all to be able to keep track of their left and their right. I did succeed in dispelling any trace of romance, though, and, as we moved towards the supper table, the room was loud with laughter and conversation. Harrie, I was pleased to see, was in close conversation with little Miss Nobody, and James was deep in a huddle of masculinity.

The supper, I remember, was surprisingly elaborate for such simple days, but I hardly touched the food. I couldn't even bring myself to sample the birthday cake, though I did blow out my candles and laugh when the ginger-haired boy sang, 'For she's a jolly good fellow, for she's a jolly good fellow, for she's a jolly good fellow, but nobody's told her mam', though by that stage I would have felt more comfortable hitting him. My heart was sinking lower as the evening progressed. I knew that I had only postponed the inevitable. James's question would take only a moment, and James and Harrie still had the night ahead of them; and if that wasn't enough, they had tomorrow and all its tomorrows.

I was beginning to accept that I couldn't chaperon their future when the miracle I had been hoping for happened. But maybe miracle is the wrong word. Miracle implies divine intervention and whatever force helped me it was certainly not divine. It was Harrie who asked for a tour of the house. She probably did it out of kindness – it was obvious that little Miss Nobody wanted a chance to impress and the rest of the party, filled with good food, was quite willing to be impressed.

'Oh yes,' they said. 'If it's not an imposition.'

'Oh no,' said little Miss Nobody. 'It's no trouble and I'm sure that my parents won't mind.'

'Well,' I said. 'If your parents don't mind there can be no harm in it.'

Harrie shot me a glare of disapproval that silenced me, and we moved off.

James walked ahead with little Miss Nobody. I think he fancied himself quite an architectural expert and he was intent on dazzling us all with the depth and intelligence of his questions. We followed in ones and twos.

I walked alone behind Harrie and Bill. We were led out of the library and around the stairwell to the reception rooms at the front of the house. We walked in silence, listening to the lecture that James was trying to tease out of little Miss Nobody.

'Do you know the architect? Do you think Gandon or maybe one of his school? I noticed the stucco work in the hall, baroque would you say? Though it would be closer in date to rococo. But as I always say, what is rococo if not a secular form of baroque? Do you have any paperwork relating to the house, any verification of the particular artists used?'

Poor little Miss Nobody had been looking forward to telling us all about the cost of soft furnishings and the ghost of an old housekeeper. She did vaguely know that the house had been designed and she knew not to slam the hall door because it was bad for the plaster, but that was all the information that James was able to dredge out of her little head. Not that he tried very hard to get her to talk – as usual he was happy with his own voice and confident of his own knowledge.

Little Miss Nobody hurried on and with obvious relief opened the door and ushered us into the drawing-room, the main reception room. Here at least she knew something about what she was talking about. The room had just recently been done up and she had assisted her mother in most of her choices. It was a very fine room, high and light with generations of delicate furniture. Its gold brocade curtains were beautiful and some of the portraits, none of which were of little Miss Nobody's ancestors, were well crafted. We stood and listened to the list of shops where certain items had been bought and then we were told the prices of the same items and then we were told about the insolence and tardiness of certain workmen and finally we were given leave to wander carefully about.

We girls did as we were told, as girls automatically did back then, but the boys had been fired by James's show of knowledge. It wasn't enough for them to be told, they had to be part of the telling and so they grouped around the terrified little Miss Nobody. They needed a focus on which to direct their learned questions.

It was lucky for little Miss Nobody that that was all they wanted. She wouldn't have been able to supply any answers but then, happily, the boys had no real interest in receiving any information, especially not from a girl. They just wanted to show that they knew what to ask as well as the next man.

Understandably, little Miss Nobody broke away as soon as she could. She led us all down to the far end of the room where a pair of sliding doors opened into an anteroom, which extended the drawing-room into a larger L-shaped reception area.

While she wrenched away at the doors, she explained how this L-shaped room was just perfect for accommodating the big

Christmas party her parents held every year. The doors appeared to be stuck, but she continued pulling at them while she told us just how much money her parents spent on their annual get-together and just how rude casual staff could be. Finally, the light of realisation dawned in her dim little eyes.

'Of course, they're locked,' she said, 'and the key is kept on the other side. I can get in through the landing and see if I can find it. Or maybe you could come with me, just in case I don't. It will save me coming to fetch you.'

And so we all turned and followed little Miss Nobody and her bodyguard of our men back through the forest of delicate furniture and on into the hall. I was just turning out of the room when I noticed that Harrie wasn't with us. She was still at the far end of the drawing-room. She was leaning against the glass of the window opposite the folding doors and staring down on the street below.

She was beautiful. She was lit from below by the soft streetlight and from above by the expensive glow of a crystal chandelier. Her dress sparkled over the curves of her body and her hair shone and fell thickly in its loose collection of curls. She was a celebration of femininity.

I turned back to her and the others clattered down the hall, leaving us alone together for the last time.

Chapter 21

I joined her by the window and she glanced across at me. 'I wouldn't like to live here,' she said. 'Big houses always remind me of institutions. A home should be a cottage. It should be low and warm and should be filled with the smells of baking. Big houses always smell of control.'

And then, as if she had just remembered our new relationship, her tone and her conversation reverted to impersonal practicalities.

'James and I are leaving soon. It was a good night wasn't it? I must say your dance steps were hilarious.'

'Leaving! Already!'

'Yes, we want a little time alone.'

'Thank you for coming and thank you for the perfume bottle.'

'You are very welcome.'

'Well, goodbye then. I might see you during the week.'

'Yes indeed. I hope you enjoy the rest of your evening.'

And I knew it was over. Harrie and I were standing side by side looking down on the workings of the street below us. When she had finished speaking I raised my head. It was over. It was no longer Harrie and I facing the world together.

I was going to leave her and go back to people and noise and defeat when a reflection in the glass stopped me.

The folding doors behind us were moving. Little Miss Nobody had obviously found the key. I was just about to turn, to be ready to face the group when they appeared on the other side, when I realised the potential of the situation. My mind froze on its main intent and I spoke without further thought.

'I think I really like Bill. What do you think of him?' I asked as I watched, in the window, the doors buckle slightly.

'He seems very nice.' Harrie seemed surprised by my sudden and personal question but I suppose she thought that she owed me a certain amount of civility if nothing else. 'I'm glad you like him,' she continued. 'We knew that you would.'

'Can I ask you something?'

Harrie nodded, resigned now to giving me a little more time.

The doors opened a crack. I could see a line of little Miss Nobody's dress. The doors were too heavy for her to pull apart alone. The line of her dress disappeared. She was going to get help. I continued.

'My mother gave me a leaflet on my birthday about how you can... you know... the doctor gave it to her. And I was thinking about me and Bill. I think I might like to... you know... with him and it seems that you can... you know... do it... without getting into trouble, if you just study your monthlies. Do you know if that's true? Does it work? Did you ever do it like that?'

I spoke in a rush. Little Miss Nobody had got help. The crack between the doors grew wider and wider. They were silently and heavily opening. They were rolling on well-oiled wheels, wheels that rolled over well-laid runners, runners that were sunk deep into the pile of the expensive carpet. I could see two black-suited legs.

Harrie answered briskly, 'I wouldn't recommend that you sleep with Bill. Apart from everything else, that method doesn't always work.'

She gathered herself to move away. I was forcing an intimacy on her that she was no longer comfortable with. But I stopped her going. I held on to her bare arm and I asked urgently, 'Yes but is it what you used to do?'

The doors were nearly open now. They had picked up their own momentum and were sliding quickly apart.

Bill and James stepped through them. I could see them mirrored in the window as they took that first step towards us.

Behind them the rest of the party was slowly moving down the foot of the L.

Harrie answered. She looked long at my hand until I removed it and she spoke slightly louder than usual. Her displeasure at being asked such a question forced her voice high with indignation. But she did answer: 'I don't see how that's any of your business.'

I barely allowed her to finish before I continued in pressing my point home: 'But your first lover, the doctor, did he not tell you about it?'

She was silent for a moment before she answered, but she answered again. She drew herself up to the full height of her dignity and snapped her reply with a finality that allowed for no further questions. These were the last words she ever said to me: 'All I know is that I have been lucky not to fall pregnant. There is no sure way of avoiding the risk and if you have any sense you will follow my advice instead of my example and you will not sleep with Bill.'

I watched in the glass and I saw James and Bill stop. I saw that they had heard everything and that they understood all there was to understand. I saw little Miss Nobody, next in line, crumple her face in confusion. I saw that she had heard, and once she asked the right questions, she would understand. I saw the rest of the party in the distance, and I saw that although they had heard nothing they understood that something had happened.

Then the murmur of conversation that came with the rest of the guests alerted Harrie and she turned. I turned with her. She expected to face the crowd as they came through the door and I will never forget her expression when she saw how close James was to her.

They didn't speak – there was no need. They looked at each other, deep into each other, and it was as if their eyes were killing each other, ripping each other's hearts open. And the hurt spread. It spread from their eyes down to their mouths, down to their shoulders, down their spines and further down, weighing them down.

It was a moment that I can never forget but it was just a moment, and a moment later the room was filled with a party.

'What an enormous room!'

'It does make a difference, doesn't it?'

'It's so much brighter.'

'How many does it hold?'

Harrie and James left immediately. Harrie didn't say a word. She just looked at James with hollow eyes while he made their excuses through thin, white lips: 'I think Harrie is a little unwell.'

He walked her out of the drawing-room. Little Miss Nobody scurried behind them. I stayed with the others, watching them go. I could only see Harrie's head, and the occasional shimmer of her dress, as James was blocking my view. It was the last time I ever saw Miss Harrie Elliott.

I stayed on at the party. I stayed later than all the others. I demanded more dancing and I ate more food. I asked to see the breakfast-room and I marvelled at the orchids in the conservatory. I kept little Miss Nobody up way past her bedtime and I only left when Bill, very firmly, put me into my wrap.

I was exhausted, and it was very late, but I insisted on walking home. I never wanted to return to number 26 Marsh Lane. I knew that it would house a horror that I was too young to comprehend, but obviously old enough to create, and that terrified me.

Chapter 22

Once we had left that horrible house and all its gaudy wealth, once we were alone, Bill asked the inevitable question. I knew he would. I had seen the glint of excitement in his eyes ever since Harrie and James had left. I no longer thought him handsome. His leering eagerness was especially loathsome.

'What were you and Harrie talking about before she left?'

'Girl things, you wouldn't be interested.'

'I heard, you know. So did James and from the look of him he was very interested. I'm interested too, and from what I heard it seems that you share some of my interests. James isn't as liberal as we are, though. I can imagine him arguing with Harrie now instead of enjoying her. What do you think? Do you see them kissing or snarling?'

I didn't respond. The thought of betraying Harrie any further sickened me.

'Is it really true what she was saying, though? Is she really all that bad, or that good, depending on your moral standpoint?'

I still couldn't answer and he rightly took my silence as affirmation.

'Well, well, who would have thought it? Actually, maybe everyone would have except for poor old James.'

I noted with disgust that Bill was almost salivating at the thought of Harrie in this new light. All the time he was talking he was snaking his arms around me, pushing his face into my hair, muttering close to my ear. I shrugged and pushed and wriggled but he held fast and as we passed a dark and deep porch he pulled me to him and tried to push me into it.

'Are you going to take her advice or are you going to take mine? Can you guess what my advice is?'

The poor man, he was confused by my supposed wanton intention towards him, my earlier, free-flowing kisses and my present frigidity. I fought my way back to the footpath and shouted at him in my outraged Miss Walsh voice.

'When a gentleman offers to escort a lady home, it is to be expected that he will act like a gentleman.'

We walked home in silence after that, Bill stalking sulkily ahead. He bade me goodnight at the top of Marsh Lane and I doubt that I even had the interest to answer him. I walked on alone.

The house was quiet – that was the first sinister sign. It was late into the night, around the time that Mrs Benson was usually singing her maudlin love songs, but the house was silent.

I climbed the stairs and stopped outside Harrie's room. A crack of light was showing. I was going to knock. I was going to go in and apologise, or comfort, or congratulate, or whatever I had to do to keep some shred of her friendship, but then I heard voices.

It was Mrs Benson, sober and competent, asking short, confident questions and a male voice I recognised as Fanny Boothe's doctor's, answering her in detail. I understood that much from their tone and I pressed myself against the door in the hope of hearing something more specific. I heard Mrs Benson ask whether it was necessary to alert her parents and I heard some of the doctors reply.

'Yes... impossible to stay here... responsibility... forms to be signed.'

It was dark in the hall. I was tired and nervous and it is a wonder to me that I didn't scream when I felt a hand grip my shoulder. I froze, but more in horror than in terror. I suppose I knew who it had to be. I turned slowly and faced Fanny Boothe.

'Come with me,' she whispered, but her actions shouted. With astonishing strength she pushed me ahead of her and I led the way to her room.

I hadn't been there in weeks but it was just as it always had been. Her centre table was still piled with wax and newspapers. Her room was still cluttered and dusty with memories.

There was only one small lamp lit, and that only lit one small corner of the room. The rest was weighed down with darkness and with stagnant heat. I stood by her centre table and watched as she carefully closed her door and advanced on me.

She didn't talk until she was within a step of me. Until her upturned face breathed its ancient breath on to my chin. Until her old-woman smell of dust and decay filled my nostrils and stung my eyes.

'And now do you know what you have done?'

I didn't respond. To shake my head would have been enough to shake the spell but I wasn't capable of even that much.

'Dear, dear little Harrie came home screaming tonight. Terrible screams they were. Heart- and soul-wrenching screams. She came in as far as the hall and there she stayed screaming. I was the first to her, but I was too late. By then she was quiet and it will be a surprise to us all if she ever makes another sound.'

She paused and moved away from me slightly. Her voice grew softer and it was as if she had forgotten who she was talking to.

'I've seen her bad before, but never like this. She was just empty. No life in her eyes and her mouth slack. I called Mrs Benson and she called the doctor and we had to wait for him before we could move her to her room. She was too heavy for us. It was as if the grave was calling her body into the ground and I don't know if she will ever be strong enough to break its hold.'

I wanted to ask but I didn't want to know. There was a short silence. I was trying to form a question and Fanny was composing herself. Once she had, she remembered me, and once again she thrust her face up into mine.

'She was never strong, our Harrie. What she was was beautiful and fragile and delicate. She had just enough for herself, but she insisted always on giving more than she was able, and she gave everything to you. I've even seen that before, but most people give something back. Harrie told me that.

'She told me that most friendships were a mingling of souls. She told me that she believed relationships grew into an entity of their own, independent of the people involved in them and that the ultimate entity was a child born from love. But there were lesser relationships, lesser entities, and life was all about exploring them. She gave so much and believed so deeply that she put herself at risk whenever she met a new person. This was probably bound to happen, she was bound to eventually meet someone like you, a combination of greed and evil.

'You just took and took until the poor girl was left as she is left now, hollow. And for what? For you! Harrie's soul is wasted in you, you've tainted it with your own poison.'

She spat the words into my face and I could feel them settle on my skin and burn through my being. I still stayed silent and immobile, even when she walked away, unblocking my path to the door.

She walked around her table and, picking something up, continued around in a full circle back to me. This time she kept her distance and extended her hand. I followed her eyes down and watched as she opened her fist on what I first thought was a lump of wax.

I relaxed slightly. That grey lump reminded me of her madness. But the relief was short-lived. She suddenly thrust the thing in my face and up close I could see that it was shaped as a woman and strands of my hair were embedded in its head.

'I swore that I would never do this again. I swore that I would never again meddle with another living creature's soul. But you deserve this. You may have taken all Harrie had to give, but I have taken it back, even if I had to take your filth with it and here it will stay. You will get no satisfaction from your crime.'

And then the mood broken, there were sounds of movement outside. We both looked to the door and I recovered myself enough to go through it. The movement we had heard had been the doctor leaving. I just caught a glimpse of him on the turn of the stairs.

I ran back up to Harrie in the hope of seeing her, but her door was locked, her light was off, and there was no answer to my continuous knocking. Finally, fear and exhaustion drove me to bed.

I wedged my door shut with my chair – I was terrified of what might come through it. It wasn't so much Fanny Boothe I was scared of – I knew that she had had her say – I was hiding from some kind of personification of my crime that I was still trying to understand. I lay on the bed still fully dressed and must have slept a little, because I remember the pain of waking. I woke cramped and sore. I had slept immobile, curled into a tight, foetal position.

That morning I wasn't even blessed with the blissful moment of confusion before reality returns. Nor was I blessed with the comfort of seeing things more clearly in the light. That morning I woke straight into horror. Still dressed in my dress of the night before, I ran down to Harrie, but again her door was locked, and there was no answer to my continuous knocking.

I returned to my room and sat in my chair, looking out at my chimney stacks and thinking and listening. The house was silent and my thoughts were dragging me into a despair beyond my years.

Time passed, maybe hours, before I moved. I washed my face in cold water and I changed into a day dress. Then I sat again.

Eventually I left my room. I passed Harrie's room and Fanny Boothe's room, both quiet, and I stood undecided in the hall. Finally, I knocked on Mrs Benson's door. She seemed to be my only option. She took a while to answer but she did eventually and, with an expression of distaste, she stepped aside to allow me into her front parlour.

'Yes?'

She stood facing me waiting for my questions and they came rushing out of the blankness of my despair.

'Why was the doctor here last night?'

'What is wrong with Harrie?'

'Has this happened to her before?'

'Can you let me in to see her?'

'Has anyone seen her this morning?'

Mrs Benson halted my tirade after that last question.

'Of course I have been in to see her this morning. Are you implying that I am incompetent? Perhaps you know better? But I doubt it. I have been in the nursing profession longer than you have been in the world.'

'I didn't mean that you were incompetent. I didn't know you were a nurse.'

'Of course I'm a nurse. Do you think these patients would be entrusted into my care if I were a seamstress?'

'Patients?'

Exasperated, she explained as briefly as she could.

'Yes, I am a nurse, a cook, a chambermaid and all for a pittance and barely a thank you. I would have done better to do as my friends advised and stuck to genteel women of independent means.'

'But they, we, are of independent means.'

'They have families with more money than compassion, but that makes them neither independent nor genteel.'

I must still have looked as bewildered as I felt, and with a sigh Mrs Benson continued: 'Who do you think looks after Mrs Fanny Boothe with her four birthdays a year, not to mention Miss Charter Thomas? It's not their families is it? Would any of them sully their hands or reputations with the care of an embarrassment? I think not.'

I listened to her rant against the upper classes and I slowly understood. Number 26 Marsh Lane was a kind of supervised halfway house and Mrs Benson was the supervisor, a supposed qualified and caring member of the medical profession. She was, I am sure, qualified – that much could be checked by the families involved – but, as is normal in such situations, the families involved would not be prepared to listen to reports that she wasn't caring. Especially as her establishment dealt mainly in what is politely referred to as 'nervous disorders'.

I doubt, however, that Mrs Benson's patients ever did complain. The situation in number 26 must have worked well for everyone. Mrs Benson's drinking gave her patients a freedom they wouldn't experience elsewhere, and their disorders ensured that their complaints, if any, would be disregarded.

After telling or implying that much, Mrs Benson asked me to leave, but I refused. It took aggressive questioning on my part, but I finally got her to give me a synopsis of Harrie's medical history.

'Certainly not. It is unethical.'

'But I am her friend.'

'And I am her family's confidante.'

'Are her family wealthy?' Desperation sharpened my wits and, using Mrs Benson's obvious bitterness, I got the information that I wanted.

'Yes, very. I'm sure even you would have heard of them in your backwater.'

'But they just dumped her here without even visiting?' I asked, appalled.

'Typical, if you ask me. And I didn't want the responsibility. I told them that this might happen again.'

I stayed silent. There was nothing more that needed to be said to elicit Mrs Benson's confidences. She was evidently very worried about the reaction of Harrie's family regarding her condition. I guessed that Mrs Benson's instructions concerning her charge had been largely ignored. She was using me as a stone to hone her excuses on. I stayed silent and listened to the whole story.

Seemingly, Harrie had suffered a severe breakdown in her early teens, and though she had recovered, she suffered relapses for the rest of her life. As a result she had spent a lot of time in hospitals around Europe, but for the last few years she had been gaining in strength and was considered almost cured.

It was Mrs Benson's responsibility to give Harrie a secure,

supervised if largely independent home. Everyone had thought that this would have been enough. Though I am sure that Harrie's family wouldn't have stretched their definition of the word 'independent' quite as far as Mrs Benson did. Harrie's condition could not have benefited from poor food, late nights out and loud nights in.

When Mrs Benson had finished her explanation, she shut the door firmly without giving me a chance to respond. I didn't mind. I couldn't think of a response to this kind if information. It was so far beyond my experience.

I was on my way back to my room when I remembered one last question. I turned and walked straight into the parlour. This was too important to knock for.

'Mrs Benson.'

She looked up from her glass, angry at being disturbed again, and despite the shock of the last few hours, still formal enough to be outraged by my lack of formality.

'Why am I here? Have my parents given you instructions about me? Do I have a medical history that I don't know about?'

'You're here because you're seventeen. I suppose they thought that you needed minding. Girls like you get into trouble every day. Shut the door behind you.'

My potential problems, as much as myself, bored her.

Later, I checked her story with my parents and they supported it. It seems that they expected the worst from me long before I took to wearing scarlet lipstick. But that was much later, that was when I brought James down to meet them.

Chapter 23

And that, basically, is the story of this old lady's life. Some people live for all the years that they breathe and some live for only a fraction of that time. I lived for a summer.

I sat in my room for the rest of that Sunday and I watched a car drive up and a well-dressed couple step out. I never knew if they were Harrie's parents or Harrie's mother and uncle but, whoever they were, they took my Harrie away. I saw the shape of her between them, but she was covered in blankets so that was all I saw of her.

When the car left I cried. I watched the day turn into dusk and I cried and cried.

The next day I went to work and at lunchtime I ate a ham salad alone in The Tea Maid, one of the cafés my co-workers frequented. That evening I sat in my room and watched the day turn into dusk again. But now the tears were gone and only a void was left. That maybe was the day I died. My life, from then until now, has just been a postponement of the burial. The next day I did the same and the next, and the next, and the following weekend I went home. It was maybe ten days later when I finally forced myself into Harrie's empty room.

It was very empty. The curtains were gone, the kimono, the mirrors, the white throw, the scarlet cushions. It was a square, dirty-white room with one, rotten window. It looked out on to a rat-infested dump of a garden and it was filled with aged, slightly grubby, badly painted furniture. It was nothing.

A few days later, I bought an ice-cream at lunchtime and I walked through the park, to the unpopular end where an old, rotten bandstand stood. I sat on its soft wood, after carefully brushing away a layer of dirt. I ate my ice-cream and returned to work still feeling hungry.

It was maybe that night that, desperate for a flicker of life, I crept in through the break in the park's railings and ran softly over to the tallest tree. I stood beneath it and stared through its thinning foliage and up into the dark sky. It looked cold up there and dangerous and I knew that no matter how high the tree was it could never be as high as the night. I walked home slowly. I walked through the park down its centre avenues. I couldn't even feel the thrill of danger or the excitement of trespass.

And every day I was worn by Miss Walsh's tongue. She was right, I was useless and lazy and I hung my head in silence while her words lashed down on me.

It was about two months later when James finally came for me as I knew he would. We had between us destroyed a beauty; we had both of us destroyed our love; we had both of us lost our way. I imagine that we had more in common than most couples.

It was James that filled in the missing pieces for me. Though I had guessed at them before. Instead of proposing to her, he broke with Harrie that night and he watched her break in response. She never spoke, she just curled over in pain and ran into the night. He followed her and watched as she flung herself through the door of number 26. He must have heard the scream but he never tried to describe it.

We stayed together, James and I, for the rest of his life. No-one else would ever understand us as we understood each other and so we had no choice.

James achieved remarkable success in his profession and I enjoyed the financial rewards that went with that. I achieved my own success as a society beauty and wit. We both did what we could to forget ourselves, or to prove ourselves as something more than we both knew we were.

We set out to prove the impossible and we failed. James died

a weak man and I will die a weak woman. I don't suppose that
we ever, either of us, for a moment, forgot that it was our
weakness that killed Harrie.

Marian O'Neill was born in Limerick in 1966.

Her family moved to Dublin two years later and she has lived there ever since. After leaving school she spent a year working in Berlin and studying the language. She returned in 1984 to study history of art in UCD.

She graduated in 1987 with an honours degree and, by then, she had also acquired a technical training in paper conservation from the Olmstead site in Boston, Massachussetts.

Since then Marian has worked in publishing and in book retail in London, Berlin and Dublin. She married Stephen Buck in 1994, and since 1996 has been writing full time.